The
Shop Girl's
Secret

BERYL WHITE

Drina
ROMANCE
PUBLISHING

COPYRIGHT

Title: The Shop Girl's Secret

First published in 2023

Copyright © 2023

ISBN: 9798387912900

CONTENTS

1

A FATEFUL ERRAND

December 1894

Young Daphne Parker hated causing a scene, but sometimes she had no choice. The local corner shop owner, Jimmy McGinty, prided himself on his dishonest self-interest. The highlight of his day was often making a bit of extra money off his customers. But Daphne wasn't going to let him get away with it this time—not when her mother would box her ears for wasting money.

"Weigh that flour again, or I'll get my ma to come and have a word with you. That bag's only three-quarters full," Daphne said, her voice tight with determination.

McGinty's scowl deepened as some of the other shoppers flinched at the girl's foolhardy outburst. Jimmy's reputation for being nasty was well-known throughout the community. However, beggars can't be choosers, and Jimmy loved to profit from others' weaknesses.

"It has been weighed properly," he replied gruffly.

Daphne narrowed her eyes and stepped closer to the counter. She looked directly at the weighing scales and the meagre bag of flour.

"It's not enough. I want my full pound!"

"You can take it or leave it," McGinty said with a shrug.

From the perfect observation point at the end of Prospect Street, the Irishman made sure all his tenants bought their provisions from his corner shop, with its poor selection, terrible product quality, and hefty prices. To make sure Daphne was in no doubt she was 'taking it,' the Irishman folded the top of the paper bag down and dropped it into her shopping basket with her other items.

"Put this on our slate, Mr McGinty. My father will settle the bill when he's paid. I'll tell him what you did and to pay a ha'penny less."

Daphne snatched at the basket handle and stormed out of the shop, leaving the stunned onlookers with their mouths agape. Once outside, she noticed a heavy stillness had descended upon the once bustling street. The weather was on the turn sending people scurrying for shelter. The plump raindrops pelting down on her tattered bonnet sent a chill down her spine. As she made her way across the glistening cobblestones, her chill was compounded by an unfathomable sense of foreboding. It wasn't because of the argument with McGinty. The girl felt as if some other dark fate was looming.

With her free hand, she clutched her tattered shawl around her slender shoulders, even though the thin garment provided little warmth against the cold. Would she make it back to the family home before she was soaked to the skin? She hoped so. Despite the gloomy feeling that had descended, she soldiered on, darting from alcove to alcove, determined to not let the rain soak her or fear to paralyse her. Before the day was out, she would fail on both accounts.

Just half an hour earlier, when her mother had given her the shopping list, it had been a beautiful sunny day. Well, sunny for London's dismal East End. Now, the grey sky blended into the grey slate roof tiles. As she approached number twenty-two Prospect Street with its familiar scuffed front door, complete with the peeling paint on the door frame, it creaked open. Swiftly, Mrs Parker took hold of the shopping basket and ushered Daphne inside.

"Come in. Quickly now. My poor little love, you'll catch your death out in this. Why didn't you borrow my nice warm coat, you silly thing, eh?"

"Because it nearly comes down to my ankles, ma. Besides, I didn't know it was going to rain this much when I went out."

Still feeling on edge, Daphne chose not to mention the sense of foreboding in her stomach. Mary Parker didn't have a superstitious bone in her body. The girl told herself the ominousness was probably caused by something and nothing. Mary looked at Daphne over her shoulder as she arranged the fresh groceries in their tiny larder cupboard.

"Your father should be back soon. I'm famished today."

"I hope he took his brolly," said Daphne as she shoved her wet curly hair off her forehead.

Daphne took a quick look in the cracked mirror above the fireplace. Even when barely damp, her locks always became bigger and curlier and she hated that. She tried to pull a tress straight but it bounced back.

"Your dad is a sensible man, so he grabbed an umbrella. You'd do well to follow his lead, instead of living in your own little world and fluttering around like a whirling dervish from one mishap to the next."

"I resent that, mama!" said Daphne, as she peeled a small sticky ginger cake out of its greaseproof paper wrapper and dropped it onto a plate with a clatter.

Mary's eyebrows lifted.

"Yes. I know cake wasn't on your list, but papa loves it. I had a ha'penny saved up from helping Mrs Bradley. Plus, I think I was a bit cheeky to him this morning."

"You were. Your papa's done so much overtime to make Christmas nice for us. He's exhausted. I'm sure he'll appreciate putting his feet up with some tea and cake. By the way, did McGinty give you any trouble about getting the shopping on the slate?"

Daphne shook her head. She decided not to mention Jimmy diddling her out of some flour. She eyed the loaf in her mother's hand suspiciously.

"I hope the bread isn't stale this time, mama. I reckon Jimmy saves the rock-hard loaves for us because we don't pay as promptly as the other folks on a Friday. He always gives us his old stuff not fit for rats. The selfishness of that man is staggering."

Mary gave the loaf a squeeze and it squished a little.

"This one's not so bad. It was odd last time I went over to the shop, Jimmy was uncharacteristically amenable. I thought he'd been drinking! That said, there was that buxom woman from Paternoster Row in there, Milly Compton's mother, Ethel. I reckon he might have been trying to dazzle her with his charm," Mrs Parker said with a chuckle.

Feeling a kick inside her belly, Mary patted her swollen stomach as she carried on with her assessment of Ethel.

"Just because she grew up in a large house in Hoxton doesn't mean she should act all haughty now. She can't be doing that well in life if she's ended up lodging on Prospect Street," Mary scoffed. "Did I tell you my grandfather's family used to have money? We'd still have it if it wasn't for my uncle wasting it all on gambling. Our lives could have been so different. Still, what will be, will be."

Mary sighed a note of nostalgia in her voice. She glanced around her forlornly, as if remembering a better time. Daphne tried her hardest to suppress an eye roll. She had heard her mother's gripe many times before, and its familiarity was beginning to wear thin. The girl changed the subject.

"Mama—talking about grandfathers, when is Grandpa returning from Portsmouth? I do hope he'll get some leave soon. I expect he'll have lots of old sea dog tales to tell us by the fireside!"

Her mother tucked a stray tress of silvering hair back into her loose bun and took a stool from under the tiny table.

"Daphne, you do know he makes most of those stories up, don't you?"

"You always say that, but I believe him. What about that giant squid that was as big as his ship and had tentacles long enough to wrap around the hull several times? Or when he saw some mermaids swimming alongside? I've seen those mentioned in books!"

Mary's only response was a snort and a shake of the head at her daughter's gullibility.

"You must have some idea when he'll be back to see us, though, ma?"

"How many more times, child? I don't know when!" Mary grizzled as she sat down. "You know what the Navy is like. They never tell us mere mortals anything."

On the range, the kettle whistled, sending out a wisp of steam—a sign that it was time to search for the least dented enamel mugs in the cupboard. The cold had seeped into Daphne's bones, and the girl was determined to get a comforting hot cup of tea in her hands sooner rather than later. Mary noticed her daughter's weary look and took on a more soothing tone.

"I'm sure he'll be back soon, love. He's been away nearly a year now. Bless him, he doesn't even know he's got another grandchild on the way! He'll be jumping up and down when he finds out, won't he?"

Mary's hand glided over the pronounced curve of her belly again.

"Mama—"

"Yes?"

"How did the baby really get inside you?"

Mary flinched.

"Oh, um—I'll have to tell you another time. We need to press on. It's nearly dinnertime, and you know how much your father appreciates a meal on the table when he gets in."

"Oh, mama—surely we can cook and talk?"

"Not this time. I'm exhausted. Now, go and make yourself useful and chop those onions."

"Yes, mama," Daphne said gloomily.

The girl had been speculating for days about the origin of babies, naively feeling her own belly to see if she was expecting too, thinking pregnancy might be contagious like cholera. All the time, her slender waist remained perfectly flat.

Daphne decided that if by some miracle she did have a baby she was certain there would be enough room in her heart to welcome the little one. Accommodation wouldn't pose a problem either. A few months ago, her brother Walter Henry—named after Grandpa but known to everyone in the family by his middle name—had joined London, Tilbury and Southend Railway as an apprentice labourer and was busily helping with their Essex bridge building and tunnel digging plans.

Henry moved to Chelmsford to begin his basic training, a good few hours away from the rest of the family in London. He and Daphne had shared a bed before he left. She thought he was a big old lump, so there would definitely be room for her tiny bairn beside her.

Suddenly, both of them jumped at the sound of a series of loud raps at the door.

"What's all that racket for?" Mary grumbled as Daphne dashed across to see who it was.

There was another set of impatient knocks.

"Alright, alright, we're coming."

Daphne was surprised to be greeted by a man looking smart in his dark, knee-length frock coat with a matching waistcoat, crisp white dress shirt, and black bowler hat. Smartly dressed folk didn't come to their neck of the woods often.

"I'm here to see Mr and Mrs Parker."

Mary groaned as she got to her feet and stood beside the girl.

"I'm Mrs Parker. Can I help you, sir?"

The man bowed his head and removed his bowler.

"Yes. I'm Mr Jepson, ma'am. This won't take long. Do you mind if I step inside?"

Mary noticed the raindrops beading on the man's clothing.

"Certainly, sir. Please excuse my daughter's woeful welcome."

Daphne's eyes narrowed to slits, but she decided against protesting when she saw her mother's troubled expression.

"Can we offer you a tea?"

The gentleman gave a sombre headshake.

"Thank you, but I'm fine Mrs Parker," he said as he put his hat under his arm. "Actually, I have some news to share with you about your son, Henry—bad news, I'm afraid."

Daphne decided this man's bad news must have been the cause of her ominous feeling earlier. Mary tried to speak but no words came out.

"Pray, sit down, Mrs Parker."

Mary lumbered over to the table and flopped on a stool. Daphne wondered what could have happened? Henry was still doing his induction with the railway company. Mary wondered if he'd done something silly at work? Played a prank on someone and got into bother with his boss? Or perhaps fallen ill? His lungs always gave him trouble. Jepson cast a sharp gaze at Mary's huge bump before speaking.

"Will your husband be home soon? I suggest we wait until he is present. I think he should be with you. If you don't mind me saying."

Daphne's heart sank as she looked at her mother, slouched on the stool. Noticing her own anxiety reflected in her mother's buckled frame, without saying a word, the girl moved closer and gave Mary's shoulder a firm squeeze. Time stood still. The only sound in the room was their own laboured breathing. Outside, rowdy workers trundled to and from the Little Drummer Boy pub who valued a bellyful of beer over keeping dry. Even though it had only been minutes since Mr Jepson knocked, the wait felt like an eternity. The clerk shifted his weight from foot to foot, then took a sharp breath. He appeared to be ready to speak at one point but then chose to remain silent. It only increased the tenseness for the awkward trio.

"Mama, would it help if I carry on preparing the din—?"

Daphne's suggestion was interrupted by her father vigorously shaking his brolly outside, then darting in and closing the door.

"I saw the strangest thing tonight, Mary. There was a nice-looking carriage parked at the end of Dean Street. The driver looks a bit worried that one of the ruffians around here will steal his wheels."

Johnny Parker stopped when he turned and saw Jepson.

"Oh! Forgive my manners."

The man shook Johnny's hand firmly.

"Good evening, Mr Parker. I'm Mr Jepson, based at your son's engineering depot in Chelmsford."

"Welcome to our humble home. I trust you are well?" said Johnny, his voice wavering.

"I bide fine, thank you, Mr Parker."

"Let me get you a hot toddy, sir. There's a real chill in the air tonight."

Johnny went to the small dresser cupboard where they kept some of Grandpa's rum, but the visitor declined.

"A cup of tea, then?" Johnny said, still fussing. "Mary, I can't believe you didn't offer this good man refreshment?"

"Mr Parker—sit down! Please."

"Yes. Sorry. Please tell us more."

Johnny was a far cry from his usual cheerful self. His frantic eyes darted over the visitor's face hunting for clues, His face drained of its usual colour, leaving his expression pale and drawn.

"I am sorry but your son has been badly injured in an accident."

The grim comment act like a weight lifted from her father's shoulders, which confused his young daughter.

"Injured. God bless you, sir! I feared you were going to say he was dead!"

Jepson didn't share his relief.

"Well, Mr Parker, the trouble is, the infirmary doctor has said it's touch and go if your lad will make it through the night."

Mary wriggled free from her daughter's grasp and leaned forward.

"What sort of accident, Mr Jepson?"

There was an uncomfortable shift in the clerk's posture.

"I'm afraid I can't comment at this time. Everything will be explained by the foreman at the depot."

Mary pleaded as she gripped her husband's forearm.

"Johnny, we need to be at his bedside."

The poor father was unresponsive, stunned with shock. Mary looked to Jepson.

"Is it your coach at the end of Dean Street? There is no way for us to get there otherwise."

"Well, Yes. But it's quite a trek by coach, ma'am, and in your condition—perhaps the train from Fenchurch Street might be better?"

"To hell with my condition, man. We have to see our son—and you will get us there right now!"

Daphne held her breath, waiting for her father to object to her mother's blaspheming, but instead, Johnny got to his feet and nodded at the suggestion.

"I agree with my wife, Mr Jepson. We are his parents. We must be with him—and we will be with him."

"What about me?" Daphne whimpered. "I want to see him too!"

"I'm sorry, Daphne, but no," Mary snapped. "A railway depot is no place for a young girl."

"But I'll be with you! I'll be safe!"

"Don't throw another one of your tantrums, Daphne. The answer is 'no'."

Her mother's use of the word 'tantrum' riled Daphne but she ignored it.

"What are your plans for food, papa? Should I make dinner for your return? I don't mind if you're back late."

"Thank you, but there's no need, child," he replied. "We probably won't be back tonight, maybe not for a day or two. Not until your brother is well enough to travel."

"What am I supposed to do in the meantime?"

"I beg your pardon! The world revolves around the sun, not you, my girl!" Johnny growled.

When her gaze met her father's icy stare, Daphne backed down but was still bristly. Mary made an attempt to placate her daughter.

"Please don't take your father's behaviour personally, sweetheart. He's under a lot of pressure, that's all."

Daphne pouted at Johnny and he looked away dismissively.

> "You can stay with a neighbour for the night. How about your friend, Sarah? Under the circumstances, I'm sure her mother won't mind."

> "Sarah won't be back from the shop yet. She works late these days."

> "While we finalise our plans with Mr Jepson, why don't you go and ask?"

Frustrated, Daphne sighed as she wrapped her damp shawl around her body. Going to Sarah's lodgings this early felt pointless and she only complied to soothe her father's simmering anger.

2

UNWANTED RESPONSIBILITY

The rain had stopped. Now, the light from a full silvery moon lit the streets, bringing a little cheer to life as Daphne strode to Sarah's house. No one answered when she knocked, so she carried on walking to give her parents some privacy. She pottered down Dean Street, the second most run-down street in Whitechapel, past the market stalls, the merchants selling jellied eels, Bert the rag man, the one-penny meat pie men, past the costermongers' barrows and tradesman's shops.

Feeling lonely and needing time to think, she sheltered from the bedlam under a huge red-brick railway arch. Rubbish filled the corners and it smelled awful, nevertheless, it offered a little privacy for a while. Above her head, the wheels of a locomotive squealed, and the engine belched forth clouds of sooty grey smoke. Having never travelled by train, she loved seeing the trail billow in the dark night sky and imagining what it might feel like to 'travel' rather than 'walk' somewhere.

Daphne's mind wandered back to thoughts of her brother. The possibility of Henry not making it to the morning filled her with dread. She would miss his playful pranks, like sneaking up on her while she was absorbed in a book or game and scaring her with a flick to her ear. Despite being furious, she would always end up giggling as Henry hugged her.

Despite his mischievous ways, Daphne cherished Henry's kind-hearted nature, especially when he was teasing her. She realised that perhaps what she would miss the most about him was their playful banter and ribbing. No one else could fill those shoes. Feeling sick when she noticed she had referred to him in the past tense as if he had gone already, she reprimanded herself not to be so thoughtless.

It was getting late and it was time to sort out where she would be staying that evening. As she made her way back to Sarah's, a gaggle of rough-looking children were sitting begging in doorways, their clothes tattered and their faces smudged with dirt. Although there was nothing in her pockets to steal, Daphne shoved her hands deep. As she passed by, one of the children tugged on her skirt.

"Excuse me, miss. Do you have any spare change?"

Daphne hesitated, unsure of how to respond. She had grown up poor herself and knew how difficult it was to make ends meet. But she had also heard stories of pickpockets and thieves preying on unsuspecting passers-by.

"Please, miss," another child chimed in. "We just want to talk to you."

"Sorry, I have to dash."

Pulling her skirt free, Daphne scurried onto the safety of number seven.

Mrs Bradley's smiling face greeted her at the door, but her expression grew with concern as Daphne explained her situation.

"That's no problem treacle. No problem at all. Course you can stay here," the woman reassured. "When are they going off to visit Henry?"

"Right away, Mrs Bradley. There's someone official from the railway here. They won't want to keep him waiting. He's come by coach all the way from Essex."

"But what about your mother? She's only a few weeks off giving birth. Darting across the country won't be good for her or the bairn."

Daphne looked down and gave a shrug. When it came to her mother's 'pride and joy,' her precious and only surviving son, nothing could deter her determination.

"Come on, girl. No time like the present. Off you go to your house. Go and get your things," Mrs Bradley ordered as she grabbed Daphne by the arm and marched her over.

Mr Jepson's carriage driver, against his better judgement, had weaved his way along Prospect Street to wait outside, keen to get away from the stench, the squalor and the small army of ragged children eyeing up his coach on Dean Street. Technically, the road was wide enough for a driver to navigate, but not when it was clogged up with envious nosey-parkers admiring the vehicle. Once parked, the driver was frantically trying to stop the kids from pulling at the horse's tail. The beast stamping its hooves and snorting in disapproval achieved nothing.

The driver started to shoo them away with his long whip. Daphne kept her distance. Her mother had always told her to be wary of strangers. Then again as he was about to take her parents miles away, she decided he must have been reasonably trustworthy. As she admired the carriage, her mother's head appeared from the doorway, adorned with her best green bonnet.

"Finally, Daphne! Where have you been all this time? You had one thing to do! Will Mrs Bradley mind you while we're gone? Well?"

"Yes, mama," she said meekly. "Do you have any idea how long you'll be away?"

Before her mother could reply, her father piped up.

"We have no idea. We'll be as long as it takes for us to know your brother's safely on the mend. Then, we'll come back."

Feeling guilty for snapping at his daughter, he put his arm around her and squeezed tightly.

"It sounds serious, papa! He's not going to—die—is he?"

Mrs Parker reached out and ruffled her stammering daughter's hair. The poor thing looked at her with tears in her eyes. Johnny stepped back inside and checked he and his wife had got everything before heading off. Mary took Daphne's hand.

"Bravery is required of us all, my love. We must ask God to intervene on behalf of your brother. The best thing you can do is say your prayers for him."

"Of course, mama. And I'll light a candle for him in the Chapel of St George."

As her father helped the driver put the family carpet bag on the luggage rack, Daphne ran over and hugged him dearly, clinging on like a limpet. He gripped her too, kissing the top of her head before pushing her away when Jepson, who had seen more than enough of Whitechapel for one day, finally put his foot down.

"Time to be going, Mr Parker."

"You be good for Mrs Bradley, now," said Johnny. "Don't let your manners slip because we're not here. Best behaviour, my girl."

"I promise, papa. You don't need to worry about me. Go and help Henry. Send him my love, won't you?"

Johnny Parker stepped into the cab as Mr Jepson took a seat next to the driver, not looking too happy about losing his comfy seat inside.

Daphne's parent's heads bobbed outside the side windows as they craned their necks to keep sight of her. She waved until they were out of view, and then her parents closed the window and retreated into their private hell.

"I just need to get some things from home, Mrs Bradley, I'll be over in a couple of minutes."

"Right-o. Just make sure you don't dawdle, Daphne. You're not too old to feel the back of my hand."

"Yes, Mrs Bradley. I'll be as quick as I can," she agreed before scurrying inside and shutting the door firmly behind her.

First, the meat went in a thick stone box in the larder cupboard. Then she popped the wizening vegetables in a pan and sloshed in some water from the kitchen bucket so they would last the night. She picked up a few tatty old copies of 'Harper's Illustrated Magazine for Girls', thinking they might provide a welcome distraction. On the windowsill, she saw her mother had got out some blue yarn to darn her father's best pair of socks and vowed to repair them herself in her absence.

She considered knitting a little jacket ready for the baby's arrival. Daphne had helped her mother unravel one of Grandpa's old pullovers, and that had gone well, but when it came to knitting, the girl was terrible. Her efforts were all dropped stitches and forgetting whether to knit or purl a row. Her last attempt left her mother tutting as she unpicked it all. Knitting was a standard part of many a young girl's education, but no matter how many hours her mother spent with Daphne, her daughter's skills never improved.

She decided it might be best to collect the yarn and needles and see if Mrs Bradley might be willing to barter a bit of knitting in return for her doing some chores around their house instead. Just then, there was another insistent knock at the door. Daphne expected it was Mrs Bradley coming to tell her off for her tardiness. She shouted as she collected her things.

"Sorry, Mrs Bradley. I was just—"

But when Daphne peered out of the window, she stopped dead. Instead of Sarah's mother, she eyed a younger woman standing with her back to the door, dressed in a long grey coat, plastered with patches. The woman turned and Daphne saw an infant resting in her arms. *'What could she possibly want?'* Curiosity overcame her fear. She raised the latch and opened the door as little as possible.

"Can I help you, miss?"

"Aye. I'm here to see Harry. This is the right place. I checked the address. And I asked about."

Daphne manoeuvred to narrow the gap in the doorway.

"I'm sorry. You're mistaken. Nobody called Harry lives here."

The woman seemed to be fighting back tears. Daphne let the door swing open a little wider. The visitor was only a few years older than her. Twenty perhaps? The twitchy neighbours stared past the pulled-back curtains, and out through their broken window panes, curious about the second unexpected event of the night at the Parkers.

"Oh, miss. Please don't cry—"

The baby joined in with its mother's wailing as the strange woman pushed the child into Daphne's arms, fleeing before the girl could finish.

"Hey!" Daphne yelled, doing her best to chase after the woman. "Hey, come back, missus! You can't just dump your baby on me! The cheek!"

Burdened by her wriggling human cargo, Daphne tried to catch up with the sobbing woman who was half-stumbling, half-running up the street. Soon, the bewildered girl lost sight of the young woman as she turned the corner into the bustling Commercial Road. The mother simply melted into the drab throng of workers making their way home.

What ought Daphne to do? She was clueless about caring for babies. A few years earlier, she had watched her mother give birth to a bairn and watched her suckle him, but he passed very soon after, so she never got to care for him for long. Asking Mrs Bradley seemed the wrong thing to do. The poor woman had only just agreed to take her in, not this screaming little thing too.

Against her better judgement, Daphne scooted back down Prospect Street, past the Bradleys and into Brooks Road, where she knocked on a tired-looking door. No one ever called around to that house uninvited, but needs must. Her arms were aching now, so she thrust out a hip and tried to rest the bundle on it as she waited. After a short while, the door opened and a craggy old face looked out.

"What's this, then, missy? Knocking on my door at this hour!" she woman growled.

"I've called about this baby, Mrs Bridges."

"I can see that. How come you've got it? It's not your ma's. Whose is it?"

"I don't know. A young woman visited and asked for someone called Harry. She dumped this little one into my arms and fled in the direction of Bethnal Green. My parents have had to go on an errand, so I don't know what to do."

"I see. Well, I'll make an exception since your parents are away. Come in."

Mrs Bridges swung open the door and dragged the girl over the threshold. As Daphne's eyes adjusted to the gloom, she looked around the cluttered room and saw rows of wonky wooden shelves rammed with rows of pill boxes and potion bottles.

"Put it on the armchair," ordered the old woman.

Daphne did as she was asked, and unwrapped the grubby shawl. As she did so, a crumpled envelope tumbled to the floor. The girl reached for the note but was too slow.

"I'll have that, thank you," snapped Mrs Bridges, as she grabbed it.

The old crone muttered as she read.

"What? What does it say?"

"One of the men in your family has been a naughty boy, or its mother mistook the address," Mrs Bridges announced.

"What do you mean?" Daphne shrieked, her voice so loud it tempted several nosy neighbours to sneak in off the street and scrabble to read the note.

"What's going to happen to the little mite?" the busybodies asked the girl. "Have you got a plan?"

"A plan?" Daphne grizzled. "I haven't the foggiest. Give me that note, now."

She did her best to decipher the words, clearly scrawled by a barely literate person.

'Baybee iz yourz, Harree. Carnt cope. Sorry. Yors C.'

"Oh, heck!" exclaimed one of the neighbours. "Is there anything else in the swaddling, have a look, Daphne. Any more clues? Who do you know whose name begins with 'C'?"

"No one!" the panicked girl protested. "Why me? Why did this have to happen now?"

Daphne teased off the rest of the blanket, revealing a ragged nightdress and a wet nappy. Despite its soiled state, the baby now gurgled cheerfully and tried to grab one of the girl's fingers.

"Ah, it looks like it likes you," cooed another young girl, Ruth.

"What is it? I don't reckon it's a girl," said one of the other women, taking the child and yanking at its clothing. "Thought as much—a boy. How old do you reckon?"

"A few months. Six maybe?" said Mrs Bridges.

"Shall I find a copper?" asked Ruth. "They might help find his mother?"

Mrs Bridges tutted.

"The police couldn't care less about abandoned babies round this way. Especially to an unwed mother. The orphanage at the mission round the corner might take him. If you're lucky."

Daphne tried to slip away and leave them to it, but Mrs Bridges spotted her.

"Oi! Where do you think you're sloping off too? He's your responsibility, not mine. Where's your mother gone?" she asked. "She'll have to help you because I'm not."

"My brother is very ill and they have gone to be at his bedside," Daphne explained. "Since mama is expecting, we have a few baby clothes and bits and pieces at home. I can manage changing his nappy I think. But what do I do about feeding him?"

Looking at her perfectly flat chest, the other women all chuckled.

"Here, I can pitch in," suggested another local lass who hadn't long arrived. "My John's almost weaned. He won't mind sharing."

She picked up the grizzling baby and cooed to it.

"I can tell he's hungry. I'll take him now," said the stranger as she opened her blouse.

"I can't begin to thank you."

As the crowd filtered out of Mrs Bridges' cramped little dwelling, they stood on the pavement mumbling and speculating about the girl's predicament. Strangely, relief flooded through Daphne. She felt much less alone. As the baby was fed, she noticed her sticky parched tongue glued to the roof of her mouth and her tummy growling. When the woman passed the nursed bairn back to Daphne, she looked down at the tot. He seemed neither happy nor sad, just a fleshy lump in her arms. Although he was a complete stranger, Daphne was filled with an immense sense of responsibility. It seemed there were a lot of decisions to be made, actions to be taken, and the poor young girl was almost paralysed with fear.

"I'd better be making tracks to Mrs Bradley's. The last thing I want is to cause her any worry. Can you look after him for just a little longer? Give me time to pack my things?"

Reluctantly the woman took the baby back.

"Alright. But just for a little bit. Then you're on your own."

3

STRENGTH IN NUMBERS

As Daphne sipped at the last of some lemonade from the larder, the thought of being with a baby at her age seemed absurd. How would she ever cope? Perhaps she could convince the lady who had nursed him that she might like another one to care for? But if she refused, then what? Panicking and bitter, she slumped at the dining table. How would her parents react when they returned?

All the women at Mrs Bridges had assumed the tot was her father's or grandfather's baby, but he couldn't be. Grandpa was at sea so much and her papa's heart belonged to her mother. Everyone said he was a wonderful husband. It had to be a misunderstanding.

Her stomach rumbled yet again, so she took a carrot from the saucepan and nibbled on it as she got her nightdress off her bed. She went downstairs and opened the front door then flinched as she saw three boys having a lively kickabout. A football hurtled towards her at head height. The ball flew inside and ricocheted off the back wall.

"Hey! Watch it!" she shouted, as she hoofed the ball back out to them.

To her horror, the ball flew towards the window of a house opposite and hit the fragile pane with a heavy thump. She was relieved when the window didn't break. The boys gave her a hard stare as they scooped up their precious ball and ran away. Daphne was thankful that nobody had come after her for her aggressive footwork, as that would have been another problem to deal with.

Finally, as she went to leave, a little girl with a mass of golden curls came to see her.

"Is that your baby me ma's been feeding?"

"Do you mean the—?"

Daphne tried to remember the appropriate word. Someone said her father was one. He'd been left in a basket in a church doorway.

"—foundling?"

"Yes, that's it."

"No, he isn't mine, I just happen to be caring for him for a bit. I was counting on your mother to keep him."

"She says that she can't do it as we can't afford to feed another mouth."

Daphne stalled for time and fiddled with the cuffs of her dress.

"My ma wants to know when you'll come over to collect him."

Her heart sank.

"Alright. I'll be over when I can."

The blonde girl nodded. Daphne had previously seen the youngster, but since her mother did not allow much socialising, she had never spoken to her.

"Tell me your name?" Daphne asked to jog her memory.

"Ivy."

"Ah, how nice."

"What's yours?"

"Daphne. Daphne Cassandra Beresford Parker."

"Oo-er! That's posh. I ain't got one middle name, let alone two. Ma says pa don't like people who have lots of first names."

Daphne laughed.

"Well, I like my names. My mother was a Beresford, and she says it's good to maintain a connection to our heritage."

Ivy pulled a face.

"Have you eaten a dictionary?"

"No," Daphne chuckled. "Do your brothers and sisters have the same hair colour, Ivy? It's like spun gold."

"Just me. Me ma says it's because I'm special. She's over there."

A woman walked towards them, clutching two babies to her waist. She tried to hand the elder one to Daphne.

"He's fed and cleaned."

Daphne's arms remained behind her back.

"Could you keep him a little longer, Mrs—?"

"Mrs Leah. And no, I can't. I don't have the space or the money. I can feed him every now and then, but that's all."

Mrs Leah gave her own baby to Ivy, and then carefully placed the bigger one into Daphne's spindly arms.

"But I can't care for him," Daphne whispered, her voice trembling with fear. "Little Johnny Junior died. I feel cursed when it comes to babies. What if this one dies too?"

Young Daphne's eyes glistened with tears as she contemplated the possibility that her inexperience might have been the cause of her brother's death. Mrs Leah placed her hand on Daphne's shoulder.

"You mustn't think that way," she said soothingly. "Your brother was sickly from the moment he was born. Although this little chap's a bit on the thin side, he looks healthy enough. You'd better get him inside. It's freezing out here."

"I should be staying with Mrs Bradley tonight. I'll check if I can bring him there. If not, I might need you to take him just for one night. Please?" Daphne begged.

"I'm sure Mrs Bradley will be alright with him for one night. Then we can all come up with a plan. His mother can't be far away. Someone's got to know who's suddenly missing a son."

Mrs Leah rushed to take her baby from Ivy, who was squirming in her small hands.

"I'll get your lad fed in the morning. There really is no need to worry. You'll be fine," Mrs Leah said as she pinched the girl's chin lightly and smiled.

"Right, let's be off, Ivy. Your father's expecting his dinner."

They left Daphne staring at the child in her arms while the girl debated her next move. Wondering where she had got to, Mrs Bradley came out to find her.

"So, it's true. They said you're with a baby. I didn't know what to believe."

"Yes, Mrs Bradley, and I don't know what to do."

Daphne looked up at the lady with a confused expression.

"Here, let me have him. It's a boy, isn't it? We'll take care of him."

The girl could not hide her relief.

"Just for a bit, mind. Not forever."

The girl felt the suffocating panic rise again but hid it.

"Thank you so much. I'd hoped you'd offer some assistance. Looks like the Lord is smiling down on me today. I'll find some clothes for him. Ma kept some upstairs. Bear with me."

Daphne went back inside and produced a baby's night dress from a drawer.

"Will this fit?" she said as Mrs Bradley stifled a belly laugh.

"No, that's for a newborn. This chap looks like he's a few months old. Don't worry. He'll be fine tonight. We'll sort something. What could his name be? What did the note say?"

Daphne took a note out of her apron pocket and read it and then passed it over.

"Nothing here about his name. Here, you take a look."

"Well, he's going to need one," said Mrs Bradley. "We can't call him 'thingy' all night."

Daphne looked around. She'd visited Sarah's house many times to play with her dolls, but she had never noticed the framed embroideries, or the squat shiny Toby jugs in the cabinet in the corner.

How about 'Archibald'?" suggested Mrs Bradley.

Daphne winced.

"Urgh. No, not that. It reminds me of a nasty uncle who was always slapping my legs for being rude when I was younger."

"Rude young girls always deserve a slap on the legs," Mrs Bradley chuckled.

The woman took the needlework resting on the arm of her chair and put it on the windowsill.

"I'll see if dinner's ready. You take a seat. My husband will be home shortly. And Sarah."

"Is there enough food to go round, Mrs Bradley? I don't want to impose. How about I bring the carrots we were going to have for our tea?"

"Don't you worry yourself, lass. We'll manage somehow. We always do."

4

A TEMPORARY HOME

Ten minutes later, Sarah returned to number five.

"What a day—," she began, then stopped when she noticed Daphne. "Ooh, hello. What brings you here?"

Before she could reply, Mrs Bradley filled her in.

"Daphne's here while her parents have gone to see her brother in Essex."

"That's a long way to go. Why's that then?"

Sarah was interrupted as the front door opened.

"Evening, papa," she said as she went over to aid the man limping into the house.

"Here, let me take your coat."

As she steadied her father, he teased his arms from the sleeves. As he bent over, he glowered at Daphne from under his thick eyebrows. Then, he scowled in silence and shuffled off to the kitchen to wash his hands. It was a pointless task, the dirt was so engrained they seldom looked that clean afterwards. The Bradleys and Daphne had a simple meal of bone broth and potatoes as they sat around the small wooden table. The lodger tucked in heartily.

"This is delicious, Mrs Bradley. My ma's food isn't this good."

Another scowl from Mr Bradley caused her to pause and then take small bites of her meal instead. Her own father had often scolded her for gobbling down her food, and she didn't want to suffer the same fate now. The only sounds that filled the room were the scraping of cutlery on plates, and the occasional grunts coming from Mr Bradley as he chewed. To Daphne, he resembled a snuffling pig she'd seen at Smithfield market before it was dispatched by the butcher. She glanced up and caught Mrs Leah's gaze, and looked away in the hope that she hadn't read her thoughts.

After the meal, a chatty Mrs Bradley cleared away the plates.

"I'm sorry, there are no desserts today. After all that's happened, I didn't have time to make one."

Reclining in the only armchair, Mr Bradley took a big swig of his ale, then wiped his mouth with the back of his hand and fought to stifle a belch.

"That's a pity about dessert, my dear. I love your rice pudding. I like the skin. All gnarly and tasty."

"Do you like rice pudding, Daphne?" Sarah asked.

"I—"

The girl stopped and then looked at Mr Bradley, wondering if she should speak. His raised eyebrow indicated he expected a reply.

"I'm not sure," she answered.

The grumpy man gave a long sigh as if he found her response deeply unacceptable.

"Before I forget, dear, I have some news. It's not just Daphne who is with us tonight."

Daphne was surprised to see Mr Bradley's face soften as he listened, not the response she had anticipated at all. Sarah clapped her hands joyfully at the news.

"A baby. That's wonderful!" she said.

"Well, I wouldn't put it like that," replied her mother.

"Where is the little darling?"

"Upstairs."

"You can go and see him if you want, girls. As long as you're quiet and don't wake him. I'll wash up while you're gone."

"You can leave that to me. I'll do it I come down, Mrs Bradley"

"No, it's alright, flower. You just concentrate on being quiet and not thumping around up there."

Sarah led Daphne up to the first floor of the little tenement. The baby lay peacefully on the floor surrounded by cushions. Sarah leant over and stroked his cherubic face.

"Isn't he delightful? A proper little angel. What's his name?"

"Doesn't have one yet," Daphne said with a shrug. "Do you think I could call him Johnny after my little brother we lost?"

"What a lovely thought. Yes, Johnny, it is then."

Downstairs, Mrs Bradley sat down and picked up her darning mushroom and began to repair a large hole that had formed under the armpit of her best cardigan. The girls took a seat at the table. Daphne smiled at Sarah as she reached for a pack of playing cards.

"Fancy a game of something?"

As Mr Bradley lit his pipe, thick smoke began to drift in their direction. Daphne found it acrid, devoid of the enticing aroma of her father's baccy. She opened her mouth to answer Sarah but found herself choking instead. A nod would have to suffice.

"That stuff honks, pa," Sarah complained as she dealt. "Do you have to smoke in here?"

The man of the house settled back in his chair and plonked his aching bad leg on a footstool in front of him.

"Are you trying to tell me what I can do in my own home, my girl? Because if you are—"

"—It's just that it might upset the little one upstairs."

"Fiddlesticks. It never did you any harm. If you think I'm going to forgo one of life's little pleasures for a foundling that's been dumped on us, well, you're mistaken!"

He prodded the tobacco in the pipe with the tip of his pen-knife, then continued to puff away. His eyes followed a neat set of six rings, proudly puffed out to enhance his enjoyment of the moment.

"I'm sorry about him," Sarah whispered.

"What was that, Sarah? If you've got something to say, say it to all of us."

"Sorry, pa."

Daphne gave her friend a discreet smile. It wasn't Sarah's fault she hated the smoke, and why shouldn't the man do as he pleased in his own house after a hard day's toil?

"How was work today, dear?" his wife asked.

The girls ignored their elders' dull conversation, choosing to focus on the lively card game instead.

"How did you get four aces, Sarah?"

"Born lucky me!" the girl chuckled. "Another?"

Daphne grinned, as she gathered and shuffled the cards. A sound came from upstairs which made her freeze. Was the baby awake? She glanced across at Mrs Bradley. Had she heard the noise? Apparently not, for she was still doing her needlework. The girl was tempted to see what was happening but stifled the urge to go and check. Her ears strained for any more clues, but there were none. Mr Bradley stood up and tapped his pipe on the hearth to empty it, then proceeded to fill its tarred and charred bowl again.

"Off for your usual pint, dear?"

"Aye. Too much female company in one go is bad for a man."

"Well, you shouldn't have forced our Bertie away, should you? Then you'd still have your precious male company."

"Oh please, woman! Stop your nagging," Mr Bradley growled as he took his coat and stepped outside.

Cuthbert's whereabouts had everyone baffled. Some years before, Sarah's elder brother had run away, but no one knew the reason. She did wonder if someone would tell her why one day, but none of the Bradleys seemed keen to do so. Daphne yawned, setting off a chain of reaction, as both Sarah and her mother followed suit.

"It's time to turn in," said Sarah, putting the cards back in their tatty printed box. "Where's Daphne sleeping, ma?"

Mrs Bradley paused and stretched.

"How about on the floor next to the baby? I'll get you a blanket and something to use as a pillow."

"That won't be very comfortable," Sarah complained. "How about sleeping in my bed? I can shuffle up. There's plenty of room—and best of all, I don't snore."

Daphne laughed. Snoring or no snoring, she didn't want to share the same floorspace as the baby. The thought of rolling over on him while he was sleeping and smothering him kept popping into her head. She'd heard plenty of tales about poor little ones meeting their maker that way and didn't want to add to the depressing statistic.

"Thank you, Sarah. You're sure you don't mind?"

Sarah yawned again.

"Stop asking! It's fine. Right, up the steps to Bedfordshire. I need to get up early in the morn."

"Good. I like to be up with the lark, too. Have you ever seen a lark?"

"In Whitechapel? Are you having a laugh? I'll just nip out to the privy. Coming?"

That night, Daphne tried to drift off to sleep, but her mind was racing with thoughts of Little Johnny's unexpected arrival and the strange young woman who abandoned him. What's more, how were her parents and brother faring? Despite her anxiousness, she held on to a glimmer of hope that everything would be alright in the end. Alas, her hope was misplaced. Daphne's future would prove to be far more tumultuous than she had ever imagined.

5

NAVIGATING THE
UNKNOWN

Daphne was pleased the baby slept soundly through the night. In the morning, Mrs Leah fed him and showed Daphne how to change his nappy. He was well-behaved for Mrs Leah when she did her demonstration but turned into a flailing ball of limbs for Daphne when it was her turn.

"I've managed to borrow an old pram for him. It's not the best, dear, but it'll make things a little bit easier for you."

"Thanks, Mrs Leah."

Alas, nothing felt easy about looking after the boy. Daphne, at a loss for what to do with the lad, decided to take him for a stroll. Even though it had been a sunny start to the day, she remembered the sudden downpour the day before. She wrapped Sarah's old but thicker shawl around her shoulders and headed out, pushing the pram towards Victoria Park at the end of Commercial Road. It was her safe haven from the squalor of Whitechapel. Little Johnny found the pram's vibrations strangely soothing and was soon fast asleep again.

The girl found a bench and relaxed there for a moment watching a flock of tiny birds pecking for scraps. She wondered if one might be a lark, but in truth, she wasn't sure what one looked like. On the cobbled lane just beyond the park's wrought-iron perimeter, ladies in fine attire sheltered from the winter sun in their Hansom carriages as they rumbled by. Daphne turned to face the sun, closed her eyes, and bathed in the toasty golden glow.

Although there were only a few weeks left of her formal education, she worried about missing school to care for the baby. The authorities would take a dim view of her absence. However, on her next birthday, she would be officially free and needing to apply for jobs. One consideration was how to make her father happy. He had expressed concern about the dangers of sending his daughter to work in one of the many match-making factories in the area and instead suggested she join a household. As her finger traced around a repair to her skirt, she fantasised about donning a housemaid's smart black uniform and pure white pinny freshly laundered and pressed.

Her daydreaming ended when a lady who looked like she might be a nanny approached. She was accompanied by a little girl in a red coat and matching bonnet. As they both sat next to Daphne, the nanny looked into the baby basket with curiosity.

"Is this your brother or sister?"

"Yes—or perhaps, no."

"Either it is or isn't, surely?"

Daphne wasn't keen on repeating the baby's story again and her sour expression made the little girl run off.

"Don't go too far!" the nanny warned, preferring to stay in her seat.

"His name's Johnny, miss."

"I have a brother called Johnny. How old is he?"

Daphne noticed the woman didn't look much older than herself.

"Mrs Bridges says six months."

"Probably."

The stilted conversation ended when the tiny girl tottered back. Alas, the infant stumbled and fell. The nanny reached out, dragged the tot to her feet, and then scolded the child.

"You stupid girl. I told you to be careful. Now, look! You've got mud all over your coat. What will I say to your mama when we get back?"

As she smacked and shook the girl, the little thing went into full rebellion and screamed even more. Daphne wanted to intervene, but decided not to. Judging by the look of fury on the nanny's face, she just might get her ears boxed too.

"What a mess! I knew this would happen! Your mother will blame me for not looking after you properly," snapped the nanny as tried to brush off the mud with her pristine white handkerchief. "It's unrealistic to expect a young child to sit still for hours on end, but I am supposed to make her comply. I thought a walk would tire her out so she'd be ready for a nap when we returned. but here we are with her disobeying me and mud everywhere! My mistress will likely not be pleased with this mishap. My wages will suffer for this."

"I am sure the fresh air is good for you both. At least the coat kept the mud off that lovely dress. A quick wash and all will be well. She won't need it when she's back at her nice warm house," suggested Daphne, as she rolled Johnny's pram back and forth, the shouting unsettling him.

"That won't help. My mistress has eyes in the back of her head. She's got a right temper on her," grumbled the nanny. "I have to go now and sort this out. It's a good thing we don't have very far to go."

In temper, the nanny picked up the sobbing stumbling girl and marched off. Daphne watched her trudge out of the park, yanking the writhing child up every time she slipped down. Perhaps being a nanny was not so great after all. It seemed preferable, in theory, when compared with the risks of the match factory, or the backbreaking toil of the laundry, perhaps? But it seemed the job came with a heavy responsibility and—if the child needed constant discipline—not a happy job either.

As a dark cloud blotted out the sun, Daphne pulled her shawl tightly around her. Checking on the rocking pram, she was relieved to see the baby had dozed off. Her gaze then flitted to an excitable brown and white puppy. The

King Charles spaniel bounded around with its fluffy tail wagging and long ears flapping. Drawn to the furry creature, Daphne tiptoed over and bent down, extending an inviting hand. Remembering her manners, she searched for the pup's owner, but there was no one in sight. Suddenly, a small horse-drawn buggy came careering along the path. Instinctively, the young girl panicked worried the dog would be crushed beneath its wheels.

"Stop!" she shouted frantically as she waved her arms.

The driver quickly reined in the horse, narrowly missing the dog by mere inches. He leaned over to her in shock.

"What were you thinking, jumping out like that? Are you alright, miss? And the baby?"

"Oh no! Johnny! She had nearly forgotten about him in the chaos and ran over to check.

"Yes, thank God," she breathed a sigh of relief. "He's fine. We're all fine. And so's that little terror."

They spotted the puppy trotting down the path unconcerned that it had just narrowly escaped death. Daphne collapsed down on the bench with a bump, clutching the handle of the pram. Things could have been very different.

"Are you sure you're alright, miss?"

The baby still looked at rest, although Daphne felt jangled.

"Yes. Quite sure. I am not far from home. You get along, sir. We'll be fine."

The driver seemed satisfied with her answer and continued along in his buggy at a more sedate pace.

So much for a peaceful morning in the park! Daphne wondered if the baby needed feeding again soon. Mrs Leah had mentioned only giving him a little bone broth at lunchtime, but she hadn't said who would prepare it, or when. With the boy still settled, Daphne took the long way back home. She strolled down Brooks Road, past Mikhail Pavlovich's pawnbroker shop and Mr Horowitz the bakers, staring at the window displays. As she rounded the corner onto Prospect Street, she peered into the pram and smiled at first. But then her heart thumped as she leaned in closer. There was no sign of life in the infant's chest, no reassuring rise and fall, no pulse showing in his little neck.

> Daphne gently stroked his cheek. It was icy cold. "'Oh, no. Please, God, don't let him be dead," she pleaded. Despite not knowing what would happen to him when her parents returned, she couldn't bear the thought of him perishing. She knew that the community would point fingers at her and that she would never be able to shake off the title of 'child killer', just like poor Ruth Nithercott. Even now, people still spoke of the death of little Billy. Babies were lost all the time, but some deaths were talked about more than others.

Running out of ideas, she pinched his cheek as hard as she could. In agony, the tot yowled. *'Thank you, God. Now, please don't do that again. My nerves can't take it!'*

Daphne realised motherhood put her firmly out of her depth and decided it would be better to spend the rest of the day amongst women who had knowledge of babies. Adjusting her shawl and skirts, she hurried along Prospect Street, passing Jimmy McGinty's shop, the hub of local gossip, and the Little Drummer Boy, where Fergus, the landlord's drinking companion and burly bouncer, had just thrown out another set of brawling dockers.

Further down the street, two men wearing long, filthy coats and tatty canvas trousers emerged from a manhole cover. Even from a distance, they emitted an unpleasant smell. As they approached, one of them gave Daphne a playful wink and said to his companion:

"Cor, Danny, don't she remind you o' your daughter?"

"Which one, Jack? I got six."

"Ha ha, 'course. Anyway, look what I found today."

Daphne couldn't make out what it was, but she wasn't overly concerned. It would likely be something pungent. Danny rubbed the soiled object against his trousers, and to her surprise, a golden yellow glint shone through. As she hurried past, she caught the tail end of their conversation.

"Blimey! Danny! A whole sovereign."

"Aye, Jack. It looks as though some posh gent dropped this—most likely his winnings from a wager he made at one of McGinty's bare-knuckle fights at the pub."

"Are you sure it's real, Danny?"

Daphne felt queasy as the man bit the thing and nodded. The traces of unidentifiable brown sludge on his lips made her empty stomach turn again.

"You must feel like a millionaire."

"This job ain't too bad, sometimes, is it, Jacky, lad? Beers on me tonight."

'How lucky are they to find a whole sovereign?' She had heard of the coin but had never seen one before. She couldn't imagine the possibilities of what Danny may be able to buy with it, but the grin on his face said it was a grand discovery.

Mrs Bradley's front door was ajar, so Daphne peered inside. When she called out there was no response. Disappointed, she realised her much-needed guidance would have to wait. She wondered if Mrs Leah was at home, but again, there was no reply there either.

The baby began to fidget, sniffle and sob, then let out a piercing cry. Daphne hurried back to her family home and left the pram outside before rummaging through the larder cupboard, desperate to find something that could pass as a meal for the bairn. Beef knuckles were a luxury, so bone broth was out of the question. Would half a slice of bread in water suffice? She wasn't sure if babies could eat that, though, and Whitechapel's water supply was rank. After grabbing a dried-up sausage, she remembered that the tot had no teeth. What about butter? Or melted butter? Could she spoon that into him? She wasn't sure.

There was no placating Johnny now. He was weary, famished and increasingly cantankerous. She picked up the wailing baby and fussed over him, but this only served to exacerbate the situation. With her free hand, she found a rusty storage tin and, after a struggle, prised off the lid to reveal oats. *'Watery porridge, didn't Mrs Bradley say that was alright for a little 'un?'* She hoped so.

She poured some of the dusty white flakes into a pan and tried to recall how to make porridge. Adding some water, she prodded the contents as they thickened with the heat. The resulting starchy mess looked unappetising, but it didn't need to be tasty. If the boy was hungry enough, edible would do.

Johnny continued to scream, his red-faced head thrashing from side to side. With no help in sight, she took the basket off the pram frame and brought it inside, laying the baby down for a moment. She poured some of the sticky white goo into a bowl. It steamed like an engine boiler and was still far too hot. She recalled putting a spoonful of stew in her mouth last week only to get her tongue seared. It still felt tender from her mistake.

"You don't want to suffer the same fate as me, do you?" she cooed at the baby. "No one likes a scald!"

As she gingerly tested the porridge with her finger a few minutes later, she recoiled in pain and had to flick the scalding mixture off once more. To make matters worse, although it seemed improbable, baby Johnny managed to wail even louder.

"No, no, please don't cry. It won't be long. We just need to wait for it to cool a little."

She plunged a spoon into the gooey mixture, then raised it to her mouth and blew on it. After tentatively testing the temperature on her bottom lip a few times, the porridge seemed to be at a suitable temperature to offer to the baby.

"Here, see if you like it."

His gummy little mouth sucked on the spoon hungrily then yelled again, as he punched her hand and forearm with his tiny little fists.

"Be patient. Here's some more."

She tried to aim the food into his gaping mouth. At the last minute, the lad pushed the spoon away. The porridge smeared all over his face. He rubbed his hands in it and covered his clothes with the sticky mess, then continued to yell for all his worth. Writhing angrily, he was thoroughly uncooperative.

"Why can't you just calm down? What can I mop this mess up with? Mrs Leah will have my guts for garters letting you get in such a state. Stay still!"

The floor was in a lamentable state, so she picked up a rag rug and laid it high on the dining table, then rested baby Johnny on top of that. She hastened to the back yard to snatch a towel from the washing line, but before she could seize anything, she heard a sickening thud, and the baby's cries ceased.

6

A BURDON OF GUILT

Running back to the kitchen, Daphne found Johnny face-down on the flagstone floor, silent. She rushed over to check on him. He didn't seem to be obviously hurt, but he was limp. Shaking the child, she begged him to respond. Eventually, the screaming resumed. She grabbed the towel and wiped his face. Too scared to leave him alone to dampen a cloth to clean his clothes, they would have to remain encrusted with food. She picked up the pan of porridge again, which had cooled by now. Sitting on the chair, she tried to feed him once more. As he swallowed hungrily, she pushed more into his mouth, praying he wouldn't choke on it. The urgent scraping of the spoon against the empty bottom of the pan was soon a backdrop to yet more yelling.

"Please stop! I can't stand it. What is wrong with you? There's no food left."

The child yelled defiantly. Daphne shook the bairn again in temper, but there was no pacifying him.

"Now what? Are you thirsty? Will a drink shut you up? Let me find a baby's bottle. There must be one somewhere."

Searching through the cupboard with a baby in tow proved more difficult than she had anticipated. After laying nearly everything in the cupboard on the floor, right at the back, she found a bottle and a few teats.

"I'll have to put you down so I can fill it, Johnny."

Ignoring the baby's cries, she carefully placed him face down on the rag rug on the floor this time. She lifted the kettle and was pleased to find it full of cooled boiled water that she filled his bottle with before adding the teat.

"Here you are, Johnny, I've got just the thing for you. Drink up now, come on."

At first, he didn't want the teat, writhing and pushing her away, but after much persistence, Daphne got him to latch onto it. She held her breath in case he started bawling again or threw it all back up, but mercifully, he didn't. *'What an achievement!'* It seemed he thought so too. Finally, Johnny smiled and returned to being a gurgly, cheerful little child again.

Moments later, he seemed to strain and a grim odour filled the room. She tried to recall what Mrs Leah had shown her. As soon as his soiled nappy was unpinned, he urinated all over her, his own clothes, and the corner of the fresh, clean nappy she had hoped to put on him. She could feel her patience ebbing away to nothing.

"I hope you're proud of yourself. These are the only clothes you have for now. You'll have to wear them wet. Perhaps you'll learn then?"

As his expression contorted with pent-up anger, she held him down and pulled the nappy into position. She stuck the safety pin through the towelling fabric. As she lifted him up to inspect her handiwork, the nappy slipped off. On her third attempt, the nappy stayed in place. She couldn't bring herself to put the urine-soaked clothes back on him. She'd have to hunt around for something clean and dry.

With the blanket from the pram swaddled around him, she carried the tot upstairs. Clutching him a little too tightly as she made the ascent, he burped loudly in her ear. Laughing as she turned to admonish the lad, she noticed a pudgy lump forming on his forehead. The earlier fall had certainly left its mark. She hoped there was no real harm done. She knew there would be trouble when Mrs Bradley and Mrs Leah saw it.

In their absence, rooting around in her parents' bedroom felt wrong. Yet, leaving the child in soiled clothing for the rest of the day was no better. She laid Johnny on the bed and tucked the bulky eiderdown around him. On opening the top drawer of the small, worm-holed dresser, she saw some of her parents' possessions. She shut it quickly. Fortunately, in the bottom drawer, she discovered a neatly folded pile of baby clothes and she took out one of the garments.

"This will have to do."

The boy fidgeted so much that it took her a while to get him dressed. She was terrified of breaking one of his tender little arms, should she force it too much. Fortunately, the garment was a perfect fit. She found a pair of socks and a knitted cardigan to keep him warm. At the bottom of the drawer, she discovered a few old nappies. Though they were cotton and hard to dry, they were a welcome sight.

> "Now that you're a bit more comfortable, let's get you safe in your pram and I'll get this room in order before my parents get back. They'll think a storm's blown through if they see it like this!"

As the girl tidied up, Johnny fell asleep in the boxy confines of the pram basket. In a rare moment of peace and quiet that afternoon, Daphne cleared out the ashes from the hearth and lit a fire to make the room more inviting for her parents upon their return. Then, she slumped on one of the stools by the table. Her thoughts returned to her absent parents. On their return, what would they make of the lad? Mama might be more forgiving, but she was sure her papa would be incensed. But what else could she do? The strange woman had thrust the child upon her against her will, and she couldn't bring herself to abandon him. He would have perished. Alternatively, if she'd left him on a doorstep, someone may have snatched him and sold him to a baby farmer. When he was contentedly purring in his sleep, he was truly endearing. She peered into the pram.

> "Maybe one day I'll grow to love you—like a sister, not as a mother, mind!"

Her thoughts turned to her elder brother. Had he survived? The clerk said he may not, but miracles do happen.

Everyone had thought Mr Bradley would perish after his railway accident when he was helping to lay a new line into Fenchurch Street station. Her mother always told her to be optimistic, even though her father was an eternal pessimist. It was always doom and gloom with him. He thought the worst of everything.

Exhausted, Daphne folded her arms on the table and rested her weary head. Soon, she was fast asleep.

*

The baby's cries pierced the silence, jolting her awake. Dazed and woozy, she quickly threw some coals on the fire to make sure it would be warm for her parent's arrival. As she grabbed the pram and headed for the door, she stopped dead in her tracks. Mrs Leah stood on the doorstep with a knowing look on her face.

"I thought I heard him cry as I walked past," she said. "He must be wanting something. You look exhausted."

Daphne felt the weight of her fear and obligation crushing her. With her parents miles away and her brother's life hanging in the balance, she was left shattered and alone. Mrs Leah's concern for the foundling and the girl deepened. The other women would be hard-pressed to help both of them on top of their own families' needs. What would become of the Parker family with the odds so heavily stacked against them? As the trio headed for Mrs Leah's house, Daphne thought it best not to share the dark thoughts in her head, for fear of them coming true.

7

DRAINED AND WEARY

As Johnny was being breastfed, Daphne wasn't quite sure where to look. She was glad Mrs Leah didn't seem too concerned about the lump on his forehead. The woman gabbled incessantly, so there was never an opportunity for Daphne to ask if she could have avoided the injury in any case.

Mrs Leah was certainly more of a talker than a listener. She droned on about her daughter Ivy going for a walk with a girl from the neighbourhood, commenting on what both girls were wearing, and how Ivy's friend had wanted to take little Johnny out in the pram, but Mrs Leah hadn't deemed either girl tall enough to see over the top of the pram to navigate. She also rambled at length about the weather and whom she had encountered earlier when she walked back from Commercial Road. Daphne felt her eyes glaze over.

"There. That's him all done," Mrs Leah said as she buttoned up her dress.

The woman placed Johnny on the thick rug on the cold floor, providing him with a simple rattle to keep him entertained. Daphne sidled up to the tot, trying to see if they shared a resemblance. Was this really a relative or a complete stranger before her? She had brown eyes, whereas Johnny's were grey-blue, but their strong noses, brows and mouths bore a family likeness. As she peered closer, the boy swung his rattle vigorously, bashing her on the head. She laughed, rubbing the aching side of the impact.

As Mrs Leah lifted the casserole lid, Daphne noted the aroma of a fine stew cooking on the range. Her stomach grumbled, and she wondered if she should make something similar for her parents' return. All her life, everything she did was centred on them. She thought that if she willed them to come back with every fibre of her being, then perhaps they would.

She took little Johnny, balanced him on her hip, hugged him close, and then thanked Mrs Leah before leaving number seven. Out on the street, she noticed Ivy walking hand-in-hand with the slightly older girl. As she was spotted, Ivy let go and ran towards Daphne, clamping her arms around her legs and shoving her face into her skirts.

"What's up with you?" Daphne inquired, unsure why the girl wanted to be so clingy.

"Nothing's wrong. I'm just happy to see you."

"And I'm delighted to see you too. Did you enjoy your walk, Ivy?"

"I did. Would you come with me next time?"

"Perhaps. Maybe Saturday. Tomorrow's a school day."

"I'll be starting school soon!" Ivy trilled.

The older girl stood by watching silently. Daphne had no recollection of her face around Whitechapel.

"Do you go to St Patrick's school up the road?" Daphne asked, judging her to be about eleven.

The unknown girl nodded, with her head down.

"I go sometimes. I started last week."

As Daphne opened her front door, Ivy shifted her weight from one foot to another.

"Can I come into your house?"

"Maybe. I'll have to see if my parents are back with my brother though."

"I'll be off, then," added the other girl.

"She doesn't have to go does she?" said Ivy. "She can come in too?"

"Why not. It's nice and warm."

Daphne wheeled Johnny's pram inside her parents' house until it was a yard or so from the hearth. Then she stoked the coals until they crackled with a burst of orange. Stretching out her arms towards the fireplace, she asked the elder girl's name.

"Finoula."

"You're new around here, aren't you? Where do you live?"

The girl pointed vaguely outside as if expecting Daphne could use a sixth sense to know what she meant.

"I just moved in with my Grandma, 'cos my pa died."

"I'm sorry to hear that. Losing him must have been terrible."

Daphne couldn't imagine the heartache that would come from losing a parent, so she was taken aback by the girl's flippant response.

"Not really. He used to get drunk and use me as a punch bag. Tuberculosis did us all a favour," Finoula said.

"My uncle died from that," Ivy piped up, sitting on the rug, cross-legged.

"Who is your Grandma?" asked Daphne, wanting to learn if she lived in one of the better dwellings on Prospect Street.

"Grandma Betty."

That didn't help.

"Where does she live?"

Finoula pointed again towards Paternoster Row, down a little alleyway, where the rough people lived. Ivy jumped up.

"How about some tea? I'd love some. With two big spoons of sugar!"

"Alright, Ivy. Let's make a brew. I don't think we've got any sugar, though."

Daphne's stomach rumbled as she heard the church bells ring. It was almost five o'clock, and the darkness outside was settling in. Her parents had been gone for a full day now, and she couldn't help but wonder why they were taking so long to return. Spending another night at the Bradleys' place didn't appeal much. She wanted some normality in her life again. Daphne preferred her own bed, no matter how soft and comfortable Sarah said hers was. Her bed-fellow had a habit of thrashing around in her sleep and kicking her several times a night. She lit a grimy oil lamp and carried it across the room to the range, then set about making the tea.

"Let's play a game," Ivy whooped. "I am rather fond of card games."

"What can you play?" said Daphne.

"Snap. I can play that."

"I'll fetch the cards, but be quiet. Let's not wake little Johnny."

There was a gentle knock at the window. It was Mrs Bradley asking to be let in.

"Are your parents home yet, Daphne?"

"No, Mrs Bradley. I don't know what could have happened to them."

"Maybe your brother's still too poorly to travel? They know you're safe and don't need to worry about hurrying back."

She glanced down at the other girls.

"What's Ivy doing here, and who's this?"

"This is Finoula," Ivy announced. "She just moved here. She lives on Paternoster Row."

"The alley beside the common lodging houses?"

When Finoula nodded, Mrs Bradley turned back to Daphne.

"Are you sure your parents don't mind?"

"Mind what?"

"Strangers in their home while they are away?"

"Why would they mind?"

Mrs Bradley gave the newcomer a sideways disapproving look as if she was trying to tell Daphne something discreetly, but the girl couldn't quite make out what it was. The woman then frowned and spoke in a hushed tone into Daphne's ear.

"Just make sure everything's tucked away if you know what I mean."

"Tucked away?"

Daphne looked around the room.

"What needs tucking away? I've not long since tidied up."

Mrs Bradley spoke to Finoula.

"It's getting dark. All sorts of folks wander up and down this street—undesirable types. Shouldn't you be leaving soon?"

Finoula stood up to go and Ivy protested.

"But we haven't finished our game, Mrs Bradley!"

"You'll have plenty of time tomorrow, Ivy."

"But Daphne says she's going to school then."

"I'm not so sure now," Daphne replied, crestfallen. "If Mama and Papa don't arrive this evening, someone will have to look after Johnny tomorrow."

"Ivy, I expect your ma will be wondering where you are. You'd better go too."

Mrs Bradley ushered the two younger girls out.

"Now, straight home, the pair of you. If I catch you in the street, there will be trouble."

She closed the door and turned back to Daphne.

"You have to be careful with folk you don't know. Finoula doesn't seem to be from around here, and you can't always trust foreigners."

Daphne hadn't observed any difference in the girl's accent or colouring. A few words may have sounded different, but her accent was definitely British.

"I heard this morning from one of my friends that she and her mother used to live up north. They're a shady bunch, those northerners. As dodgy as foreigners, if you ask me. You've got to be careful and make sure that nothing valuable is left on show if you catch my drift?"

Daphne wondered why Mrs Bradley kept saying that? What valuables did the Parkers have, anyway? The only thing she could think of was her metal brooch and her mother's pair of dangly cut-glass earrings that looked a bit like amethysts. Mary always kept them wrapped up and hidden in an upstairs drawer. They had belonged to Daphne's grandmother, and her mother never wore them in case they ever got lost. Mary sometimes took them out to show Daphne how affluent her elders had been. She always said she would give them to her daughter on her twenty-first birthday, although the girl thought she would probably never wear them either. They were an heirloom to be treasured, and perhaps something to be pawned in times of need. Surely, Finoula wouldn't be rifling through her mother's belongings, even if she did live on the wrong side of the street? In the end, it was easier to agree with the woman.

"Thank you for the advice, Mrs Bradley. I shall put the valuables away. Erm, one quick question. Will Johnny and I be able to stay with you again tonight?"

"Aye. Come round at about six. Dinner will be ready. I'd better rush back before Mr Bradley arrives. He doesn't like it if I'm not there when he gets home."

As the worried wife hurried out, the oil lamp spluttered and flickered by the larder cupboard. Daphne lit the spare one just before she was plunged into darkness. She stoked the fire again thinking there wouldn't be much point using more coal to heat an empty home. She threw on a few pieces hoping it would last until the morning, in case they came back late that night.

Just before it was time for Daphne to leave for Mrs Bradley's, the little one awoke. His wailing filled the room, causing the girl to pause and consider what he needed this time. As he latched onto her finger, she let him suckle on it and felt the growing bond between them as well as the weight of his reliance on her for his every need. While he began to settle, Daphne couldn't help but dread his birth mother having a change of heart. The thought of the Parker family losing another precious baby was soul-crushing. With three infants already in the ground, Daphne couldn't face the possibility of a fourth. She began to dread every knock at the door. Would the woman return and cruelly separate them? Or could she hold onto this unexpected happiness?

8

A BOND FORMS

In the morning, Daphne awoke to find her parents still absent. Back at the family home, in the hearth, the previous night's glossy black coal had been replaced with a thin layer of powdery ash, and while she set about preparing the fire, she hesitated to light it. What was the point if no one might be there? The thought made Daphne glum. The good news was Mrs Leah kindly offered to feed Johnny again. The girl was overwhelmed with gratitude. What would she do without Johnny's wet nurse? She didn't want to think of the consequences.

Ivy called round. Daphne wondered if Finoula would drop by too. Should she hide everything, like Mrs Bradley had hinted? One thing was certain, Daphne was going to keep her eye on the newcomer to the street and find out more about her grandmother.

"Ivy, do you know where Finoula lives?"

"Yes. With her grandma."

"Yes, but where exactly?"

"No idea. She runs off through a side passage. Ma's told me not to go down there. Please let's play cards again, Daphne? My parents always say they are too tired to play with me."

"Alright. Let's play something else. I'll show you a new game. It's called Old Maid."

Daphne explained the rules which the young girl picked up quickly.

"You're clever, aren't you, Ivy?"

"Pa says that. He says I could be a doctor or an engineer when I grow up."

"I agree. I don't know what I'll do yet when I leave school. Mama says I should be working now, but pa wants me to finish my education first. He earns good money as a clerk down at the docks. Ma's got a job altering dresses for posh ladies which pays quite well, better than usual seamstress work. They buy the cheap ready-made ones from the factory warehouses, then want her to make it fit just right, and add a few trimmings, so it looks more expensive."

She told Ivy about the nanny in the park the day before.

"I don't want to be like her. That's not a job for me."

They finished the game and Ivy won the first hand.

"Can we play again?" the girl chirped as she gathered up the cards.

"I suppose so."

Daphne stood up, pushing back the tattered curtain to scour the road for any sign of her parents. Light and delicate snowflakes floated in the air, beginning to settle. The huddled men outside the Little Drummer Boy puffed on their pipes, drawing their coat collars up and their cap brims down. Daphne opened the door and peered up and down the street. A blast of cold air whistled around her knees. The bad weather would make her parents later still. She wished they would send a telegram or a letter, something to let her know what was happening. Meanwhile, Ivy was lost in her own little world, clapping her hands in glee at the sight of the snow-covered cobbles.

"I love snow. Let's build a snowman!"

"I love it too. But not now. Mama and papa can't get home with Henry if it falls too heavily."

Ivy looked up at Daphne.

"You miss them, don't you?"

"I do. I've never been alone for this long before. Even when we went with Henry just before he started his engineering apprenticeship, they took me with them."

"Is Henry dead?" Ivy blurted out. "My ma says he is."

Her childish honest was a shock.

"I don't know. I hope not," Daphne said then gulped as her throat tightened. "But even if he is, Ivy, they should be home with the body by now."

There was an awkward pause.

"Oh, Daphne! Baby Johnny's awake. May I play with him?"

The door closed with a groan, accompanied by Daphne. The boy was a real handful when he was awake. She took the tot out and put him on the rug holding him upright. Inexperienced, she had only just realised he could sit on his own quite well. Ivy crawled over and softly stroked his chin making him giggle.

"Ah, ain't he lovely!" she said, tickling him again. "My baby brother won't let me do that. He snaps at me like a yappy little dog."

The infant gave a toothless grin. Daphne remembered her late younger brother who had passed away with only one little milk tooth in his head—a tragic reminder of life's fragility. She hoped her elder brother was made of sterner stuff.

"Can he walk?" asked Ivy, lifting him to his feet.

Daphne lurched and caught him before he fell.

"Do be careful Ivy! What if he falls and bangs his head. He's got a bruise already!" she snapped. "No, I don't think he can walk yet. Although I have just found out he could sit up on his own, so maybe he will soon?"

Daphne lifted him just enough to stand him up. His legs staggered and wobbled even with the support. Ivy badgered her to experiment further.

"If you let go, you'll find out."

"No. It's wrong, Ivy."

"Go on. I dare you! Are you chicken or something?"

"No!"

"Go on," said Ivy, pulling at Daphne's fingers. "Let go."

The moment Daphne released her grip, the tot toppled over. At first, the infant chuckled, but a minute or two later his mood shifted and the wailing resumed.

"What is it this time? Why do you always have to scream and shout? Please, just shush!"

"Urgh! I know what it is. He stinks," said Ivy. "Needs changing, see. He's like my brother. My pa says my brother can crap for England some days."

Daphne gasped.

"He doesn't use those types of words, does he? You shouldn't either!"

"Why not?"

Daphne couldn't bring herself to use swear words. Ivy taunted her.

"My pa says it all the time. Cra—"

Daphne lurched forward, her grip on Ivy's wrist firm, as she spoke in a clipped, authoritative tone.

"Stop swearing, Ivy. If my mama comes in and hears you, she'll tan your backside good and proper."

Ivy began to cry. Daphne frowned with guilt.

"I'm sorry, Daphne. I didn't mean any harm. I was just trying to be more grown up. People outside the pub talk like that all the time."

"What labourers say outside The Little Drummer Boy is by the by. You are a young lady. Please don't repeat words like that, or you won't be welcome here anymore."

"I'm sorry. Please let me stay."

"Very well, but only if you're on your best behaviour."

Daphne undid the nappy pin and recoiled at the odour. Johnny was screaming and thrashing wildly.

"Urgh! You were right. He smells. Hold his legs up while I clean him with this rag."

The little girl pinched her nose with one hand and held one of Johnny's feet with the other.

"What do you call it, then, Daphne? That stuff you're wiping up?"

"Does it really matter?" the girl said sharply, making Ivy fall silent. "Blast! There are no nappies down here. I'd better see if there are any clean ones upstairs."

Daphne left a naked and shrieking Johnny propped up by cushions and ordered Ivy to keep an eye on him while she went rifling upstairs in the dresser. Then, the girl heard a blood-curdling cry and saw Ivy dragging Johnny towards the base of the stairs by one of his arms.

"Stop that right now, Ivy. Can't you see you're hurting him!"

"He kept crying and I couldn't carry him. I was bringing him to you. You need to look after him. He's not my responsibility," said the youngster with an angry pout.

With a sigh, Daphne examined the boy. Other than some dirt on his legs where they had slid along the flagstones, he seemed fine. She wrapped him in a shawl and then went out to the shared washhouse to launder the nappies.

"I hope I can get you clean and dry at some point today" she griped as her neighbour appeared.

"Och, I thought I heard ye out here," the woman said, grinning warmly and showing her one blackened front tooth. "How are ye managin'? I gather yer parents are nae home yet?"

Mrs Irvine hailed from Scotland and used strange-sounding words from time-to-time, which the young girl managed to guess from the context mostly.

"I'm doing quite well, and no, my parents are not back yet."

"If ye need clothes, lassie, just let me know. I've got a wee drawer full of them, tucked away in case another bairn comes along. I'd be glad tae help out."

"If they fit, I'd be very grateful."

"Do you mind if I—?" asked the neighbour, reaching towards little Johnny.

Daphne gladly passed the boy over, then shook her aching arms. A sheepish Ivy appeared at the communal wash-room door.

"Would ye like me to look after him for a wee while, lassie? Give ye a break? My boy, Mark, is ten now, and I'd love to have a little 'un to fuss over again."

"Ah, thank you. That would be a help. I've got mountains of nappies to wash."

Daphne rolled up her sleeves, the heat from the scalding water stinging her arm. She looked for a wooden dolly, but there were none. Ivy crept up beside her.

"His pram is in the front room if you'd like to take him for a stroll, Mrs Irvine. It looks like the snow's stopping."

Ivy started to say something but was interrupted.

"Nay lass. I just want to cuddle him a bit. Come and see me when yer washing's done, aye? Ta ta for now."

When they were alone, Ivy snarled at Daphne.

"Are you mad? You shouldn't have let that woman take Johnny!"

"Why not? I've got chores coming out of my ears."

"Because she murdered her baby."

"That's not true. He died."

"Well, my ma says she killed him."

"And mine says she didn't."

Daphne didn't have the time or the inclination to argue with the naïve young girl. Wasn't it obvious the woman didn't kill her own flesh and blood? The thought of it!

After scrubbing the soaked and soaped nappies relentlessly on the washboard, she ran the dripping fabric through the mangle over and over again.

"Can I help? Go on. Let me?" Ivy begged.

"No. And I suggest you keep well clear!"

"But that's not fair. I want to help."

"Just stand there and be quiet, then. Keep your hands to yourself. Last year I had an awful accident with one of these things. Got my finger caught in the rollers, and the nail came clean off. With everything else going on, Ivy, I don't want you being maimed on my conscience."

The mangle removed a lot of the water, but the nappies would still need pegging out. She shooed a sullen-faced Ivy away and went outside to the courtyard to check the weather. It was much cooler than the washroom but less humid and there was a gentle breeze. The two girls trotted over to the washing line, with Daphne praying she wouldn't drop her big bundle of clean laundry on the mucky floor. She was pleased the heavy grey snow clouds had moved on, and now the sun was beginning to emerge again.

"Ivy, can you pass me that peg bag?"

"Of course!"

Soon, the line across the courtyard was sagging under the weight of Daphne's clean laundry. Ivy still seemed gloomy, but Daphne reasoned if she wasn't happy she could always go home. Nobody was forcing her to stay. Much as she enjoyed the younger girl's company at times, she didn't want Ivy sulking about in a miserable mood. It was hard enough for Daphne to be cheerful as it was. Ivy perked up when a fluffy tabby kitten padded across the courtyard, appearing from the blackened-brick ginnel that separated their tenement from the one next door. She bent down to stroke it.

"Ah! Look at this little fella. Ain't he sweet, Daphne?"

"Urgh! I hope the mangy thing doesn't have fleas! My ma says fleas are dirty. The woman at number twenty had nits a while back. Forever scratching she was. And they jump."

Ivy tried to shoo the animal away with a big sweep of her arms. Daphne crouched down on her haunches behind the girl and then jumped up, terrifying her. Once Ivy's shock subsided, they fell about laughing.

Now that the nappy situation had been dealt with, the two girls went back down the alley and gazed along the road. One or two delivery boys glided past on new-fangled two-wheeled contraptions, and a few cart horses trudged by, but there were no Hansom cabs. The endless waiting was such a frustration for Daphne. A woman approached with a pram, this time Mrs Leah with her own baby.

"Ivy, are you behaving yourself? If not, you should come home now."

With a worried face, Ivy looked up at Daphne.

"Yes, Mrs Leah, wonderful. She's been a big help to me today."

"We found a tabby, ma. It was really cute."

"Well, I hope it wasn't infested with fleas."

"That's what I said, Mrs Leah. You can never be too careful," the girl added, giving Ivy a smug look.

"Many of the houses around us are infested with mites, Ivy. We don't want them infesting ours. Where's baby Johnny? Is he still with you or has his mother come for him?"

Ivy motioned to Mrs Leah to bend over, then whispered into her ear.

"She lent him to—"

The girl nodded her head towards Mrs Irvine's door and Mrs Leah's eyes widened.

"You mean—the child-killer?" she said, mouthing the last words, careful not to let anyone overhear.

"See, Daphne!" Ivy tutted as she turned to her, "I told you so!"

"My ma says the baby just died, and I'd rather believe her. A mother wouldn't kill her own baby, would she? Disease kills little 'uns around here, not people."

Daphne heard the rumble of coach wheels.

"Could that be ma and pa!"

Mrs Leah took Ivy's hand in anticipation. The coach passed without stopping.

"Wait!" Daphne called out. "Stop!"

Alas, the glossy black cab continued on and then turned right towards Tynedale Hall.

"Why didn't it stop? Why weren't my ma and pa in it?"

Tears rolled down Daphne's face, her disappointment and exhaustion finally taking their toll. Mrs Leah laid a comforting hand on her shoulder.

"Try not to fret, love. I'm sure they won't be away much longer. How about I make you a cup of tea?"

Daphne popped in, grabbed the coats and closed the door to number twenty-two.

"I'll just let Mrs Irvine know where I've got to."

When the girl knocked on her door softly there was no reply. There was no response to her louder insistent knock either. Daphne bit her lip as she went over to number seven.

"I mustn't stay long, Mrs Leah because Mrs Irvine won't know my whereabouts when she brings Johnny back."

Ivy gave her mother another one of her grim stares.

"Do you really think she killed her baby, Mrs Leah?"

"Well, that's what the folks around here say about Mrs Irvine. But there's no way to prove it. Otherwise, the courts would have her in prison by now."

"We learned about prison at school," Daphne said.

Ivy stopped fiddling with a loose thread on her sleeve and looked up.

"I'm going to school soon, ain't I, ma?"

"Yes, I hope you can learn more than I did at a few Sunday School sessions. There wasn't really any proper education when I was a girl. Not like now."

Mrs Leah's baby began to cry. She picked him up and began unbuttoning her blouse.

"I'd better be going," said Daphne. "Thank you for the tea."

As the girl walked home, the snow began to fall again. She sighed, knowing her laundry would never dry. It hung on the line, all crisp and crunchy, so she unpegged it outside, shook it, and then pegged it back up again inside, where it was hung on twine stretched across the room. Then she relit and stoked the fire, and the nappy material began belching steam as the heat penetrated it. Her mother detested drying the washing inside during the colder months as it worsened the mould problem, but it had to be done.

Daphne sank onto the stool, pondering the consequences of her parents' lengthy absence. The kitchen cupboard was almost bare, with only a few staples for the dinner she would prepare for their arrival, plus a few jars of applesauce her mother had made over the autumn when the fruit had been plentiful. The vegetables in the saucepan were on the turn and the coal scuttle was almost empty. Scrounging a few pennies from the neighbours was an option, perhaps in return for doing a bit of laundry or some other chore. It was best not to dwell on the possibility of ending up in the workhouse, but sometimes it was hard to push the dark thoughts away.

Teary-eyed, her fingertips caressed the dog-eared photograph of her parents on the day of their wedding. Mary had told her the memento had cost a fortune, even though her cousin had kindly taken it. In those days, photography was a new occupation, but he had got an apprenticeship at a studio at just the right time and had a talent for it—until he perished from the dreaded tuberculosis. She looked up at their happy expressions, longing to see them again. Silently, she pleaded for them to come home soon, then took the worn photograph and clasped it tightly into her chest. But would her wish come true? As she held the photograph close, she could only hope and wait.

9

RELIEF AND RESPITE

The sound of someone fumbling with the door handle made Daphne's heart skip a beat. Torn between hope that it might be Mrs Irvine or her parents, and dread that it could be Johnny's birth mother, she was unprepared for who she saw when she opened the door. With a shriek, she recognised the greying beard and sparkling eyes of a very special man standing on the doorstep.

"Grandpa!" she squealed as she ran into his burly tattooed arms.

"That's the kind of welcome I like," he said in his deep voice, delighted to be reunited with his beloved granddaughter.

He tried to ease her away, but she held on to him.

"Eh, my girl, Come on now, let's be having a goosey at you."

She took a step back.

"My, how you've grown since the last time I saw you."

"Oh, Grandpa, I'm so happy to see you. You won't believe what's happened."

"Put the kettle on then and you can tell me over a nice hot cup of tea."

He took off his deep blue sailor's coat and hung in on the hook on the back of the door with the others.

"Where's your mother?"

"I was going to tell you," Daphne replied as she made the tea. "Sit and I'll begin."

"Looking at you, you're too big to sit on my knee now. And I have so many nautical tales to share as well," he chuckled.

"Oh, how I've missed you and your stories, Grandpa!"

"I've missed you more. All those days on the high seas. Anyway, fire away—," he said before sipping his tea, "—What did you want to tell me?"

The happy mood in the room changed as she explained about Henry's accident. He tilted his head to the side and met her eyes.

"So, you don't know when they'll return from Essex?"

Daphne shook her head.

"No. And it keeps snowing. And there's something else too."

"There is?"

"Yes. A woman dropped off a foundling the day they left. Just thrust him at me with a brief note then ran away. She was convinced he belongs here, but I don't see how."

Walter Beresford examined the cryptic note with a puzzled expression while Daphne smoothed her apron.

"Did she say anything else?"

"Just that she insisted the father lived here. She said she'd double-checked the address apparently."

"I assure you I'm not the father," the silver-haired sailor joked.

"Tell me something I don't know. Shall I make you some dinner, Grandpa? I'm sure you must be hungry after your journey from Portsmouth."

"Famished. What's in the cupboard, Mother Hubbard? More than last time I visited I hope?"

Daphne checked the dried sausages in the stone box. They didn't look too shabby and there were just enough fresh root vegetables for two, even with her grandfather's large appetite.

"Fried sausages and veg all right, grandpa?" she called out as she chopped up the ingredients.

When she received no response, she went to check on him. There he was dozing beside the table, she tenderly draped a small blanket over him, then put the pans on the range. After wiping her hands on her apron, she left the house to inform Mrs Bradley that her grandfather had returned and she would not be staying the night, then called in at number twenty-four to collect baby Johnny. The door was ajar.

"Mrs Irvine, are you there?"

There was no sign of anyone. She looked around and called again, then decided that the woman must have taken Johnny for a stroll after all. She hastened back home. Grandpa was still dozing. She checked on their dinner and winced when she saw the sausages had turned to charcoal on one side and were pinkish, squishy and raw on the other. Biting her lip, she flipped them over and prodded at the crispy black bits to see if they would fall off. Then she gasped as she saw wisps of smoke coming from the vegetable pan which had boiled dry. She sloshed in some more water and hoped for the best. She wondered if she should wake Grandpa and ask him to keep an eye on the food as she looked for Johnny. There was also the question of when to let him know she was out of money and they needed to buy more food. It would be awful when her parents and recuperating brother arrived after their long journey and there was not a scrap of sustenance left.

As Grandpa slept, her stomach growled. She gazed at the sausages and then at the old man. She told herself he would never know how much she had cooked for dinner. Giving in to temptation, she popped one of the burned bangers into her mouth and bit off a chunk, deciding it was delicious despite the charring. She chewed slowly, relishing the gloriously fatty, meaty taste and ignoring the burnt notes on her palate. Her eyes sparkled with delight.

"I hope that isn't one of my bangers, missy?" came a voice from behind her.

She turned, the half-eaten sausage still in her hand.

"Caught in the act, young lady."

Luckily, the twinkle in his eyes told her he was joking, as usual. Swallowing quickly, she placed the remains of the sausage back on her grandfather's plate. Her mother loved to call sausages 'mystery bags' because she said you never quite knew what the butcher had put in them. However, since they tasted so good, Daphne didn't really care what they consisted of: beef, pork, chicken, offal, or even horse, she didn't mind.

With the meal finished, Daphne began clearing up. Now he was rested, it felt like the right time to ask her grandfather for some housekeeping money. There was no way Jimmy McGinty would allow a child to add any more items to the slate. The bill had to be settled on Fridays, and since her father wasn't there to collect his wages or pay the balance, she would have to find another way to cover the hole in the family finances. Fortunately, the solution presented itself when Grandpa looked in the larder for one of his favourite biscuits and found none.

> "Do you know what, I quite fancy a ginger snap as dessert? How about you go get some supplies, lass?"

Walter produced a tatty leather wallet from his trouser pocket.

> "Here, this should cover it. And why not treat yourself to some humbugs as well, while I nip up the stairs and unpack my bag. How are we doing for coal?"

He peered into the coal scuttle and examined the three meagre lumps hiding inside.

"Order a sack from the coal merchants. Get a big one. We don't want to freeze to death."

"Are you certain, Grandpa? Can you afford all this?"

"Aye. I wouldn't offer otherwise. And there's Pavlovich's if we get really stuck. I can pawn my pocket watch."

She rose onto her tiptoes and kissed his cheek, her soft face rubbing against his wiry sideburns. He jingled some coins into her hands and she felt the weight of her financial troubles lift with each clink.

"Thank you, Grandpa. I won't be long."

With a determined spirit, she made her way to the coal merchants and then braved a short stop at McGinty's. Despite her worries, the warmth of her grandfather's love and his unwavering devotion to their family filled her with hope. Little did she know, fate had more hardship in store for them than just the biting cold.

10

HEARTBREAK AND TRAGEDY

Despite their modest surroundings, the warmth of the range and the sweet aroma of hot cocoa created a cosy cocoon for Daphne and her grandfather. As they sipped their steaming cups of cocoa, Walter regaled her with more of his fanciful tales, transporting her to a different time and place. The church bell tolled again. It was getting late.

"I'd better check with Mrs Irvine again, to see if she's done with the baby," she said, not at all eagerly.

"A girl your age shouldn't have to worry about a baby."

He took out his pipe and lit it. The baccy smelled sweeter than Mr Bradley's.

"If this little 'un stays with us, there will be two babies, Grandpa."

"Two?" said Walter, sitting up and leaning forward.

"You didn't think to tell me your mum was expecting? By Jove, girl. This is important news."

"Oh, I'm so sorry. What with everything else happening it slipped my mind."

"Ah, don't you worry yourself, flower," he said as he leaned back.

"I named the foundling after my little brother Johnny, and pa, I suppose. Do you think ma will mind?"

Shrugging, he banged his pipe over the hearth.

"I think she'll be more worried about him being here, than the name you pick. Anyway, I'm nipping down to the Little Drummer Boy for a pint and a catch-up with a few mates. I'll see you later."

"Night, Grandpa. Don't get—what's the slang the labourers use for drunk? Brahms and Liszt?"

"Who taught you that expression?" he chuckled. "And, no I won't. One pint and I'll be back."

Walter got his coat and continued to chuckle at his granddaughter's comment as he headed out. Daphne walked through the back yard and over to Mrs Irvine's back door, lifting her dress to avoid the mud. She saw the woman singing softly to baby Johnny on the doorstep.

"Ah, Daphne. I dinnae expect ye so soon!" she said, lovingly cuddling the tot to her bosom. "I've had such a grand time looking after this wee one! He's been such an angel. Not a hint o' trouble the whole time."

For Daphne, it felt like ages since she last saw Johnny. Mrs Irvine's wide grin revealed the lone black tooth once more.

"Thanks for your help. Grandad's back now, so things will get easier for me."

"Och, that's nice. I was just thinkin' if it turns out he's not part o' yer kin—could I keep him for myself?"

"For good, you mean?" said Daphne, with suspicion.

"I've wanted another babbie for the last few years, but God hasn't blessed me with one. This little chap is like a gift o' heaven."

"Do you think so?"

"They say all babies are gifts o' heaven, Daphne."

The conversation came to a halt. Daphne couldn't decide whether she wanted the boy back or not. Her grandfather had said she was too young to be concerned about a baby, and her father had plans for her education. Furthermore, would her mother be willing to accept another child, especially if it turned out to be her father's or husband's? However, the cute little baby was worming his way into her affections, and she feared that her heart would be shattered if she had to part with him for good.

Mrs Irvine lifted the lad up and gazed into his cheerful little eyes.

"This wee chap is so happy and healthy. Did his ma say anything when she handed him over?"

"Um, she just asked if Hank was home. When I said I didn't know anyone by that name, she dumped him in my arms and ran off anyway."

"I reckon he could be your grandad's. He's a widower, yes?"

The girl appeared confused by the question.

"That doesn't add up. Gramps has been at sea for nearly a year. And he's three times that woman's age!" her shocked voice concluded.

Daphne reached out to retrieve the boy, but Mrs Irvine held onto him while turning her back as if to shield the child.

"Let me keep him. I promise, if your kin wants him back, I'll return him immediately. Please?"

"You will take care of him, won't you? You wouldn't hurt him, would you?" asked Daphne, worried about the accusations against Mrs Irvine.

"Och, why would I ever do that?" she said indignantly, but then softened. "Ach, I can't blame ye, lassie. You've heard what the loose-tongued folk have had to say, no doubt?"

Daphne nodded. Mrs Irvine, cradling little Johnny in her arms, explained tearfully.

"I didn't kill my child. He died in his slumbers. Nothing was wrong with him. He hadn't had any illness and I didn't do anything to him. He just died. The Lord called for him, that's all there is to it,"

Daphne gazed at the woman sympathetically, seeing the pain etched on her face. She knew the gossip that had circulated about Mrs Irvine, but looking at the poor woman now, she couldn't believe that she was capable of such a horrific act.

> "How about this? You can look after him until my parents get back, then we can decide? In the meantime, Mrs Leah has offered to wet nurse him so you'll need to arrange that between you two."

Mrs Irvine nodded gratefully, looking down at the baby in her arms. Daphne could see the love and care in the woman's eyes and knew in her heart, the bairn was in good hands.

As she made her way up Prospect Street, she hoped God wouldn't object to her giving the baby away. Mrs Leah didn't seem convinced when Daphne told her of her decision.

> "Well, there's no smoke without fire," the woman said as she watched the two girls do battle with a jigsaw.

> "But there wasn't a fire, ma? He just died."

> "You silly girl, Ivy. That's just an expression. Anyway, people don't just die, not even babies. There's always a reason. That's why the doctor or the coroner gets involved—to find the reason."

Daphne watched as Mrs Leah changed her own baby's nappy, and she felt a weight lifted from her shoulders. Although she adored Johnny, she was grateful that she wouldn't have to do such a disgusting job for a while.

"Oh, there's some good news. Grandpa arrived home today. He's seen us right for supplies and coal."

"That's good."

"I'd better be going back now. Gramps said he wouldn't be long at the pub. He's just having one pint."

Mrs Leah raised an eyebrow.

"One pint, you say? Since when were sailors on shore leave known to limit themselves to one?"

"Bye then," said Daphne, not wanting to get drawn into the debate.

In the street, she saw Sarah Bradley ahead and hurried to catch up.

"I've got some good news. Mrs Irvine wants to keep Johnny for a bit, so I don't have to worry about him. Will you tell your ma?"

Sarah's eyes opened wide.

"Yes, I know what everyone thinks. But I don't believe she's capable of killing her child. And she seems to love and care for Johnny. I've seen it with my own eyes."

"Do you want to come in for a bit, Daphne?"

"Just for a minute. Will you be around tomorrow? I could do with a bit of light relief from all the worry."

"No. But I am free on Sunday. We could go somewhere nice after church?"

"We'll see. It all depends on— you know—things."

"Of course, I understand, treacle. Keep your chin up."

"I will. Night."

As Sarah closed the door, Daphne rubbed her hands to warm them. Arriving home, she was pleasantly surprised to see her heavily pregnant mother also warming herself by the fire.

"Mama, thank goodness you're home. I have such much to tell you."

Mary gazed at her with reddened eyes, wearily got to her feet, and embraced her daughter with a powerful grip. Daphne was taken aback. Her mother was not one to show her emotions openly. After struggling for a moment, the young girl finally managed to wiggle free.

"Where's papa?" she asked, looking around as she stepped away. "Has he gone to the corner shop? And my brother? Can I go and see him?"

"No, well, err."

Her mother pulled a handkerchief out of her sleeve cuff and dabbed her tear-stained cheeks.

"You see—" Mary began again. "Oh, Daphne, my darling girl. It's so awful. I can't begin to explain."

Daphne looked around the room for signs of them, but could only see her mother's belongings.

"Is papa still with Henry?"

Mary shook her head.

"Henry's not dead, is he? Has papa stayed to make the arrangements? Or escort the body back?" Daphne croaked.

Sniffing, her mother shook her head.

"Sit, child."

All sorts of ideas swum around Daphne's brain as she slumped on the stool.

"When we arrived, your father was distraught. We had missed the chance to see Henry before the Lord had taken him. Your papa, not in his right mind, visited the workshop to try to learn more about the accident. The foreman felt sorry for him and kept plying him with drinks. Your father wandered off in a melancholic stupor, and they believe he fell from a bridge near the station. Two days later, they found him washed up on the riverbank, drowned."

"No! You must be wrong!"

"The funerals are tomorrow. Both of them, at Bethnal Green Cemetery. The bodies are coming back to the undertakers tonight or in the morning. The railway company is organising that."

The scene was surreal, almost dreamlike. Was it all a figment of her imagination? Daphne blinked and pinched herself, but the reality remained unchanged. Her mother, grief-stricken and desolate, sat silently on her stool, wringing her hands and staring at the floor. Despite Daphne's own desire for answers, her heart went out to her mother.

"Why didn't you call for me? You were all alone for days?"

"There wasn't time. It all happened so suddenly, one disaster after another. And you're still so young. I should be taking care of you!"

"But Mama, I'm sixteen!"

"Anyway, it's too late now."

Daphne leapt to her feet.

"I'll go find Grandpa. He's got shore leave, and he's at the Drummer Boy."

Her mother's mood brightened briefly.

"How fortunate for us in this darkest of hours. I'll come with you."

Before they could leave, Mrs Irvine called round.

"Oh, is that you, Mary? You're back. Can I have a moment, please?"

Daphne recognised that it was not the right moment for little Johnny's existence to be blurted out. She quickly made her way over to the woman to stop her from spilling the beans. Daphne and Mrs Irvine had a whispered discussion on the doorstep about the tragic news.

"By Jove, Daphne! My heart breaks for you."

"We're just off to find Grandpa. Will you excuse us, please?"

"Of course, of course. Please give your mother my sympathies. Don't worry about the baby. He'll be in good hands with me."

"Thank you, Mrs Irvine. Bye for now," she said, closing the door in the woman's face.

"What did she want, Daphne?"

"Nothing much, mama. She just heard you were back."

"Did you tell her anything?"

"I'm sorry, I had to. I don't like keeping secrets."

Guilt stabbed at the girl. Not mentioning Little Johnny was a very big secret.

"Good. If you tell that woman anything the whole street soon finds out. Now I won't have to inform everyone individually. Come on then. Let's find your Grandpa."

The mother and daughter arrived at The Little Drummer Boy and stopped outside.

"We can't go in there. It's not a place for women," said her mother, as she looked inside. "Listen to all that noise."

The smoky, booze-laden place was raucous, with laughter and ribaldry streaming out of the crack between the heavy double doors guarding the entrance.

"Shall we ask Fergus to go in and look for Grandpa?"

They both took a deep breath as the bulky Irish doorman came closer.

"Hello, ladies," the man greeted. "You're not the usual sort of, err—ladies—we have in our establishment. Can I help you at all?"

Fergus made sure he pronounced the word 'ladies' in a derogatory way.

"No, sir," replied Daphne, unsure what sort of ladies he might be referring to, but keen not to be lumped in with them.

"Please would you ask if Mr Walter Beresford is inside?"

"Old Walt, is he back from his travels?"

"Yes. Now, would you just check for us?"

"Since you asked me nicely, I shall do as you ask. Who might I say requests his presence?"

"For goodness' sake, man, just go," cried her mother, losing her patience. "It's his daughter. And it's important."

Seamus's head poked out to find out who was shouting and why.

"You're supposed to be dealing with trouble, Fergus, not causing it! Bejeezus!"

The doorman grimaced as he went in to look for Walter. The Parkers stood outside the pub, watching numerous questionable men stumbling in and out of the establishment. It took quite some time before her grand-father finally appeared.

"Daphne! Mary, you're back!" he exclaimed, moving to greet them but sensing that something was amiss.

"Hang on, my love. I'll fetch my coat," he said, picking up on his daughter's dark demeanour.

Grandpa gave Daphne a glum look when her mother's back was turned.

"Right then, let's get you two back home," he said when he reappeared moments later.

"I'll put the kettle on." Daphne offered.

Grandpa hung up their coats, and her mother sank back on her stool, unable to speak. He followed his grand-daughter to the stove and cupped his gnarled seafaring hand over her ear.

"Well? What's happened?" he whispered.

"Oh, Grandpa!"

She rested her head on his shoulder, her favourite place of refuge.

"Let mama tell you. Sit with her while I do this."

Daphne saw the ginger cake, completely untouched. Silently, she broke down, knowing that her papa would never have the chance to enjoy it. After wiping away her tears to conceal her sorrow from her mother, she took a deep breath and brought the drinks over.

For Walter's benefit, Mary began the fateful tale, explaining how they had arrived less than an hour after Henry had been taken by the Lord. The railway company said he never regained consciousness after the accident.

"They were blasting through some rock to lay more track, and he was hit by some flying debris," her mother explained, her voice heavy with grief. "I've been advised that two other engineers in charge of using the dynamite are to be formally charged with manslaughter."

The news stunned Daphne and Walter was shell-shocked too. Gramp's focus quickly shifted to his son-in-law.

"Is Johnny helping the railway company with the funeral arrangements?"

Walter had a barrage of questions. Mary broke down, unable to continue. Daphne had to explain her father's fate although she didn't fully understand everything herself. As the seadog sat in silence, staring off into space and tugging at his wiry beard, a heavy question hung in the air.

"When are they bringing the bodies?" he finally asked, his voice flat and empty.

"Tonight, or in the morning, I think."

Mary stood up, groaning and holding her belly as she spoke. Silence settled over the room once again, broken only by Mary's deep, sharp sniffs as she tried to boost her resolve.

"It's time to start preparing for the wake," Mrs Parker said, her voice firm. "I'll have to go to McGinty's in the morning. If Jimmy finds out I chose someone else for the catering, it won't end well."

She looked at Daphne and Walter, her eyes pleading.

"Will you both sleep in my room tonight, my dears? I don't want to be alone."

As they gathered in Mary's cramped bedroom, the weight of the impending double funeral was almost suffocating. The Parker family had faced many challenges in life, but these last few days felt particularly soul-crushing. How much more could the family endure before they broke under the strain?

11

FACING THE
UNTHINKABLE

The morning arrived all too soon. Daphne rose quietly from her bed, mindful not to wake her grieving mother. She slipped into her best dress, then came downstairs to find her grandfather in the kitchen busy with chores. He had struck a deal with Jimmy's corner shop and set to work making sandwiches for the wake, carefully arranging them on the family's few plates. Even the leftover ginger cake was given a second lease of life with some icing sugar dusted on it. Normally a tedious task, preparing a mountain of food brought them a sense of purpose and normalcy to an otherwise bleak and trying time.

"Take your ma up a cup of tea," Grandpa said after he had checked that everything had been prepared.

There was no need to go upstairs. Mary had shuffled down when she heard the kettle whistle.

"You are good to me! Thank you."

As she sipped her tea, Daphne leaned towards her grandfather.

"Should we tell her about—?" she whispered as she nodded towards Mrs Irvine's. "I think we should tell her before someone else does."

"What are you two plotting and scheming about?"

Walter told Mary about the foundling.

"Is this true, Daphne? The mother asked for Harry?"

"Well, I'm sure I ain't that baby's father. I was thousands of miles away for one thing. And your Johnny? Never. She must have the wrong address."

"Indeed. And Mrs Irvine is happy to keep the baby until we decide what to do? Perhaps we can sort out this mess after the funeral."

Daphne nodded then slumped beside her mother and rested her head on her bony shoulder.

"Poor child. You've had to cope with all that on your own. Well done you for not abandoning him like his heartless mother. What's he like, this baby?"

"A cheerful little thing, if I'm honest, ma. I called him Johnny. After Johnny Junior."

"How bittersweet it is to hear that name, my love."

"—But Grandpa says you might want to call the new baby Johnny. We can call him something else."

"No, petal it's fine. No point getting all sentimental. Life goes on. Besides, I think this little one will be a girl," Mary said, stroking her belly.

"How do you know?"

"Just a feeling in my bones. Right, we better get a wriggle on. The undertakers might be here soon."

Daphne's determination appeared to dissipate at the mention of the undertaker.

"Oh, Gramps, how will we bear it?"

"I'll be here for you," he said as he stroked her curly tresses. "I've been thinking. It's time I stopped sailing the high seas. I'm getting on a bit for such a demanding job. From now on, I'll be around to look after you all."

"You'd do that for us?" Daphne said as she looked him in the eye. "Grandpa, that'd be a real sacrifice. You love your life at sea."

"Yes, I do. But I love you more."

Mary smiled weakly.

"Are you sure, pa?"

"Never more certain, my dears. I have a small amount of savings I've kept over the years, and there's my sailors' pension from the Navy, so we'll get along just fine—. Gosh, look. The hearses are coming."

Mary tried to stand but looked woozy. Her eyes were glassy and her breathing shallow. Walter forced her to sit down on the stool. He crouched in front of her like a coach speaking to his bare-knuckle boxer, cupping her face in his hands to focus her attention.

"I know you want to go, Mary, but I think it's too much strain. Your bairn's due soon. Look at the size of you. You and Daphne should stay here. You don't want us organising your funeral next."

"Mama!" Daphne said with a pout.

Mary fought to free her head.

"Whether you think it's right or wrong, I'm going to the service, Walter Beresford. And so is Daphne. If you're serious about caring for us, you can start right now!"

Begrudgingly, the old man yielded and helped them into their coats.

The Parker family emerged from number twenty-two. Grandpa respectfully bowed his head and held his hat. Daphne helped her mother step outside. The neighbours filed past and offered their condolences. Two coffins, one plain and one fancier wrapped in a railway company flag were carried on small wooden hearses pulled by two mangy black horses. Clearly, the railway company was comfortable with cutting corners with the service.

Those closest to the deceased took their place directly behind the hearses, followed by most of Prospect Street's residents, the Thornhills, the Cavendishs, the Leahs, the Bradleys and even old Lydia Kirkham. Daphne had expected only a few to attend since it was a weekday. She hadn't anticipated such a large turnout. Standing on her tiptoes, she whispered in her grandfather's ear.

"Let's hope not everyone can attend the wake, Grandpa. We don't have enough to feed them all!"

The snaking line of mourners grew and grew. The less able-bodied stood in their doorways, hats in hands, heads bowed. At a respectful pace, the procession marched out of Prospect Street, up Commercial Road and onto Bethnal Green towards the cemetery. Despite their poor condition, the horses plodded forward with a solemn determination. The creaking of the wooden carts added to the heartbreaking atmosphere. A long line of mourners trailed behind the hearses, shuffling their feet in unison and lowering their heads in respect. The sound of their hushed whispers and muffled sobs was barely audible over the clip-clop of the horses' hooves and the bustling city beyond.

Daphne noticed her mother wincing and heard her mumbling to herself.

"Mama, are you alright?" Daphne whispered.

Her mother nodded bravely, but it was clear that something troubled her deeply. As they arrived at the graveside, Mary gave another sharp intake of breath. Grandpa took his daughter and granddaughter by the elbows and guided them to the far side of the plot as the other mourners dispersed around the grave. It was a peculiar situation. The turnout was impressive, given that Daphne's father was pleasant but not particularly popular. He had impeccable manners and solitary habits.

"Ashes to ashes, dust to dust," the priest droned.

Gazing into the dark abyss before her, Daphne found it hard to accept that she would never again see her father and brother again. No more practical jokes. No more birthdays. No more Christmases. When her grandfather offered her the wooden box of soil, she threw a few handfuls into the grave and watched as they thudded and scattered on the lids. When her grandfather went to talk to another mourner, she let a few tears fall. Her mother stood motionless, except for cupping her belly again. Daphne's eyes stung as she observed her mother's expression of numbed sadness. The girl reached for her mother's comforting hand, but instead of affection, Mary stiffened and pulled away.

"Mama, come on, let's go. It's all over now," Daphne urged.

"It's only just begun," her mother whispered, her voice tight.

"What do you mean? What has begun?"

Mary said nothing as Daphne felt her hand suddenly grasped and then crushed by her distraught mother.

"Mama, come on. Let's get home and have a cup of tea."

"I can't, my love. It's the baby."

"But he's at Mrs Irvine's. You don't need to worry."

"Not that baby, this one," Mary gasped as her knees buckled.

She gave a strangled cry, then gripped her belly. Daphne held her mother up with a steadying hand under her armpit, but she was like a dead weight. Help was needed—and soon. Father Lane strode towards them, his hands clasped reverentially in front of his crisp black cassock.

"Mrs Parker, it's freezing out here. It's time we got you home."

"I think she's having the baby, father" cried Daphne, struggling to keep her mother upright. "Please! You've got to help us."

The priest's eyes widened in a momentary panic.

"You mean—?"

As the cleric flapped and fussed Daphne's grandfather reappeared.

"It's alright. I've found a midwife. I recognised her among the crowd."

"How did you know, Grandpa?" asked Daphne.

"Never mind how I knew. Let's just help your mother."

The rugged old sailor took Mary's arm and put it around his neck, and then he put his arm around her waist.

"Come on, love. You've been so brave and done your duty today. Let's get you home now. You can't give birth outside in a cemetery, can you?"

"But I can't walk, pa. I'm in too much pain. And I'm worried the slightest movement and the bairn might slide right out. You've got to help me!"

She groaned, her eyes rolled and her brow beaded with more sweat. The midwife gently placed her hand on Mary's stomach.

"Do you feel like you want to push, dear?"

Mary nodded weakly.

"Oh, dear. This really isn't the place," grizzled the midwife, as she looked around. "Hey! You there! Stop!"

She spotted the carts that had transported the coffins were trundling towards the wrought-iron gates that lead out of the churchyard.

"Run to them, girl. Tell the drivers to stop."

The drivers turned as Daphne hurried towards them, her skirts flapping and hair billowing as she yelled.

"I know the funeral's over, but we need someone to take my mother home quickly. She's having a baby."

"What? Now? This very minute?"

"Yes! Please help."

Mary was manhandled towards the nearest cart as it rolled to meet her. As she lifted her leg to stand on the small footplate, she screamed:

"Quick, it's coming. I can feel it. Oh, please not here!"

"I don't think you've got much choice in that, my lovely," cooed the midwife.

Mary used the last of her strength to flop onto the hearse. The men looked away as the midwife lifted the woman's skirts to begin the delivery. Less than ten minutes later, Mary Parker saw a blood-soaked wrinkly baby screaming before her.

"Congratulations! You have a bonnie baby girl, Mrs Parker" the midwife announced as she lifted the bairn and cut the cord. "Here, you go. Meet your daughter."

The midwife wiped the child with Mary's dark grey shawl and handed the wriggling tot across to her exhausted yet relieved mother.

"She looks like your Johnny. Got his eyes, so she has," said Walter.

Daphne heard a muffled cry followed by cheers from everyone, including the men who still stood politely facing the other way. Walter covered the mother and daughter pair with his thick woollen greatcoat.

"You need this more than me, my love."

"God be praised," preached Father Lane. "As one life ends, another begins. Hallelujah."

"Hallelujah," the crowd replied.

The midwife elbowed her way over to the mother again.

"You all can do your fawning and admiring later. Walter, we need to get your daughter home right away so I can clean her up properly. We don't want her getting infected, now do we?"

The midwife settled into a seat next to her patient, while the old man slipped a coin to the driver before proudly climbing onto the small wooden carriage next to his daughter and newest granddaughter.

"Please take us to Prospect Street, would you, my good man?"

"Certainly, sir."

"I'll catch you up," Daphne said with a wave.

"Well, not everybody who's born on a hearse," her grandfather said as the vehicle pulled away. "You're going to be a very special girl."

The clip-clopping of the horse's hooves drowned out Mary's faint reply.

"What a turn of events," exclaimed one of the mourners, as the throng walked back.

Daphne turned from watching the cart to see Mrs Bradley respond.

"Well, I didn't think she was due any time soon. I was wrong! The wonders of nature. Fancy turning tragedy into triumph. I remember once—"

Daphne chose not to engage in the mourners' chatter, craving some time to herself to make sense of the day, and pretended to pay attention as she followed along down

Commercial Road. Walking alone when most of the street had turned out to support the Parker family would have seemed very odd indeed.

"Daphne! Daphne, are you listening to me?" snapped Mrs Bradley. "I suppose you'll be going out to work now that your mother will be laid up for a bit?"

"I hadn't really thought about it," the girl muttered.

"Well, your grandfather won't be able to support the four of you on his wage, and your mother won't be fit for work for a few weeks yet. It's time for you to bring in some extra money. Our Sarah enjoys her job at the department store. Would you like me to ask if they need anyone else?"

"I haven't finished my education yet. My father wouldn't have wanted me to leave early."

"He should have thought before he—"

Daphne halted in her tracks.

"Before he what?"

The older woman continued to walk briskly, and Daphne hastened to catch up. She wasn't about to let the comment go unnoticed.

"Before he jumped off the bridge, do you mean?" Daphne asked.

"I didn't mean anything. I should keep quiet," Mrs Bradley replied.

"Is that what everyone thinks? That my father took his own life? He wouldn't have, not my papa. Father

Lane says it's a mortal sin. Papa would have gone to hell if he did, and he doesn't deserve that. He was a good man. Besides, Father Lane wouldn't have given him a proper burial if it was suicide."

"You Catholics," scoffed Mrs Bradley, stopping to look in a milliner's shop window. "Gosh! What a stunning bonnet. Isn't that the most adorable thing you've ever seen?"

Daphne glanced at it, thinking it looked rather drab. Without replying, she carried on alone. There was no way her father had killed himself. Her ma would have told her for one thing. Then again would she? What if she wouldn't want her daughter worrying about his soul, lost forever, tormented in the darkest depths of hell.

Staring up at the blanket of cloud cover, there was no chance of catching a glimpse of her father up in heaven. With a sigh, she continued walking. Mrs Bradley had disappeared. Daphne correctly guessed the woman had gone in to try on the hat, even though she couldn't afford it. What was the point, Daphne wondered? She had forgotten most of Prospect Street's residents had a habit of admiring things they knew they could never buy. It made them feel better, providing a diversion from their wretched lives for a fleeting moment.

Still wanting time to herself, she decided to take a more indirect route back home and consider her work options. Working at the library at Tynedale Hall or in a shop using her mental arithmetic skills both seemed viable. As she stopped outside a cake shop, she watched the staff in the open kitchen baking and boxing up the doughy treats. The thought of working there and being able to bring home leftovers for her family was appealing.

Before her nerve could desert her, Daphne swung the door open with such gusto the little brass bell nearly swung off its wall fixing. Behind the counter was a cheery woman with a warm expression. Daphne seized the moment. It was time to support her family, just like Grandpa was.

12

A CLASH OF OPINIONS

"Please, Mrs—err—I don't suppose you have got a job going for a baker's assistant, have you?"

"And who might you be?" asked the woman, startled by the girl's forthrightness.

"Daphne Parker, ma'am. I need a job. The thing is, my pa just died and I reckon working here would be just right for me."

Daphne sniffed the aroma of freshly baked Victoria sponges. It was glorious.

"And you thought you'd be able to stand around and eat cake all day, did you?" asked the woman.

"No, ma'am, certainly not. I'm a hard worker."

The girl looked at the tempting array of delicacies on the counter, knowing full well that she would nibble on anything and everything if she could get away with it.

"Well, we don't need anybody, missy, so you'd better be on your way. Go on, shoo!"

Daphne thought there was no need for such rudeness. So much for the kind face. Her frustration with the assistant got the better of her.

"Well, that's for the best. I wouldn't want to work for someone as miserable as you, anyway!"

Daphne ran out, tempted to grab a cream cake to compensate her for the woman's derogatory comments, but didn't in case the matronly woman came after her brandishing a rolling pin.

What other local shops were there? There were a few on Brooks Road: Mr Pavlovich the pawnbroker, Mr Jones the blacksmith, and Berry's the ironmongers, but they weren't options. They would never employ a girl. But maybe the haberdashery shop on upmarket Wellington Road could work. Daphne pictured herself measuring out pretty ribbons and buttons, and cutting bolts of fabric to length with some razor-sharp scissors. It was a bit of a walk, but the girl made good use of her 'alone time'.

"Is there anything else I can assist you with today, ma'am?" Daphne rehearsed, adding a fake upper-class twang to her diction.

The first try wasn't quite right, but with a bit of practice, she believed it could work. Despite having only visited a haberdashery shop once, many years ago, she remembered all the buttons and bows on display vividly. The array of colours and textures had been mesmerising.

Determined to support her family in their time of need, she smoothed down her skirt, tucked her curly hair into her black bonnet, and reminded herself not to barge in like last time. With a broad smile on her face, she opened the door to the haberdashers. She strolled over, pretending to be interested in a luxurious tartan cloth while waiting for the sales assistant to finish serving another customer. Once she was free, she approached Daphne.

"Can I help you with anything?"

The assistant stood in front of the tartan, stroking it like it was a pedigree cat. Daphne attempted to sound polished once more.

"Good day, ma'am. Could you please inform me how I might contact the proprietor of this fine establishment?" she asked, hoping her eloquence would impress the woman.

"And what if I do?"

"I was wondering, ma'am, if the owner had need of an assistant? Since this is such a popular and well-stocked shop."

"Don't waste my time, you little ragamuffin. I've just chased off one of your light-fingered chums. I'm the proprietor if you must know. And I'll tell you something for nothing—you know where the door is. Go and steal from somebody else's shop. Now, hop it."

"Please, madam. I mean no harm. I am a good worker. Are you sure you don't need a little extra help from time to time?"

Daphne's arm made a sweeping arc across the masses of cluttered shelves. In truth, the woman was tired of long hours and lost sales. It was often too much for a single staff member. The shopkeeper scanned the jumbled merchandise. It was never as neat as she would like. There simply wasn't enough time to keep on top of everything. The girl picked up on her mood and appealed to her conscience.

"The thing is, my father passed away this week, and my mother has just had a baby, so she can't work for a while. Our landlord, Mr McGinty, isn't a patient man when it comes to the rent. If we fall behind, I don't know what we'll do. I promise I'll work very hard. My mother is depending on me. Please, ma'am, is there any chance you could give me a job? Even just a trial. I'll work for free. Go on. Please!"

"Perhaps. What references do you have?" said the woman eyeing the girl suspiciously.

""As it stands—err, none."

The woman frowned, irritated that her time was being wasted.

"You see, my father used to work as a clerk at the docks. It paid well enough for me to stay at school, so I didn't need to get one. However, I do have a talent for sewing. My mother often says that I'm the best needlewoman she's ever seen. And when it comes to mental arithmetic, I can add up like nobody's business. Would you like to test me?"

The woman raised a sceptical eyebrow.

"Okay, let's see how good you really are. What's eight multiplied by eight?"

"Sixty-four," the girl replied promptly.

"What about six sixty-fours?" the woman fired back.

Almost instantly, Daphne's face lit up with a smile.

"Three hundred and eighty-four!"

The woman nodded, impressed.

"Not bad at all. Alright. I'll give you a trial, but don't expect any special treatment. And one hint of bother and you'll get your marching orders. Understood?"

As Daphne was about to respond, the loud tinkle of the brass doorbell halted their bargaining. Two women bustled into the shop, their voices boisterous and their presence commanding. One of them pointed to a roll of exquisite blue silk.

"Oh, look, Loretta, do you think that silk would match my eyes?"

"It would be perfect, Maria. Just perfect!"

Moments later, the doorbell rang again and more customers trotted in with lengthy shopping lists. Daphne observed from a discreet distance as the shoppers were served but still cast her keen eyes and ears on all the prices quoted. The girl totted them up in her head as the shopkeeper wrapped the goods in fine sheets of crisp white paper.

"Two shillings and thruppence," she whispered to the owner.

The shopkeeper nodded at her new underling with a hint of a smile. As soon as all the ladies left the owner swung the sign on the door to 'closed'. She looked Daphne up and down again, her lips pursed to one side.

"Hmm. If you're going to work here, you'll need to change into something a little more—how shall I put it?"

Daphne's heart sank. She hadn't thought about her appearance. She didn't own anything good enough to wear, and neither did she have any money to buy something better. Her funeral attire would be the smartest she'd ever look.

"I have a dress that doesn't fit me anymore," the woman said as she patted her midriff. "I've gained some weight since marrying my husband. He loves puddings after our evening meal. But it looks like it would fit you. Come back at five o'clock this afternoon and I'll dig it out. If it fits, you can wear it tomorrow."

"Thank you, ma'am. My mama will be pleased. This is such a worry off our minds. You won't regret this I promise."

The lady flipped the door sign back to 'open'. As Daphne rushed out to tell her mother the good news, she remembered she had not asked the lady's name. She stuck her head round the door.

"I'm sorry, ma'am, forgive my manners. I'm a little flustered today. May I ask your name?"

"Miss Lawson. Lillian."

"I thought you said you're married."

"I am, but I keep my professional life separate from my personal life, so I use my maiden name for work."

Daphne stared at her, surprised.

"But all women take their husband's name when they get married?"

"Not all of them. Anyway, what's your name? I can't employ someone called 'thingy', can I?"

The mercurial woman's eyes twinkled, putting Daphne at ease. The lady looked too old to be recently married. She guessed her employer was in her early thirties.

"Miss Daphne Cassandra Beresford Parker at your service, ma'am."

She gave a curtsey, which triggered a broad smile on her employer's face.

"Stop all that nonsense. And there's no need to call me 'ma'am' either."

"Sorry, ma'am. I mean Miss Lawson."

"You said Beresford?"

"Yes, it's my mother's maiden name."

"My mother's too, Daphne. I wonder if we might be related?"

"Oh, I doubt that very much."

"What part of London does your father hail from?"

Not ashamed of her roots, but not wanting to admit that these days the family lived on Prospect Street either, she wondered how to reply. As Lillian's look became more insistent, she was saved when another customer came in, sparing her from the awkwardness.

"Please excuse me. I must be getting back. My mother will be worried. I'll see you later," she said then strode off down Wellington Road.

When she got home, she announced her good news.

"Mama! Grandpa! You'll never guess what I've done!"

"Quiet, child! Don't be so loud," her grandfather growled from the kitchen. "Your mother's trying to rest."

"I'm sorry, Grandpa. I am excited."

Her jaw dropped when she observed the man more closely, for he was holding not one, but two babies.

"That other one's not Johnny. Why are there two newborns?"

"This little fellow was born on the way home. On the hearse as well. You couldn't make it up."

"What do you mean?"

Grandpa shook his head at her naivety.

"Good grief. Did they teach you anything at that school of yours? They're twins, Daphne. Your mother had twins."

"On the cart?"

"Yes."

He handed one of them to her.

"Now, we have two more mouths to feed."

"Three, if Mrs Irvine doesn't keep Johnny," Daphne added forlornly

"Let's hope she will. She came earlier and asked to look after him for another night. Or maybe the mother will realise her mistake and come back and collect him? Or we get five minutes to go to the mission."

Daphne peered at the sleeping baby's face.

"Have I got the boy or the girl, Grandpa? I can't tell the difference yet. All babies look the same to me."

"I think that's the girl, you've got there."

"I hope they survive, not like Emma and Edmund. Your poor mother. They didn't live a week."

"I don't remember them. They arrived when I was little more than a bairn myself, didn't they?"

Walter nodded solemnly.

"What's mama going to call these little ones?"

"I haven't asked her yet. I doubt she knows. Too sad to think about it at the moment, I reckon. Although, I think she'd want to call the boy Johnny, in memory of your father."

"But we already have a 'Johnny.'"

"I know, but he isn't really ours, is he? Anyway, why were you so excited when you came in?"

After the latest revelation, Daphne felt her news had lost its steam.

"A job, Gramps."

"Who for? Your mother won't be able to work for a while yet."

"For me, silly. I thought that I'd need to work, seeing as papa's wages won't be supporting us anymore. I went into a shop on Wellington Road. I asked if there was any work I could do. The lady, Miss Lawson, said I could start tomorrow. Although she isn't really a 'Miss', she's a 'Mrs'. Anyway, she said I can start in the morning as long as the dress she's lending me fits. I've got to go back at five tonight to try it on."

"Slow down! I never understand you when you jabber on at that speed. Start again."

Daphne took a deep breath.

"It's true, Grandpa. I have to go back at five o'clock today, and she said she'll give me it, or did she say lend it? I don't remember—."

The torrent of information baffled Walter and he gave up trying to follow it all. The bairn in his arms began to doze off, so he gently laid the lad in the wooden drawer from the bedroom dresser that had been placed by the range. It was decked out with the softest blanket they owned.

"Looks like this one's tired too, Gramps. Where shall I put her?"

Walter took the child and laid her gently next to her sleeping sibling.

"Aren't you pleased about the job, Gramps?"

He said nothing so she tugged at his sleeve. Why wasn't he pleased for her?

"Grandpa?"

"Want a cuppa, lass?"

"Please. I'll take one to mama, too. I bet she'll be glad when she hears my news."

Walter picked up on her frustration.

"Look, love, it isn't that I don't care, it's just that your father thought it was important you got an education. He was so proud of you when you started attending school. To leave now, well, he would be disappointed."

"I know, Grandpa, but what do you always say? Needs must? This feels the right thing to do."

Walter fell silent. Saddened by his response, Daphne picked up a cuppa and carefully carried it upstairs. She paused half way up and peered over the handrail.

"I can always tell Miss Lawson I am not allowed to work there, Grandpa. If that's what you want."

As her sad little face vanished out of Walter's view, guilt tightened his throat.

Her mother was asleep, so the girl laid the cup gently by the bedside without waking her. Mary looked exhausted. Daphne was desperate to give her the news, to see her reaction, but her ivory-white face looked so peaceful in sleep she couldn't wake her. Coping with the twins would require all her energy. Daphne wondered why the first set of twins had died. She prayed these two wouldn't perish. After losing her husband and adult son, it would surely break her poor mother's heart.

13

EMBRACING A NEW PATH

Mary wouldn't get the peace she needed. There was a knock at the front door accompanied by a crowd of voices. Daphne sped downstairs and joined her grandfather in greeting them, hoping her mother would sleep through the wake's commiserations and occasional celebration of the arrival of the twins.

As the wake rumbled on, Daphne began to question the wisdom of taking the haberdasher's job. Her grandfather had not spoken to her since she had revealed her news. Growing weary of the visitors, she carried the crotchety babies upstairs. Mary could only nurse one at a time, so the twin who had to wait its turn bawled even louder. The whole situation gave Daphne a headache. Unable to speak with her mother, the girl left to walk the mile or so to Miss Lawson's shop, planning to arrive a little early to demonstrate her eagerness.

As she passed by the Leahs' place, Mrs Leah came out, holding Ivy by the hand.

"How are you, petal?" she asked, patting Daphne's shoulder. "It's so sad, what happened. And yet, that little one arriving just after the service. As the bible says, 'The Lord giveth and the Lord taketh away'."

Ivy wrapped her spindly arms around Daphne's legs, pinning her in position.

"I'm doing quite well, Mrs Leah, thank you."

"And your mother? And the baby?"

"You'll never believe this, but she's had twins."

"I beg your pardon?"

"My mother had twins, right after the funeral. Grandpa says the other one arrived just before she got home."

Mrs Leah put her hand to her mouth.

"The funeral was only a few hours ago. And now this. What a shock. I'm so sorry I couldn't make it to the service. My bairn was restless, and there was nobody to leave him with."

"Don't worry yourself., Mrs Leah. Please forgive me, I must dash. I am on an errand."

Daphne prised Ivy's arms off her thighs and turned towards Commercial Road. She refused to be late and risk Miss Lawson changing her mind about the job offer due to tardiness.

"Send my regards to your mother and tell her I'll drop by in the morning to see if she needs anything."

"Thank you. I will. Good day, Mrs Leah"

To avoid any further delay, Daphne swiftly departed from the woman's company. Mrs Leah had good intentions, but Daphne simply didn't have the time or energy to indulge in her chit-chat.

As Daphne stood outside the shop doorway, she found herself staring at the handle, feeling too afraid to go in. What if Miss Lawson had changed her mind? What if the dress she promised didn't fit? The endless possibilities made the girl's anxiety soar out of control. She hovered around outside awkwardly. The two ladies, who had been in the shop earlier, popped back for some more of the sumptuous blue fabric.

"I just had to get some more. It's perfect," the one said to the other, pushing past the girl as if she wasn't there.

Daphne wondered if she could remain polite to such snobbish customers. Could she hold her tongue if they were rude or cruel? But why would they be rude? If she were behind a counter looking presentable, she would be someone who would command respect. Miss Lawson looked impeccable, and Daphne decided her old cast-offs would be a significant improvement on her current attire. Alas, thirty minutes later, the girl was still pacing outside. Finally, Miss Lawson came to the door.

"Am I late? Please tell me I'm not. I'm sorry for my tardiness. Although, actually, I was on time. The shop seemed very busy and I didn't want to impose. So, I just stood here and lost track of time," Daphne said nervously.

"Well, don't just stand there, girl, come inside. I must confess I am rather disappointed. I thought you had changed your mind," the proprietor replied curtly.

"Gosh, no, Miss Lawson. I promise I haven't. I got a bit waylaid, but there is a good reason. My ma's had twins, not just the one baby I told you about. She had another one on her way back home on the hearse, so I really need this job more than ever."

"Twins? Today?" Miss Lawson asked, surprised. "— And two funerals?"

"Yes, miss, I promise. That's the truth. Cross my heart."

Miss Lawson surveyed Daphne, her brow furrowed. Did she believe the girl? After all, it was rather far-fetched. Thankfully, the shopkeeper's puzzled expression came from weighing up Daphne's dress size rather than the legitimacy of her mind-boggling story.

"I'll get the dress. Wait here. On second thoughts, come with me. I wouldn't want to leave you alone in the dark."

Was that a cover story? Was Miss Lawson wary of Daphne being light-fingered? It was understandable, given the number of rough characters that lurked in Whitechapel, Stepney, and Bow. Shopkeepers were right to be wary. London's notorious female gang, the Forty Elephants, were highly skilled at storing merchandise in secret pockets in their hooped skirts and absconding with it. They had even pulled off a heist at a Bond Street jeweller right under the nose of a trained security guard. Leaving an unknown girl in a shop full of valuables was a risk.

As they made their way upstairs, Miss Lawson and Daphne began to search for the dress that the former had in mind. The piles of cardboard boxes made the task a little difficult, but the shopkeeper was able to clear some space on the cluttered floor.

"I lived here once, would you believe?" she said, seemingly nostalgic for a moment.

As Miss Lawson swung open a wardrobe door, Daphne was taken aback by the colourful array of dresses within.

"Which one would you like?" Lillian asked.

Daphne trailed her fingers along the dresses, admiring their beauty.

"My goodness! And none of them fit you anymore?"

"I'm afraid not."

Miss Lawson pulled out a lovely damson dress and held it up against the girl.

"This one should do nicely."

Daphne hesitated. She needed something appropriate for mourning but didn't want to offend the woman.

"Silly me. You need a mourning dress. I do apologise. Mind like a sieve sometimes. So, we need black or purple then. Fear not, young lady, I'm sure I have something that will be perfect."

Lillian rummaged through the dresses and produced a dark-coloured one that looked promising. However, as she turned it around, Daphne spotted a huge bustle at the back, clearly thirty years out of style.

"It's—um—"

"Too old-fashioned? You're right. Nobody wears bustles anymore, Daphne. What else have I got?"

Daphne was amazed at the number of dresses and wondered why Lillian didn't sell them and buy something new. They took up so much room.

"How about this one? It can be altered if needed. It wouldn't take me long," Miss Lawson suggested, holding up another stunning garment.

The deep mauve dress looked perfect, with its high-necked collar and pleated ruffles. But this was such a tailored garment. How could she wear it? She was used to shapeless shift dresses and pinnies.

"Here, try it on."

"Now?"

"Yes. How else will we know if it fits? I shan't look if it's your modesty you're worried about."

Daphne's primary concern wasn't her modesty but her tatty underwear. Her best dress was of passable quality, but her undergarments definitely weren't. The girl kept pulling the dress around her to test the fit rather than get changed.

"Let me help. Come here."

Daphne had no choice but to give in, and thankfully, Lillian seemed unconcerned about her underclothes. A few minutes later, the girl looked in the mirror with a sigh of relief. Could that smart-looking lady really be her, Daphne Parker, the haberdashery assistant staring back from the looking glass? Yes, it could.

"I love your curly hair," Miss Lawson remarked, picking out a spiralling tress and twisting it around her fingers. "My hair just hangs down like curtains, all lifeless, lank and straight. That's why I like putting it up in a bun most of the time. It doesn't matter what it wants to do then."

"At school, the kids teased me and called me Medusa. The nuns who taught us kept telling me to tuck my hair into a bonnet."

"Well, I won't tell you what to do. You can have your hair hanging down your back, with just a few pins to keep it off your face if you want."

Lillian stood back to admire her assistant's new outfit.

"What do you think about the dress, Daphne? Very becoming, I'd say."

"Yes, it is. But—erm, it feels too grand for someone like me."

"Fiddlesticks! Never say that. It needs no altering at all which is a blessing. It's perfect."

Lillian helped her undo the buttons, and Daphne quickly darted behind the wardrobe door and donned her old dress.

"I suppose you're wondering why I keep them?"

Daphne nodded.

"My husband insists that I only wear the outfits he buys for me. These are remnants of my single days. They don't fit me anymore, but they hold sentimental value, so I hang on to them. I know it's silly, but I like to pull them out and look at them every once in a while. We're a bit of an odd couple. He's a few years my senior. Well, if I'm honest, he's well over pensionable age."

"How old is that?" Daphne blurted out before regretting looking terribly nosey.

"Sixty-eight."

"Blimey! That's older than grandpa, and he's that old I sometimes worry he'll die one day."

"Oh yes, I know that feeling," she chucked. "Every time I see him slouched in his winged armchair with his eyes closed I wonder if he's shuffled off this mortal coil. But I don't worry for long. Without wishing to sound mercenary, I shall be a very wealthy lady when he does pop his clogs. I am sure that will take the sting out of it."

"Are you expecting that soon?" the girl asked meekly.

"No, not at all. I love him dearly. There's plenty of life left in the old fool yet. He enjoys driving me round the bend too much to slip away before his time."

"I feel a 'but' coming, Miss Lawson?"

"No buts," the woman giggled.

"You'd better be getting back, Daphne. Your family will be wondering where you've got to. Would you like to take the dress with you, or would you prefer to change in the morning?"

Even though Daphne would have loved to show off her finery to her family, she decided it would be better to wait a week or two. She couldn't bear the thought of anything happening to the dress while it was in her care. They returned downstairs. Miss Lawson locked the premises and wrapped her shawl around her shoulders.

"Until tomorrow then, Miss Parker. Good evening."

"Night."

The owner smiled and then headed in the opposite direction away from Commercial Road. Daphne stood outside the shop for a moment, peering through the dark window. After failing to decipher any of the price tags, she made some up and then did some mental arithmetic to make sure her brain would be fighting fit in the morning. With a heavy heart, she turned to leave, wondering what she would find when she got home. Would anyone care about her exciting new job?

14

A DAUGHTER'S PRIDE

When Daphne returned home, she checked on her mother. Mary, who was now awake, moved her legs and patted a spot on the bed for her daughter to sit down.

"You look cold. Have you been saying goodbye to people on the doorstep?" her mother asked.

"No, mama. I've been doing something more important."

"Is that so?"

"Yes, I've found a job as a haberdashery assistant at Lawson's on Wellington Road. I thought learning a trade and earning a wage was better than us all relying on Grandpa's money and me staying in school."

Her mother blinked hard, in awe of the responsible young girl in front of her.

"Your poor father and brother are barely in the ground, and you've already got a job."

"Well, you've been busy too, ma. Giving birth to twins. Grandpa told me he helped the midwife deliver the second one!"

In her weakened postpartum state, Mary just about managed a laugh.

"Your poor grandfather. I don't know who was more embarrassed."

On hearing his name, Walter popped upstairs briefly and carefully handed the fidgeting tots up to their mother. Daphne stroked one of them on the cheek.

"Which is which?"

"You can tell them apart because he's slightly bigger," said her mother pointing to the boy.

"What's his name?"

"I haven't decided yet. I discussed the matter with your grandfather. He wanted the same as the ones we lost, Emma and Edmund but I'm not sure. It seems a bit cursed given our luck recently."

"Let's choose something more cheerful like Rebecca and Ronald?"

"Rebecca seems fine, but not Ronald. I knew a man called that when I was a little girl. Ronnie was a nasty piece of work. I'd rather not want to be reminded of him each time I see my boy."

"Well, how about Walter?" suggested Daphne after a moment. "After Grandpa?"

"Walter it is. Walter Johnny."

"I'll give Grandpa the good news," she said, jumping up. "Maybe he won't be so cross with me for finding the job then."

"Why would he be cross when you've used your initiative and possibly saved us all from the workhouse?"

"He thinks I should stay at school"

"Well, I think it's fabulous news. Many a girl would give her right arm for an opportunity like that."

"Are my ears burning," said Walter, as he appeared with a bowl of steaming hot soup.

"Ah, that smells nice, Grandpa. Did you make it?"

"Yes. Proof my time peeling veg in the Temeraire's galley was not wasted. This is parsnip by the way."

Her mother took a sip, but the golden liquid burned her lip.

"Ouch, it's scalding."

"Good. You always complain when it's cold."

Mary blew hard on the next spoonful.

"Mmm. This is delicious. I didn't know you had so many hidden talents, pa."

"There's a lot you don't know about me."

Between mouthfuls, Mary pointed at her daughter.

"She's done well, hasn't she, pa? Finding a new job at her first attempt?"

"She should be at school. You know that's what her father wanted, Mary."

"Well, that's the pot calling the kettle black, pa. You left school at thirteen to run off to the Navy!"

The debate continued back and forth between father and daughter about the pros and cons of earning and learning. Daphne sat and listened to the pair, not wanting to interrupt. As the bickering continued, the atmosphere became icier and soon there was no conversation to interrupt anyway. Mary finished her soup and handed the bowl to Walter.

"I'm not criticising you for running off, papa. There's no need to be so defensive. It was merely an observation."

"Well, it's too late now. What's done is done. Not that I would want to change anything anyway. I lived a good life at sea and enjoyed every minute of it."

"And you told your granddaughter some amazing stories—mostly made up, I'm sure."

"Really, mama? I thought they were all the gospel truth?" Daphne piped up with a grin.

He laughed as he turned to leave.

"Maybe I exaggerated a little, but the stories were mostly true.," Grandpa said as he ruffled Daphne's hair.

"Rest now, my daughter, before it's feeding time for the bairns again. Keep your strength up, eh?"

Daphne shuffled on the bed to face her mother.

"How did you meet papa? You never told me."

"We both worked at the same mill. I was fifteen and, er—"

Mary began to blush.

"—well, I was quite well-endowed—buxom. When we first met he said he was drawn to my eyes, the cheeky monkey. It was only when we were man and wife he confessed he was drawn to my figure. I'd got my friend to tell him I liked him, you see. It took us a few weeks of eye-contact to pluck up the courage to finally speak face-to-face. I was working on the weaving machines, and he was a packer in the warehouse."

"So, what did you say to each other? When you finally spoke?"

"I remember it well. It was just after a poor lad I worked with caught his arm in a loom. He was supposed to scramble under the machine all day. It was no life at all. Anyway, his poor arm was severed at the elbow. Johnny was working on our floor that day. He raced over to free the boy, and I summoned the courage to speak to him once the lad was carted off to the hospital. From then on, I was hooked. We met after work and talked and talked, and walked and walked, anywhere, just happy to be together, with his mother acting as chaperone. After we were married, he got a job here at the docks managing the delivery paperwork for the chandlers. It was a lot safer. People were always getting hurt at the mill. It was sickening really. We were glad to move away.

And secretly, I think your father was glad to be free of his meddling mother-in-law."

Mary loved reminiscing. Even in the darkest of times, it gave her strength. Her laughter was so loud that it woke up one of the babies, so she untied her nightgown and prepared to feed, which Daphne took as her signal to leave. She went downstairs and hoped Grandpa would be in a better mood about her job. Why couldn't he just be pleased for her good fortune?

15

TAKING A LEAP OF FAITH

For most of the night, Daphne lay awake, afraid of over-sleeping. She arose early to leave the house with what she hoped was ample time. She regretted not timing the journey to the haberdasher's the night before. Prospect Street lacked any churches, train stations, or coffee shops with public clocks, leaving her with no point of reference. With no church bells to guide her for a while, she had no clue how much time she had left before her first proper day of work began.

Breathless and with her legs burning, Daphne raced through the streets, relieved to find the 'CLOSED' sign hanging behind the locked shop door. After a few deep breaths, she steadied herself, ready to face the day ahead. If yesterday was any indication, she knew it was going to be a busy shift in the little store.

Daphne chuckled as she inspected the items in the shop window more closely than the night before. The arrangement of two skeins of red embroidery silk gave the impression of a heart, which was an odd choice since Christmas was fast approaching and Valentine's Day was still weeks away. There were no glistening glass baubles or decorative paper chains to give a festive feel. She decided that her first task would be to improve the arrangement to attract even more customers. Given that a thick white cobweb hung precariously between a roll of green fabric and the slender neck of a dressmaker's dummy, Miss Lawson had clearly neglected the showcased items for months.

Sweat trickled down the girl's back. As she stood waiting, shivers ran down her spine. Seeking refuge in the small shop doorway, she watched as the raindrops began to fall and the number of passers-by scurrying on their errands decreased dramatically. A nearby church clock chimed nine. Where was Miss Lawson? Moments later, the shopkeeper appeared, panting.

"Ah, Daphne," she gasped. "I hope you haven't been waiting too long?"

"No, Miss Lawson. I just got here."

Daphne struggled to hide her shivers as they hurried inside. Miss Lawson promptly lit all the gas lamps. The cloudy skies made the interior of the shop seem gloomy. Before they had a chance to remove their coats, the doorbell clattered, and their first customer of the day walked in—a refined lady.

"Good day, ma'am," greeted Miss Lawson. "Would you like to browse for a few minutes while I—?"

Impatiently, the customer didn't give her a chance to finish.

"I would like those velvet gloves in the window if you please."

"Yes, ma'am, certainly, ma'am."

Wriggling her arms back into her coat sleeves, Miss Lawson quickly moved to the window and retrieved the gloves.

"These ones seem to have a stitching issue," the lady said as she took one off.

Just as Miss Lawson was examining the gloves, the bell clattered once more, and a young girl ran in.

"Mama, why didn't you wait for me?"

"You should keep up," replied her mother while handing the faulty glove to Miss Lawson who examined the label inside.

"Forgive me, ma'am, but you didn't buy these here, did you?"

"I didn't say I did. I'm just showing you the problem."

"I do apologise."

Daphne felt the precocious girl staring at her. It had to be what she was wearing. Subtly, Daphne gestured to Lillian about her clothing.

"Excuse me, miss. Shall I go upstairs and—?"

"Of course, off you pop, Miss Parker.."

Daphne yanked off her dismal shift dress and swapped it for Miss Lawson's close-fitting mauve one, smiling to herself. Soon after, Lillian came to see if the girl needed a hand with the buttons.

"Golly, that woman was a sourpuss, wasn't she?" the girl remarked, as Miss Lawson looked up.

"Who?"

"The glove lady."

"I've had far worse customers over the years, Daphne," Lillian chuckled. "Come, let me do you up properly. Your buttons are all skew-whiff."

Daphne hoped she wouldn't smell after running most of the way to work and was relieved she had taken extra care to wash even though she didn't have time to heat the water for her basin. If she had reeked of sweat, it would have been embarrassing to have such a refined lady touch her. She was relieved when Miss Lawson didn't roll her eyes or make any comments.

"I'm in a bit of a pickle, Daphne. I've been pondering ways to make a bit of money. I've got so much money tied up in old stock. I think I'll have a clearance sale after Christmas when everyone is holding onto their money."

"Won't slashing prices bring in less money and make the losses from the unsold stock worse though?"

"Yes and no. I'll have more space to fill with the profitable lines. I'll make the money back that way."

Daphne considered the proposal.

"I see what you're saying. Now, I have no idea what sells well and what doesn't yet. But as I looked at the window display this morning, I thought we could change things a little. Make it more Christmassy, if you like? People love to treat themselves at Christmas. You might be able to sell the slow-moving items at full price with a bit of luck. It's worth a try for a few days, I think. Shall I start my review of the arrangement?"

"Splendid. Yes, start right away. I've been neglecting it lately, and a Christmas display would cheer us all up. How about we start with a cup of tea first?"

"Yes, that would be lovely, thank—"

Miss Lawson's eyebrows rose.

"Oh, you want me to make it. Sorry, miss."

As the girl scurried off, her boss gave a wry smile. There was clearly a lot of fun to be had with her new recruit.

Daphne had been so eager to make a start on the eye-catching display she forgot there would be more menial duties first. She started putting the kettle on the hob and organised the cups and teapot then went back to the shop to find several customers. She wondered if she'd be allowed to serve them, but not knowing the prices, or how to deal with customers, she thought it best to stay in the shadows.

Half an hour later, she decided to tackle the window, even though the shop had been too busy for her to discuss the finer details of the plan with her superior. She tried not to panic when a customer poked her head into the display area and asked to view the crochet hooks and Miss Lawson was tied up dealing with another enquiry.

"Um, crochet hooks? Let me see."

She waited until Miss Lawson finished speaking to approach her. The shopkeeper pointed to another set of drawers covered in a mass of boxes filled with buttons. None of the drawers had a 'crochet hooks' label. It was potluck until she found them. Daphne returned to her customer and put on her most dignified voice.

"Here is our selection, ma'am. What size are you looking for?"

The lady muttered as she picked up a chunky hook.

"Not quite. A bit too heavy."

"How about this one?"

"Too light."

"Or this one?"

"Too slippy."

Daphne feigned a smile as she worked through every type of crochet hook Miss Lawson stocked, with each one roundly rejected.

"Never mind," said the lady, tying her bonnet ribbons. "I'll check at the next shop down the road."

Out she went, leaving Daphne feeling terrible for failing at her first attempt at serving, and worrying she wouldn't be kept on if she couldn't sell.

"I'm so sorry," she confessed when the shop emptied. "She left without buying anything."

"Fret not, my dear. We can't help everyone."

"But I need to earn my wages?"

"Carry on with the window and leave me to worry about that. Everything will be fine. Trust me."

"Thank you, Miss Lawson. Since it's quiet, shall I make the tea?"

"Yes, and do call me Lillian, Daphne. Not in front of customers, but on our own it would be fine."

"Of course," said the girl, beaming at the news that their relationship was deepening.

As she poured the drinks, she reflected on how fortuitous it was to have such a good job with such a friendly employer. After all the problems and heartache at home, it was a genuine relief. Later, Daphne started with the display, beginning with giving the glass a good clean with some vinegar and newspaper, then began making some selections to showcase.

Several hours later, the girl's stomach rumbled. She hadn't had breakfast, nor had she considered lunch. She'd thought nothing of it. The Parkers frequently skipped meals due to financial constraints. She wondered what Lillian did for lunch and pondered if her husband organised something? She hadn't summoned the courage to call her boss by her forename yet, preferring to say it in her head instead. Despite the rain that was still falling heavily, she went outside to inspect her display.

"Well, you've done a grand job there, Daphne," the girl mumbled as she took a pace towards the road to see more of the frontage.

As she moved backwards, she was horrified to realise she had collided with a towering grey-haired gentleman who relied on a walking cane. She hoped Miss Lawson hadn't spotted her mistake.

I'm so sorry, sir," she replied, her face burning.

"It's nothing, miss. Don't worry yourself. I'm fine."

Daphne expected him to carry on towards Whitechapel so she was horrified to see him open the door to the shop. He held it open for her.

"After you," he said, with his other arm outstretched, herding her into the premises like a shepherd.

"Percival!" exclaimed Miss Lillian, turning to see who it was. "I wasn't expecting to see you today."

He glanced over at Daphne, then back to his wife.

"I came to make sure everything is alright."

Daphne wondered what Percival meant by 'alright'. She hoped he didn't think she was planning to steal from the shop or the till while Miss Lillian wasn't looking.

"Why wouldn't it be?" asked Miss Lillian "Everything's going well. Just look at the magnificent window display Daphne has been putting together. I've been run off my feet. All my customers must have heard that I have a new assistant because they keep popping in to take a look at her. Not that I mind as long as they make a purchase when they come to have a gander."

Daphne hadn't realised the customers had been inspecting her, She was far more preoccupied with where to place the Christmas decorations in the new display.

"Please don't use such words like 'gander', my dear. You already know my thoughts on the use of slang."

The man took off his rain-soaked hat and placed it on the counter. The water soaked into her order book and the ink began to run.

"Please, dear do try to be more careful—" she grumbled, but with one icy look from him, she stopped. "May I introduce my new assistant, Miss Daphne Parker? Daphne, this is my husband, Mr Johnson."

Daphne walked forward, debating whether or not to curtsy, then did a small one just in case. Lillian's husband was not at all as she had expected. There was no rapport to be had with him, and he lacked his wife's warmth. Thin lips were a sign of meanness, her grandfather told her, and he was right. She found Percival to be a very belligerent man.

"She looks very young."

"I am sixteen, sir, and—"

His eyebrows formed a contour that seemed to forbid her to utter another word.

"But she is very willing," continued Miss Lillian, in the girl's defence, "and has shown a talent for arithmetic and an eye for presenting the stock. And her tea-making skills are excellent."

She took his sopping hat from the counter and hung it on the coat stand behind her just as three ladies walked in. Mr Johnson reached out for it and snatched it off the peg.

"I won't keep you, my dear. Farewell for now."

He swept out of the shop without giving Daphne another glance. Daphne waited until the ladies finished before voicing her opinion.

"I hope you don't mind me saying this, but your husband was not what I was expecting."

"Maybe not. I try to describe him favourably as a wife should, but—"

Lillian twizzled the spare fabric back onto the roll from the last lady's order.

"I wanted to ask him to take us for a spot of lunch, but seeing as he didn't seem in a pleasant mood, I decided not to."

"Does he come around often?"

"Rarely. He engages himself in other ways, thankfully. Otherwise, he'd want to interfere with how I run the place. I know him. He wouldn't be able to help himself. It's better if he stays away."

"I suppose it would be difficult with him breathing down your neck."

Instantly, Daphne regretted the comment, but Lillian didn't seem to mind.

"Very difficult. Anyway, grab your coat, my dear. We are closing for dinner. It's my treat. Thank you for being so thoughtful and brightening my window. It looks so much better."

Daphne was relieved that Lillian was paying since she didn't have a ha'penny to her name. Miss Lawson locked the door after flipping the sign from 'OPEN' to 'CLOSED'. She surveyed the tasteful display with the products now dusted and perfectly positioned. The paper chains and baubles added a cheerful festive touch. She gave Daphne a broad grin.

"Wonderful. This should bring in even more customers—and there will be two of them to serve them. Simply perfect."

She leaned in and peered a little closer at the girl's handiwork.

"Ah, look at those little lambs you've put around the manger. How adorable. I love them. Not that I see any these days here in the city."

"I've never seen a sheep, except in books."

"We should take a train to the seaside for Easter. I'm sure we'd see plenty in the fields. Margate, perhaps?"

Alas, before Daphne could take advantage of the thrilling offer, Miss Lawson's flighty mind had already moved on to another topic

"Lunch? Let's go to that lovely little tea shop round the corner."

Daphne agreed it was lovely which wasn't difficult when it cost an arm and a leg.

The remainder of the day passed quickly, with Daphne starting to put the shop interior in order. Miss Lawson introduced different sorts of fabric, from silk to taffeta to velvet. Daphne organised them by type, and then into colours, using the colours of the rainbow as her guide. The racks of cotton reels were arranged in the same way, as were the drawers of embroidery silk. By the end of the day, everything was neatly arranged, although Daphne did worry Miss Lillian might struggle to find anything, having been used to everything being in a muddle for so long. Still, the woman seemed positive about the changes.

"It looks much more professional now that it's organised, Daphne. You've done a fine job. Tomorrow—silly me—I mean on Monday, you can start on the storeroom and weave your magic there too."

The enthusiastic girl was exhausted but pleased with her progress which, for her first day, had been stellar.

"Did you have a good day?" asked her grandfather when she got back.

"Oh, yes, Grandpa," she trilled before sharing every detail at a breakneck pace and making his head spin again.

"Well, it all sounds lovely. Better than working in a factory, I suppose, although—"

"Please don't bring up the topic of going back to school again. Miss Lawson has allowed me to take a few minutes off on Monday to inform them that I won't be returning, and I shall take her up on that offer. I am learning a trade and practical skills that will be far more useful to me than reciting Shakespearean sonnets, discussing ancient battles, or knowing what the capital city of Spain is," she said with a touch of defiance.

"It's up to you, lass," he said with a shrug. "I won't say I approve. I'm sure your father would have an opinion on it, but I'm proud of the sacrifice you've made for the family."

The thing was her job didn't feel like a sacrifice. It felt exciting and grown-up. Daphne thought it was time to let the simmering feud go. Neither was going to back down, so with a hug, she inquired about dinner.

"Shepherd's pie, lass."

"Mmm! It smells lovely. How's mama? May I see her?"

"She's feeding the babies, so check first before barging in like a bull in a china shop. You get far too excited at times."

"Yes, Grandpa."

She crept into her mother's bedroom and warmed her hands by the fire. There wasn't much warmth from it though. There was barely enough coal to keep it going.

"That's Walter taken care of," her mother said, holding out the baby to Daphne to place back in his makeshift cot. "The girl is still asleep so I'll leave her. I haven't had much peace today. As soon as one falls asleep, the other one's wailing about something."

Daphne took the boy and studied the little face looking up at her. The more she looked, the more she could see a likeness to her father, and perhaps to little baby Johnny.

"Hello, Walter. How are you today, young man? All sweetness and smiles, I see."

He burped as she lifted him up above her head.

"Urgh. Maybe not that sweet," she confessed as she put him down.

Mary invited her daughter to sit down, patting the eiderdown.

"Tell me, how was your day? I want to know everything," her mother asked eagerly.

"It was rather good, actually. This grown-up lark is fun," Daphne replied, beaming.

"That will wear off, trust me," her mother warned, but the girl ignored the comment and continued to recount her milestone and every morsel of minutiae of the day.

"Miss Lawson sounds kind. I hope she keeps you after you've finished all the tidying."

Daphne looked like she'd been punched.

"Oh, mama! I didn't consider that. Should I slow down a lot on Monday and let things get messy again? Then she'd have to keep me on?"

"No, dearie, I don't think that's a wise idea."

Mary was chuckling but Daphne looked glum as she gazed at the twins.

16

HARSH REALITIES

Daphne would normally sleep later on Sundays but one of the screaming twins woke her early.

"What's wrong this time? You do know you'll wake up the whole street if you keep this up," she grizzled, rocking the little one on her lap. "Shush, now. Shhh."

It was no use. Soon, her groggy mother sat up with a groan.

"Again? Good grief."

Little Winnie still bawled as Daphne hugged the baby close and bounced her gently. Soon, the tired little one's head was quietly lolling on her shoulder. Daphne thought things were going well until the little body tensed up suddenly and then threw up on her.

"Ugh, ma!"

"Dear, oh, dear. She struggled to take in some milk in the night, and now she's brought it all back up again. I'm so worried about her—"

Daphne watched as her mother grabbed Winnie, wiping the little one's mouth clear and trying to force her to suckle.

"But what about my nightshirt, ma?"

"Daphne Parker! You can be so selfish at times. It's a most unattractive trait. Can't you see how ill your sister is? Go and get changed instead of sitting and complaining. Your grandfather can help you with the laundry."

"He will?"

"Yes, he's a canny old thing. He'll probably ask one of his friends down the pub if their wife will do a bit extra and then pretend he did it all himself."

Daphne pulled the smelly garment over her head trying her best to keep the sick away from her face, then changed into her Sunday clothes. The dress was a bit thin and she started to quiver with cold. She went to stoke the fire and as the poker jostled the coals, they crackled and popped.

"I should have done this before I got changed," she moaned. "I hope I keep the coal dust off."

"How many times have I said to put my apron on when you're doing that? I feel like I am talking to myself in this house sometimes."

With the fire flickering merrily once more, Daphne went downstairs hoping to see Gramps who was usually the first to rise, but there was no sign. She prepared some tea and took it up to Mary. These days Walter had moved into a tiny cot bed that used to be Daphne's, wedged in a small curtained-off alcove, while the girl shared with her mother. Daphne peered round the drape and saw him all cosy, tucked under a crocheted patchwork blanket.

"Do you think Grandpa will go to church with me? We ought to pray for pa and Henry."

"I don't know. You'll have to ask him when he surfaces. He used to attend when he came home on leave, so he might."

Feeling bored, Daphne went downstairs and began moving the table and stools to one side, thinking she would help her mother and sweep the floor. Mary poked her head into the stairwell.

"Thank you, dear, but it's very distracting hearing you banging about. Go and find something else to do, preferably outside."

Frost and fog enveloped Prospect Street that morning. Daphne wondered what quiet activity she could do at such an early hour. She decided to work on her arithmetic by doing some calculations on her chalk slate and sharpening her skills. About an hour later, she was interrupted by her grandfather burping loudly as he staggered downstairs, clutching the handrail.

"Goodness me, this cold weather is playing havoc with my arthritis," he said with a grimace. "You're up early."

He scratched the back of his head and yawned.

"Winnie decided to be my knocker-upper this morning. Gramps, will you come to church today?"

"Of course, we need to say prayers for your father and brother, don't we?"

"Oh, that's a relief. I was dreading having to face everybody on my own. All that pointing and whispering. It's going to be awful, I just know it."

She knew from experience that the bereaved were always encircled by the congregation as they filed out of the nave, with everyone clamouring to know what had happened to the recently departed. She couldn't face that interrogation alone.

"My belly's empty. I fancy a quick bite," he said as he put the kettle on again.

"No, Grandpa, you can't eat. Not until Holy communion. That's what Father Lane told me."

"Am I not exempt for being old?"

"You're not old. You'll have to manage."

"Well, I feel old this morning."

He stretched his creaking bones, his arms almost touching the ceiling.

"You shouldn't really have tea, only water."

"I'll have it black with no sugar then. It's murky water then, isn't it?"

With a lot of puffing and blowing, he sat in the rickety old armchair he'd bought off Fergus at the Little Drummer Boy. Any time someone needed something on the cheap, the landlord was always an excellent source. Just don't ask him where it came from.

"See if your mother's awake and take some tea, there's a good girl."

Daphne had been about to say Mary had already had one but then realised that nearly two hours had passed, such was the distraction of the sums. Deciding her mother would probably appreciate another, she watched the sugary tea steep with anticipation. "It will taste all the better for the wait," she muttered to herself. However, her throat stung as she recalled the phrase. It was something her father would say every Sunday. But not this Sunday, and not ever again.

As Daphne sat in her pew listening to Father Lane's sermon on forgiveness and reconciliation, she couldn't help but feel as though the priest was staring directly at her. His warning against going to bed angry after an argument struck a chord, causing her to reflect on her last conversation with her father on a rainy day before he left for work. Was it a proper argument or just a bit of back and forth? She couldn't quite recall, but she did remember his abruptness. Now that he was gone, she was left with the weight of those words.

Daphne's heart was heavy as she walked home, her thoughts consumed by her father. She didn't even notice if the young man who had caught her eye was present which was odd. Despite knowing nothing about him, she found herself eagerly anticipating their weekly meetings. His special wink never failed to quicken her heartbeat.

As the congregation filed out of the church, Father Lane stood at the door and offered his condolences to the

Parkers once more. For a brief moment, Daphne entertained the idea of telling him to 'stuff it' since he seemed to trot out the same spiel to every grieving family, but she bit her tongue instead.

"And how's your mother coping? I hear she's had twins, Daphne."

"She's alright, I suppose. Grandpa and I are looking after her, and a few neighbours pop in."

"Will she be coming back to church soon?"

"I don't know, father. She isn't quite ready yet."

"Well, tell her to hurry back soon. There are the christenings to consider."

Did the cleric have an ominous premonition about the twins' future? Daphne's mother appeared troubled by Winnie's difficulty in feeding. As Father Lane turned to greet another parishioner, Walter took hold of her arm, and they slipped away into the crowd. Eager to return home, Daphne hurried ahead until she noticed her grandfather trailing behind, struggling with a slight limp.

"It's nothing," he reassured her when he managed to catch up. "Come on, let's head back."

It was an unpleasant reminder he was getting on in years and she hoped he still had plenty of time left. To lose another loved one so soon would be devastating. She reflected on the Prospect Street residents who had made it well into their seventies. One of Jimmy McGinty's aunts had been eighty-four when she died. Even Miss Lawson's husband was sixty-eight. She feared that the loss of her grandfather might be more painful than the loss of her father, such was the strength of their bond. Instantly, she felt a twinge of regret. *'No, no, papa. I didn't mean that! The thought just popped into my head. I would never think something so awful. Please forgive me.'*

"Hey, Daphne!"

She turned to look far behind her.

"Oh, sorry!"

Lost in her own thoughts, she had quickened her pace and had left poor old Walter far behind. She slowed down and waited for him to catch up.

"Shall we sit in St Bartholomew's Gardens and rest for a while, Gramps?"

He nodded. She spotted an empty bench to sit and talk. Walter sat down with a faint groan and rubbed his hands together.

"Brr, it's cold."

Ignoring the coldness in her own fingers, she took his hands in hers to warm them.

"You would think you'd have thick skin from being at sea all your life. You're going soft, Grandpa."

He shrugged, giving her a smile as she wrapped her scarf around his hands. They sat in silence for a while, Walter glad of the rest and Daphne wondering if he was really alright. They watched the world go by until she felt herself starting to stiffen up with the cold. The girl stood and bounced on her tiptoes to warm her feet up.

"We'd better get a wriggle on. Mama might need us. I should also see Mrs Irvine to check how she's getting on with little Johnny."

"Yes. Now life's getting back to normal, we should really get him to the mission. I have no idea if we'll ever find his mother," Walter said as Daphne helped him up. "Tell me what the woman said again, exactly."

So much had happened since that day, it was hard for Daphne to recollect.

"She asked if 'Harry' was home and left the note. That's everything, I promise."

"Perhaps she'd lost her mind?"

"Well, she must have gone mad to abandon her child like that. I've never had a child, but I'm sure I wouldn't want to abandon it."

"Maybe she didn't want to. People do odd things when they're desperate."

They continued their journey home in silence, each lost in their thoughts about Johnny's parentage. Daphne could hear Walter becoming breathless, perhaps the walk had been too far for him today. It hadn't been a problem in the past, but this trip was different. He seemed a little frail. His recent stroll to The Red Lion had posed no problem, and that was about the same distance, but then, she hadn't gone with him, so maybe he had struggled. She'd never know if there was an issue because there was no way Walter would ever speak of any personal weakness.

When they got back, she made him a little cheese sandwich and a cup of tea to warm him up. She then went to check on her mother, who had managed to feed the babies and was now engrossed in an old copy of The London Illustrated Journal.

"I'm popping next door to see Mrs Irvine, ma."

As she put her coat on Walter lit up his pipe and puffed at it hard.

"That doesn't help with your wheezing, Grandpa. Maybe you should give it up?"

The reply he gave was not what a young lady should hear. Mrs Irvine greeted her with tears in her eyes.

"Och, Daphne, thank goodness yer here. I was about to come round."

"There's nothing wrong with Johnny, is there?"

"No, no, he's doing well, I give him some boiled milk, so I don't have to bother Mrs Leah. Look at him, lass. He's thriving. Seems to have put on some weight. See?"

The two of them looked in the old pram and there he was, gurgling cheerily and kicking his legs. Mrs Irvine covered him up, then leaned in towards the girl's ear, and spoke with her voice breaking a little.

"But I can't have him any longer. It isn't that I don't want to—."

Daphne swallowed. She had hoped Mrs Irvine would keep him for a while longer. Since the arrival of the twins, her mother wasn't really in a position to decide what to do with him in the long term.

"It's my old man. He says—"

She blew her nose as tears streamed down her face.

"He says we cannae afford him. He's just lost his job. And then there's my boy, Mark. He's got such a jealous streak. Says doesn't like him, and he never will."

Sobbing harder than ever, she gazed at the baby. Daphne patted her shoulder, but she was inconsolable and her body continued to shake as she wailed.

"It's fine, Mrs Irvine. I'll take him. Now mama's home, we'll manage. And I'll bring him round whenever you want."

Her offer didn't help the distraught woman.

"Och, no—that would—make it—worse," Mrs Irvine stammered between sobs.

"I do hope we can find his birth mother at some point.."

Footsteps descended the stairs. Daphne was desperate to leave before Mr Irvine arrived, but she was too slow. He appeared, wearing chocolate-brown trousers that were threadbare in places, his braces hanging down. A grimy grey string vest covering his chest still left a mass of thick curly grey hair poking through the holes. Daphne expected him to snap at Mrs Irvine for her tearfulness, but he swung his arms around her instead.

"Don't be upset, Mary. You always knew it was only temporary."

"Yes," agreed Daphne. "I didn't expect you to keep him forever. Let me take him now."

Mr Irvine nodded in agreement. As his wife's pained cries cut through the still air, Daphne carefully negotiated the back door, wobbling the tiny pram over the threshold and out into the yard. Mrs Irvine looked on as the girl pushed baby Johnny up the narrow ginnel between their houses before disappearing into the Parker's lodgings.

In the armchair sat Walter, fast asleep with his chin resting on his chest. She settled Johnny by the range then crept quietly upstairs. Mary sat up when her daughter appeared.

"Is everything well? You look troubled, treacle."

"I'm fine, mama," Daphne said, unable to look her in the eye.

"Come on, what is it? I may be tied up with the twins a lot, but I am still your mother. I know when something's not right. Tell me, child."

"It's baby Johnny, mama. Mrs Irvine says we have to take him back."

"We really must get him to the orphanage. He's not our responsibility. I'll be strong enough in a day or two. Your grandpa can pay for a bit of extra milk, or Mrs Leah can help feed him in the meantime."

"How will you cope with three babies when I'm at work?"

"I'll rope in your grandfather. Don't you worry."

"But—?"

Daphne thought better of confessing her concerns about his health and told a white lie instead.

"—are you sure he'll have time?"

"We'll manage. Worse things happen at sea, so they say."

"I'll bet Grandpa has said that a few times," Daphne chuckled.

"We'll survive. We always do. We're a hardy bunch. I'm sure someone, either Mrs Bradley or Mrs Leah, will help if it gets too much for me."

"Do you want anything? Because I was thinking, I might go and see Sarah for a little bit?"

"That's fine, dearie. You run along and have a bit of fun. Where's Johnny now?"

"He's downstairs. Should I bring him up?"

"Actually, if you do want to help, there is something you could do. My chamber pot could do with emptying. If you wouldn't mind?"

Reluctantly, Daphne slopped the contents of the pot into the outside privy, then went to check on baby Johnny. After that, she made her way to the Bradleys.

"I bet Mrs Irvine returned him because she was afraid she might murder him," said Sarah.

"That's awful, Sarah! Don't be so cruel! She was heart-broken. You didn't see her. I did."

After quite a debate, the two girls agreed to disagree.

"Let's take a walk, maybe to Victoria Park?" Daphne suggested, keen to smooth things over.

"If you like. Will your grandfather look after Johnny? Someone should be keeping an eye on him," Sarah said as she put on her winter coat and scarf.

"I'm sure he will. Let's go and tell him we're going out."

Her grandfather snored in the armchair, and he didn't respond to some gentle prodding in the ribs, so they decided to take the pram with them.

"Hopefully, Johnny will sleep all the way, so he'll be no trouble," Daphne assured her friend.

"Well, if he starts crying. I'm off. I can't deal with screaming infants."

"That will change when you have one of your own, Sarah."

"I can hardly wait," Sarah fibbed, rolling her eyes.

Daphne looked at her friend quizzically.

"Don't you want children of your own?"

"Definitely not!"

"But that's unnatural. Every woman should want children."

"Perhaps I have different aspirations," Sarah said with a shrug. "I can't help how I feel. I don't like babies, and that's all there is to it. Noisy, smelly, demanding things. Don't tell mama. She got angry when I mentioned it once."

"I'm not surprised. But what will you do when you're older? Who will take care of you?"

"My handsome, but aged husband," Sarah joked.

"But you looked happy when I first brought Johnny to your house."

Sarah stepped through the gates to the park.

"That was different. He isn't mine. I can give him back when I've had enough. Can't do that as easily when it's your own. Talking of husbands, I wonder if there will be any nice eligible bachelors promenading today?"

"That contraption is guaranteed to scare off any potential suitors," Sarah grizzled as she jabbed at the pram.

"If you're so peeved being seen with us, why did you come at all?"

"Sorry. I'm just a bit tired. It's been a long week. Blimey! Look over there.

"Where?"

"By the bandstand. It's the man I told you about. The one I saw last time."

"Which of them? The one with the top hat, or with the frock coat?"

"The frock coat. Isn't he lovely? Don't let him catch us staring. Look away."

"He's rather old for you, isn't he?"

"Are you forgetting I'm two years older than you!"

"I bet he'd want babies, Sarah. Will you tell him you don't?"

"Will you shut up about babies? You know I don't like them. Crikey! Look. Oh no!"

"Do you want me to walk away?"

"No, don't leave me alone," Sarah muttered, grabbing her friend's sleeve. "They're coming our way!

"I thought you said baby Johnny would put men off us?"

"I was wrong, alright? You win!"

The two men got closer and closer. Sarah held her breath. Then they walked past without paying any attention or pausing their conversation.

"He looked at me, didn't he?" gushed Sarah, once the two chaps were out of earshot.

"Did he? I didn't notice."

"Well, you wouldn't. You're too young. Oh, he's so dashing in that smart coat. I wonder if they'll turn back."

Sarah watched as the men went out through the gates.

"Ah, Daphne, it doesn't seem like it. Poor luck. At least I've seen him. What could his name be?"

"How would I know? I'm not even allowed to notice him, let alone know his first name!" Daphne chortled. "What would you like to call him?"

"Something like—"

She pulled a face, pondering deeply.

"—Arthur? Do you like that?"

"Not particularly. It's a bit old-fashioned. How about—Oliver, as in that book about the orphan boy in the workhouse?"

"Now you're being silly. Why would I want that?"

"I just like the name. I reckon you could call your first son Oliver," Daphne teased.

"I've told you. I'm not having children. Will you just drop it?

"No. What if you have a girl? What would you call her?"

"Olivia. Happy now? Gosh, I'm bored with this game. How many more times? I don't like children."

Soon, an awkward silence fell upon them. Eventually, Sarah spoke.

"Look over there, Daphne. What a handsome pair of horses."

Two black stallions were pulling an even glossier black coach, the passengers inside dressed to the nines. The girl thought the horses looked a lot healthier than the nags at the funeral, then gulped when she recognised the people inside were: Miss Lawson and her husband. Daphne wondered what the etiquette was. Should she acknowledge them or pretend not to have seen them at all? When the carriage came to a stop a few yards in front of her and a head turned to face her, the decision was taken out of her hands.

"Daphne, good to see you taking some air," Miss Lawson called out.

Her husband looked like he would rather have continued on their journey. He leaned forward and muttered something to the driver. Lillian tutted at Percival.

"Let's not pull away just yet, thank you, Mr James. Honestly, Percival, you can be so rude at times. I'm sorry, Daphne. Is that one of the twins? Do let me see."

The elegantly dressed woman leaned out from the carriage to get a better look, which only made Mr Lawson's impatience flare up even more. Daphne feared Lillian might fall out of the carriage as her husband ordered the driver to pull away. As it trundled into the distance, the girls noticed the two silhouetted figures arguing animatedly.

"How on earth do you know people with a posh carriage like that?"

"That's my employer, Miss Lawson."

"Ah, the haberdasher. But you called her Miss? I thought she was married? Was that man her father?"

"No, her husband."

"Really! Well, I never!"

"I suppose he is a bit older. Anyway, she inherited the shop before marrying, so she prefers to continue using her maiden name professionally. She said he was happy with that."

"Well, it all seems a bit strange to me. He seems to like ordering her around yet doesn't care if she takes his name or not."

"It's none of our business, Sarah. Can we change the subject please?"

The baby opened his eyes and began to fidget. Sarah winced.

"I bet you he's going to start balling again, isn't he, Daphne?"

"Oh, dear, it looks like it. He's probably hungry."

Daphne halted in her tracks.

"I forgot to check if we have any milk left for him at home. What shall I do if we don't? I can't buy any until tomorrow."

"I'm sure the neighbours could donate a dribble each, if you ask them nicely," Sarah suggested, mimicking dainty pouring movements that made Daphne laugh.

"Or maybe your mama can spare a little?" the girl chuckled, cupping her bosom with her hands and swaying provocatively.

"Stop it! That's so rude!"

Daphne yanked Sarah's hands away from her chest.

"To answer your question, mama complains that she doesn't have enough for the twins as it is. Winnie isn't too demanding, but Walter Johnny likes a lot."

"That's rather a mouthful, Walter Johnny, isn't it? Why not shorten it to Wally or something?"

"Papa didn't like to shorten names. He thought it was common. But I agree. Wally might be more practical."

"Blast," Sarah blurted out after her head spun around like a barn owl.

"What's wrong? Have you lost something?"

"No, silly. There don't seem to be any handsome men left worth gazing at. Come on, let's get back."

"You are terrible, Sarah, you really are!"

Daphne pushed the pram faster when Johnny started to yell. Sarah's temper began to flare up as they reached Prospect Street. She'd had enough of his bawling. A few curtains twitched as they went by with the screaming infant.

"I'll come round later," Daphne called out as she fought her way inside at number twenty-two, pushing the pram over the threshold with all her might.

Walter was in the kitchen.

"My, my,! What a noise, young man!"

Daphne found the milk jug and saw there were about two inches left in the bottom. She sniffed at it and decided it was fresh enough for the tot.

"Please keep an eye on him while I boil this."

Without waiting, she grabbed Johnny and then thrust him into his great-grandfather's arms.

"He's got a good pair of lungs," said Grandpa, trying to pacify the lad.

The milk boiled up like a geyser. Daphne just pulled the thick iron pan off the range before it boiled over.

"It's coming, it's coming. Will you stop that wailing, Johnny," she pleaded, although it achieved nothing.

The milk was scalding and would need a good ten minutes to cool down.

"Why not get him some scone. I picked a few up earlier as a treat for later," her grandfather suggested. "That should quieten him."

"Is he allowed cake?"

"Why not? You were eating it at his age."

Daphne looked in the cake tin. She broke off a tiny piece of scone which she held against his lips until they opened, and then she shoved the morsel in. His little jaws chomped on it, and he gave a big smile. Thankfully, that kept him quiet until his milk cooled.

"What would I ever do without you, Grandpa?" she chirruped, giving him a bear hug.

"I have my uses," Walter said with a smile as he broke free of her vice-like grip.

17

A TENSE REUNION

On the Monday, when Daphne got back from the haberdashers, she was surprised to find her mother cooking. The aroma drew her towards the range. She lifted the lid and sniffed at the pan of stew.

"Oi, missy! Leave that alone."

"Sorry, ma. I couldn't help it. I'm famished."

"It's just what the doctor ordered. Not that we can afford one of them, of course. Talking of home visits, I thought the midwife would have called in by now. She hasn't been since yesterday—I mean Saturday. Gosh, I am losing track of the days."

Daphne laughed at her confusion as Grandpa served up the tasty meal. In between mouthfuls, Mary quizzed her daughter.

"How was your day, dear?"

"Good. I got there before Miss Lawson. She likes that I'm punctual."

The girl was just about to explain more when there was a knock at the door.

"Who could that be?" grumbled Grandpa. "People always seem to visit just as you settle down to your evening meal. Damned nuisance it is."

"I'll get it, Gramps. Don't let yours get cold."

Daphne let the door swing open. She saw a young woman in the dim light, wearing a grubby grey dress with torn lace. She was holding onto a threadbare shawl that covered her head and shoulders. Daphne's eyes were as wide as saucers.

"Who is it? It's not Mrs Irvine is it?" called her mother.

"No, ma. It's—"

"Well don't let them stand in the cold, girl! Please excuse my daughter. Do come in."

Daphne stepped aside giving her mother a clear view of the visitor. Instantly, the penny dropped for Mary.

"You're the one who brought the baby, aren't you?"

The visitor nodded.

"'How is he?" the woman asked.

"Well, I must say, young lady, you've got some nerve to come back here as if nothing's happened," moaned Grandpa, as he picked up his pipe. "Dumping him on us without a by or leave, then asking how he is. What about us? We've been left with a stranger's child. Taking advantage of my granddaughter when she was on her own. Shocking, it is."

The shawl covering the woman's head dropped down as she walked over to the pram, revealing a scraggy thin neck and bony shoulders.

"Why you're only a scrap of a girl yourself!" he exclaimed. "How come you left your child like that? You'd better start explaining."

With tears in her eyes, the girl looked inside the pram and began stroking the baby's cheek. Then she picked him up and cuddled him.

"It was either that or let him starve."

"You're lucky he didn't starve here. We're only just scraping by ourselves most days," grumbled Walter.

The woman went over to the mantelpiece and picked up another of the battered photos on the mantelpiece.

"This is your grandson, isn't it? This is him. The father. I swear. My Harry."

"No. There is no one by that name here. So, sling your hook, and take your baby with you."

"Father!" cried Mary. "Don't be rude."

"Well, she comes, dumps her brat on us and it's at the wrong house."

Grandpa lunged forward, trying to snatch the photo from the woman's grasp as she pointed at Daphne's brother.

"I am not in the wrong house at all!" she protested. "This is Harry. Right there, on the right."

"Ah," Walter grumbled. "Now it's making sense."

"But--?" began Daphne, confused. "Are you saying you knew my brother?"

The girl looked surprised. "Walter was my brother. Walter Henry Parker. He never called himself Harry."

Mary looked puzzled until Grandpa spoke up.

"Harry's an old form of Henry, Mary. Henry the Eighth called himself Good Prince Harry as a lad. It looks like my grandson wanted to play the field without letting on who he really was, perhaps?"

"Why do you keep saying 'was'?" asked the woman.

"Well, my grandson is dead. Killed recently in an accident. Which means no one can confirm your story. So, you can take your child and—"

Mary gasped in shock as the woman let out a heart-wrenching wail.

"Walter Beresford! Why are you so horrible sometimes? It's clear she knows a lot about Henry. The baby looks like him. That baby is my poor boy's flesh and blood and we will do the right thing. You ignore this miserable old fool, lass. By the way, what's your name?"

"Celia."

"Well, Celia, why did you come here today?"

"I just wanted to see my baby."

She stroked the baby's cheek again, her body still trembling as she tried not to sob. Walter's eyes narrowed as he watched her.

"I miss him so much. You're doing a good job with him. He looks lovely and plump."

"That's because we've had to spend money on feeding him," Grandpa growled.

"I had no money. What was I supposed to do?"

"Let's get this straight," said Grandpa, looking at the photo. "You say my grandson here is the father of your child? So why haven't you been here before? Why wait so long to show up?"

"I haven't seen him for months. I wasn't sure where he was. He vanished."

"That's because he's been working in Essex," Daphne explained. "He got an apprenticeship."

"That makes sense. He told me he always wanted to be a railwayman. We lost touch when he got that apprenticeship, so he never knew about the baby. He was always moving from depot to depot. I did try to find him. I really did, but it wasn't meant to be."

The more the woman shared about Henry's background, the more the others believed it was true. Henry Parker was indeed the baby's father.

"How did you meet him?"

"'He used to come to my house a lot. Him and my brother were pals. Thick as thieves, too. Always laughing and joking. We got on loke a house on fire."

"So, you thought you'd trap Henry and get yourself a meal ticket and move out to the country with that nice railway career ahead of him?" Walter snapped.

"No, it wasn't like that. I—we—"

The girl looked like she would pass out.

"Daphne, let her sit down," said her mother. "She doesn't look like she's had any food in ages. Is there any stew left?"

"Mama!"

"Don't fuss about me, Mrs Parker," whispered Celia as she eased herself down.

Grandpa went over to the range and came back with a small plateful of food.

"Here, girl, there's a scraping left. You have it."

The girl stared at the congealed stew for a moment and then tucked in. The meal vanished in seconds. Daphne wondered if the girl would lick the plate clean she looked so hungry. Mary checked on the twins who were getting restless in their cot.

"So, where is your brother? And your parents? You look like you've been living on the streets," Grandpa continued.

"My mother kicked me out for having the baby. It's not been easy."

"Your own mother?"

The woman nodded.

"She was so ashamed. The judging eyes and gossiping wore her down. And he's got a good set of lungs on him when he wants something."

"So, where have you been living?"

"Here and there. Wherever I could get a bed really. Pa left a year ago with some strumpet from down the street. Half his age she was. Ma was heartbroken. I haven't seen him since."

"My goodness, and do you have other siblings?" Mary asked.

"Three younger sisters and my older brother I told you about, Harry's chum. My mother found herself another fella when pa upped sticks. I was actually a bit relieved when she threw me out because I couldn't stand her new bloke. He had a nasty temper when he was drunk and used to beat me up. Mind you, at first, getting a walloping some of the time seemed better than being on the streets all of the time. Eventually, though, I got sick of the beatings. My brother visited once and I asked where Harry was, but they had lost touch too."

"You poor girl," said Mary as she picked up one of the twins.

Daphne held her breath, anxious that her mother might weaken and ask the woman to stay. She guessed the woman was infested with fleas, and her long, damp hair was full of lice.

"We called your baby Johnny after my boy who died last year," she heard her mother say. "What did you name him?"

"Harry after his pa."

"This little chap's called Walter, after his grandad," said Mary rubbing her baby boy's belly affectionately. "Have you had him christened?"

"I never got round to it."

"So, we can carry on calling him Johnny. If that's alright with you?"

The woman shrugged. Daphne couldn't understand why her mother was talking as if there was a future with this girl and the baby. How would the seven of them all squash in the little bedroom upstairs?

"You can call him what you like, Mrs Parker. His name is the least of my problems."

Celia stood up to leave.

"Um—I—"

"You sit yourself down, girl," said Walter, finally dropping his guard. "If you're telling the truth, and the baby is really the son of my grandson, then, he's staying here, and you with him. Can't have my great-grandchild sleeping in a doorway."

Daphne couldn't bite her tongue any longer.

"But, Grandpa, where will this woman sleep? We're all crammed in as it is?"

"She can have my cot bed in the annexe. I'll sleep down here in the armchair."

Celia turned to stare at him.

"No. I can't have you doing that. I'll doss in a doorway or in one of the lodging houses down the street. As long as I get to see him a bit, I can cope with anything."

Daphne shook her head as her mother made Celia an offer.

"You're doing no such thing, my dear. But if you are staying here, you'll have to take a hand bath and scrub down with some carbolic soap. You're in a shocking state. Daphne, pop over to the washrooms and get some hot water, will you?"

With a firm shake of her head, Daphne turned up her nose.

"I shan't. You've all gone mad. Why should she sleep in a bed when Gramps is forced into the chair? I'm going to Sarah's."

"How dare you!" her mother growled.

Daphne grabbed her coat by the door and went out before she'd finished putting it on. As she stormed off, she couldn't shake off the thought of Celia moving in. What would people think? What would Jimmy McGinty say about people lodging free? How would they manage all cooped up, living just above the breadline as it was? She needed to talk to Sarah about it.

"I suppose I'll have to go and get some then," grumbled Grandpa, unaware of the storm brewing in his granddaughter's mind.

18

STRAINED RELATIONS

Daphne sat in the Bradley's house, complaining bitterly.

"She's a trollop, Sarah, barely older than me, and they are welcoming her like the prodigal son. We won't see a penny of housekeeping money from her, you mark my words."

"Watch your mouth, Daphne Parker," said Mrs Bradley. "Show a bit of compassion. She's the mother of your nephew. And having the baby around will soften the blow of losing Henry for your ma."

"Yes, but why have her in the house as well? Reverend Bennett can find a place for her at the Young Women's Christian Mission round the corner. That's close enough."

Mrs Bradley looked up from her sewing.

"I thought Catholics preached good will to all men. You're not acting in a very Christian manner."

The woman was right. She should feel compassion for the girl. Celia hadn't chosen the rocky path she walked.

"You know, some men will tell a girl anything to get their way with them, even your brother. He used to knock about with Lydia Kirkham's son, Henry. I'm sure that lad's tried it on with every girl on the street. Your brother probably promised to marry her. They all say that, and some silly girls still fall for it."

Daphne pouted.

"Besides, it's almost Christmas," added Sarah. "That's not the time to leave someone on their own."

To lighten the mood, Sarah rummaged behind the dresser in the kitchen and pulled out an unfinished scarf.

"I'm making this for pa," she said, holding up the colourful yarn.

Daphne recalled the Christmas card she'd been making for her father. There's no point finishing it now.

"He will love that. Looks nice and warm," Daphne said dejectedly.

"Oh, forgive me, I'm so sorry. Here's me talking about my pa, when yours is—"

Sarah put back the knitting where she'd found it.

"What about your ma? Are you making her anything?"

"I made a little tapestry. But I haven't got anything for the twins. They weren't due 'til after Christmas. Grandpa's got nothing either because I didn't know he'd be home with us. With everything that's happened, I forgot. What shall I do now?"

She burst into tears and Sarah put her arm around her.

"I'll help you. What would you like to make?"

"I'm useless at making most things, and I am at work during the day, so I don't have time to learn new skills!"

"Don't fret," replied Mrs Bradley, as her needles seemed to fly into action. "I'll run you up a few things to help. It won't take long to run up a pair of booties for the little 'uns. But your grandfather, now he's a different matter."

"I should be paid soon then I can buy him something—if I've earned enough. I promised to give him all my wages for the housekeeping."

"I am sure he'll let you keep a few coppers back for some treats."

Daphne wiped her eyes.

"I suppose. Thank you. I'm glad I came."

"Let's play a game of cards, Daphne?"

"Won't you want to finish your pa's scarf while he's not here, missy?"

Sarah looked at her mother in hope.

"—And don't ask me to do it, my girl. I still have enough to do as it is."

Daphne looked glum again.

"I'll still have time to help you, Daphne. Goodness knows your family needs a break. It's been a while since I made baby clothes and Sarah doesn't seem to be in a rush to meet a husband and give me a grandchild."

Daphne remembered the conversation with her friend in the park. Mrs Bradley would be in for a long wait if Sarah had her way. Mrs Bradley stretched and then stood up.

"I'm off upstairs for a lie-down. Don't make a racket playing cards."

"We won't, mama," Sarah promised as she dealt. "Let's not play Snap. That gets a bit rowdy. How about Old Maid?"

After four games, Daphne suggested playing patience for a change.

"Isn't it getting close to your bedtime, Daphne?" said Sarah, noting her friend's yawns accompanying her own.

"I don't want to go back in case Celia is still there."

"I'm really sorry, but I'm shattered. I could fall asleep standing up."

"Sorry, Sarah. I'm being selfish. I'll go."

"You'll just have to grin and bear things for a while. She might be a nice girl when you get to know her? If your brother loved her she must have some good qualities, I expect?"

Sarah helped her friend into her coat.

"Celia never said they were in love."

"If she had his baby there must have been some connection. Just be patient. Give the girl a chance."

Sarah opened the door to number five and manoeuvred the girl through it.

"Good night, Daphne. I'll wait to hear what happens. Come after dinner tomorrow? Yes?"

Even though it was the last place she wanted to be Daphne's only choice was to return home.

When she returned, a girl with sparkling eyes, luscious locks, and perfect skin was sat in the armchair, dressed in one of her mother's old frocks, feeding baby Johnny a bottle. Could it be the same girl? If it was, she certainly scrubbed up well! Daphne stood holding the door wide open, taken aback by the sight. Walter, ever the raconteur, was regaling Celia with some of his old sea dog tales, and the room was alight with laughter and cheer.

"Were you born in a barn?" called her grandfather. "Shut that door. You're letting out all the heat."

"I'm sorry, Grandpa," she replied, still staring at the girl.

It had to be Celia, but where was all the filth?

"Now you're back, I'm turning in, Daphne. You two better get yourselves upstairs. Don't wake your mother or the twins."

"You girls can share Daphne's old bed. It's just about big enough," he said, before swapping places with Celia. "Little Johnny can stay down here with me in his pram. Thank you for your company this evening. We've had a giggle, haven't we?"

"Oh gosh, yes," said Celia with a grin as she tucked Johnny under his blanket.

"Goodnight, Grandpa," said Daphne, making a point of not acknowledging the girl.

"Goodnight, sweetheart."

Daphne felt crestfallen as she noticed that Gramps didn't watch her go upstairs. She had always thought she was his favourite person in the world, but it seemed that he was more preoccupied with Celia and the boy. She felt usurped or upstaged, or whatever the right word was.

The following morning, when Daphne went downstairs, she heard shuffling by the stove. It was Celia. She peered over the bannister, hoping she might catch the woman doing something untoward. What that might be, she didn't know. The main thing was it would give her an excuse to blab to her grandfather and get rid of her.

"Cuppa?" said Celia.

"No."

Daphne was desperate for a sip of tea but declined. She sat at the table to tie her bootlaces.

"I was going to make porridge," Celia added. "Would you like some? It's a long time to lunch."

The tasty hot breakfast would have been welcome, but Daphne wasn't about to indulge the woman. She'd rather starve.

"I don't have time. Some of us have work to get to. And we can barely afford to feed ourselves, let alone lodgers staying rent-free!" Daphne snapped.

"Your folks said I can stay here. But it seems you're not happy about it."

"Not happy? I'm livid!"

At least Daphne knew she would be at Miss Lawson's shop that day, far away from Celia, even if her hard work was earning money to pay for the interloper's keep. She wondered if the woman would ever contribute something to the household coffers. She didn't seem the most employable of people.

"When are you going to get a job, Celia? Ma should be able to look after Johnny, so you can get out and start looking today."

"I'll get one."

"When?"

"Soon—"

"Morning. Everything all right?" Walter asked, looking at Daphne with mild disapproval as if he had overheard her berating Celia.

"I'm off to work, Grandpa."

"Have you had breakfast? You shouldn't go out in this weather without something hot."

"I'm fine. I seem to have lost my appetite today."

Her stomach growled as she trudged towards Miss Lawson's haberdashery, regretting her stubborn decision to turn down breakfast. If Miss Lawson didn't offer to take her for lunch, her belly would feel like her throat had been slit all afternoon. Her papa always warned that her stubbornness would land her in trouble. He had a point.

In her haste, she arrived at the shop too early, so she perused the other shop fronts along Wellington Road, comparing them to Miss Lawson's, and decided they weren't nearly as beautiful. She felt chilled to the marrow, having forgotten her shawl. In her rush to leave, she had only pulled on her coat and bonnet. The coat was protective, but the straw bonnet was next to useless against the bitter northerly wind. Stamping her feet and clapping her hands did nothing to warm her. By the time Miss Lawson arrived and apologised for her own poor punctuality yet again, Daphne was like a block of ice. Freezing cold and shivery, she could barely move.

"Goodness, look at you, girl. Let's light a fire and put the kettle on to thaw you out!" Miss Lawson said as she noticed Daphne's shivering form.

As she poured the tea, Daphne explained about the uninvited guest at home.

"I don't want to sound petty or selfish, Lillian, but I don't see why we have to look after her. I can just tell she'll never contribute anything to the rent or food. Without my wages from here, as a family, we'd be really struggling."

"But isn't it a good thing that this little boy has been reunited with his mother? You don't seem pleased?"

"I'm being silly, but Grandpa seems to like her more than me."

"Ah, the green-eyed monster," Miss Lawson chuckled knowingly.

"What's that?"

"Jealousy," Lillian explained as she flipped the sign to 'OPEN'. "You've been the apple of your grandfather's eye your whole life. Now you think Celia could replace you in his heart, yes?"

"Something like that."

"She won't, Daphne. He's just looking out for her. She's in desperate need of help. You should be glad to have such a kind and caring grandfather. Not everyone is capable of such compassion. She's the mother of his great-grandchild. There's a blood connection there, even if you don't want to recognise it."

"Yes, I see your point. Ignore me. I'm just being silly," Daphne lied, disagreeing vehemently but wanting to retreat from the debate.

The young woman strode purposefully across the storeroom and snatched a pair of heavy black scissors from the cutting table. For a fleeting moment, she imagined driving the sharp blades into Celia's chest, but the shears slipped from her hands as if she had been burned. *'How depraved I've become!" she whispered. "Please save me, Lord, or I'll end up in hell.'*

"Everything alright?" asked Miss Lawson, hearing the loud clatter.

"Yes, Lillian. I knocked something over. Everything's fine." she replied in monotone.

"Cheer up, petal. You'll sort this out. You're lucky to still have your grandpa around. Think of those girls who never knew their grandfathers and how they must feel."

"You're right. I should be more grateful for what I have. Do you still have a grandpa?" she asked as an afterthought.

"Yes. He lives up in Derbyshire. He's so far away I hardly see him, though. You're fortunate to have yours there every day for you."

"How's the storeroom coming?" said Lillian as went to survey the back room.

She eyed up the neat rolls of fabric.

"Gosh, look at this place. We must make sure all your hard work is maintained. I've never seen the stock looking so tidy. You're a star."

Puffing out her chest, Daphne returned to the back room in a much brighter mood than when she first went in. She tackled another disorganised corner. Numerous boxes of ribbons and bows that had not been opened in years were covered in dust. She attempted to blow it off, but it billowed up in tiny clouds, causing her to sneeze repeatedly. Miss Lawson darted in.

"Dear me, I hope you're not coming down with something."

"No!—" Sneeze. "It's—just the—." Sneeze. "Dust."

Daphne thought she had her handkerchief with her, but after poking her fingers up the cuffs of her sleeves, she realised she didn't. The dust irritated her eyes as well, making them scratchy and hot. Blinking did nothing. Miss Lawson pushed a hanky into her sneezing underling's hands, but even after Daphne blew her nose harder than a foghorn, the sneezes continued. The doorbell tinkled and Miss Lawson went back out to the shop. A dozen incapacitating sneezes later, dizzy and weak at the knees, Daphne collapsed on a tea chest, her head aching and her eyes watering. A couple of minutes later, Lillian came to check on her.

"You look like you could do with a cuppa! Go and make one. It'll give you some time to recover. You'll frighten the customers looking all red and puffy like that."

Daphne added three teaspoons of tea to the pot as she pondered over her feelings towards Celia. Was it because her brother had not mentioned he had a secret girlfriend? They had been so close. What if he did know about the baby? Was he afraid to tell the family? She and Henry had always confided in one another, but Daphne had no clue about his involvement with the woman. She carried the drinks into the shop, lost in thought.

"Better now, lass?"

"Yes, thanks. I don't think I've ever sneezed that much in my whole life."

"I'm sure it's just the dust, Daphne. Nothing to worry about."

"I hope so. One of the girls who lived a few doors down from us recently died from diphtheria. I bumped into her just before she fell ill. We were in the corner shop. You don't think it's that, do you?"

"No, child. My mother died from that awful disease last year, God rest her soul. I don't recall her ever having a sneezing fit, just a very sore throat before the fever took hold."

"I'm sorry to hear about your mother," the girl said, then swallowed a few times to check that her throat didn't hurt, just to be on the safe side.

"Thank you for your kind words, Daphne. That reminds me. our mothers share the same maiden name. I wonder if we could be related?"

"I doubt it. It's a very common name, Beresford."

"Yes, but it's strange. I feel such an affinity for you, Daphne. I can't put my finger on why. And you did say your parents came from one of the cotton mill towns in the Midlands. I mean, it might be unlikely, but it's not impossible. Perhaps it's fate you asked to work here? Perhaps we belong together? Ask your grandfather about his parents and grandparents."

"I think they came from Ireland? Not England?" Daphne said, "Us being Catholics, and all that?"

"Just ask him!" Miss Lawson insisted as she went off to serve a customer. "I need to know."

Daphne was amazed. Could it be true? Wouldn't it be amazing if she discovered they were distant cousins? With renewed vigour, Daphne went back to her tidying task.

After finishing work, Daphne hurried home, eager to ask her grandfather about their family history. She was excited at the prospect of discovering a connection to Miss Lawson. To the girl's relief, Celia was not home when she arrived.

"Come and warm yourself, love" Mary greeted.

"It's good to see you up and about, mama."

"Yes, I can't stay in bed all day looking at the same four walls reading the same newspaper. I'll go round the twist. As long as I don't overexert myself, I'll be fine."

"Where's Gramps?"

"He went for a walk—"

Her mother hesitated.

"—with Celia and Johnny. They should be back shortly."

Mary put a cast-iron pan on the range as Daphne thumped about setting the table.

"By the way, Miss Lawson has asked me to inquire about Grandpa's parents' names."

"Well, Grandpa's family name is Beresford. As for your father, he was a foundling. He got the name Parker from his adoptive parents. No one ever knew his birth name."

"Oh. That makes things trickier. Did I tell you Lillian's husband's first name?"

"No."

"It's a strange one—Percival."

"Percival? Wasn't he one of those Knights of the Round Table?"

"Oh, mama! You mean Lancelot," Daphne chuckled. "I wouldn't call him a knight, though. Percival doesn't seem remotely chivalrous, just cold and calculating."

"Miss Lawson must love him, or she wouldn't have married him," said Mary, looking tired as she prepared to peel some potatoes.

"Let me do that, mama. Why don't you go back to bed?" Daphne offered.

"I'm fed up with lying in bed, that's why. I'll be fine."

"Alright, I'll finish dinner. You can sit in the armchair. Is that a deal?"

Daphne tried once more to prise her mother off the stool, but the obstinate woman wouldn't budge, preferring to do battle with the spuds instead. A gust of icy wind blew in through the door as her grandfather and his walking companions returned. They were giggling like Daphne used to giggle with him. It felt most unfair.

"Ah, Daphne," Walter said with a warm grin. "We were—"

Daphne couldn't care less what her grandfather had been doing with Celia, and interrupted him gladly.

"Dinner's almost ready, Grandpa. Hurry up."

"Good day to you, too, Daphne," he grumbled.

"Mama, shall I dish out the dinner when it's ready?"

"Yes, please, if you would."

Daphne gave her mother the largest portion because she needed the extra to feed the twins. Her grandfather had the next biggest because he was a grown man. Daphne had a bit less than him. She made sure the scrapings were left for Celia.

They sat down at the table and Grandpa said grace. When he opened his eyes, he noticed the variable portion sizes and gave Daphne a glare from under his wiry eyebrows.

"Is this all there is? Isn't there a little more for our guest?"

"She can scrape out the pan if she wants. It's over there."

Daphne looked down and pushed her food around on her plate.

"This is plenty, Walter. Please don't worry about me."

"You need to build up your strength, Celia."

Walter fetched the saucepan.

"Humph! There doesn't seem to be any left. Here,
I've got too much, take some."

He spooned some off his plate onto Celia's and Mary did
the same.

"Me, too. I'll never eat all this."

Daphne continued to eat, her head bowed in case her
grandfather was scowling at her. There was no way she
was going to offer any of her food. At that point, Celia had
more than she did. The meal was finished in silence. As
the last fork clattered on the plate, their house guest
jumped to her feet to wash the dishes. Daphne, who now
considered herself the breadwinner, was pleased that no
one said it was her job to do the clearing up.

Her mother pushed herself away from the table, so exhausted that she could hardly stand. Walter went to her
rescue and offered a steadying hand.

"You don't mind if I leave you all to it? I'm bushed."

"Of course not, Mary. You should have gone back to
bed earlier."

"I'm fine, stop fussing."

"You're still as stubborn as a mule, even when you're
tired," Grandpa muttered.

"I'll come and tuck you in, mama."

"You will not. What did I say about fussing?"

Once Daphne was sure her mother was asleep upstairs, she padded over to the twins, sleeping soundly in their cot and sat watching them for a while. She still couldn't tell Walter from Winnie. She stroked the cheek of the one she thought was the girl. The child tossed its head from side to side, angry at being disturbed.

"No, little one. Please don't wake up. Mama's only just gone to sleep. I only wanted to keep you company."

Luckily, the baby settled down again, and with a sigh of relief, Daphne went back downstairs. The place was immaculate. With Grandpa commandeering the armchair, Daphne sat on one of the stools next to Celia after pulling it as far away as she could. Her grandfather watched her as he puffed away at his pipe. As she settled, Daphne remembered the conversation with the Bradleys about Christmas.

"Grandpa?"

"Yes, child."

"You know when I'm paid my wages on Friday," she said, emphasising the word 'wages' to make a point.

He nodded, taking another deep puff.

"Well, can I keep a few pennies back to buy some presents?"

"Of course, child. It's only right that you keep a little money for yourself."

"Thank you," she said, glad that the conversation had been easier than she'd anticipated.

Celia looked nervous as she lowered her head and began picking intently at the skin around her fingernails.

"Tomorrow, I am going out to look for work, " she muttered. "All day if I have to. Until I get something sorted. I don't want to be a burden, Walter."

"That's good news. You'll be able to save up quickly and get your own place since you're staying here rent-free." Daphne snapped.

Celia cast her glum eyes across to Walter and then returned to picking at her fingernails. Walter cut into the dispute.

"She'll stay as long as she wants, Daphne. As the proverb says,' Whoever despises his neighbour is a sinner, but blessed is he who is generous to the poor.'"

"I've heard jobs are going for women sorting dead horse hair down at Mr Gould's knackers' yard. I suggest you pay him a visit," Daphne said coolly. *"'Beggars can't be choosers'*, to quote another proverb."

Celia flinched at Daphne's suggestion of the ghastly job, but before she could respond, there was a knock at the door, and Mrs Irvine could be seen peering through the window.

"I hope I'm not putting ye oot, but I had to see wee Johnny."

She saw Celia and stopped.

"Och, I'm sorry. I didn't know ye had a visitor."

"She's not a visitor. This is Celia, Johnny's birth mother," Daphne blurted out. "She arrived unannounced yesterday."

The woman's eyes seemed to grow larger and her one jet-black tooth became clearly visible again.

"Oh, I see."

Daphne turned to Celia.

"You nearly lost your baby to Mrs Irvine here. She wanted to keep him since you abandoned him."

"So, are ye taking him away, Celia?"

"I don't know what I'm doing yet."

"She is staying as long as she wants, Mrs Irvine," said Walter as he settled back in the armchair. "She is the mother of my great-grandson. Not many men get to be so blessed."

"So, he's Henry's? My, oh my. Now that ye mention it, I can see he's got his dad's eyes. That's a silver lining for ye, Walter. A part of Henry living on. Could I give him a cuddle? I've missed the wee laddie."

"Of course," Celia cooed as she took him from his pram and put him in the woman's arms.

The look of ecstasy on Mrs Irvine's face as she cuddled him melted Daphne's heart. How could one woman be robbed of a baby and yet have so much love for one? It didn't seem fair, especially with the cruel accusations following her too. It was so sad. After a few minutes, the woman handed Johnny back to Celia, blinking hard to hide the tears in her eyes.

"Och, I'd better be off. Lots to be getting on with. Please give my regards to Mary. I hope she bides well. Bye."

Even after Daphne shut the door behind Mrs Irvine, the poor woman's sobs could still be heard.

"I'd better turn in," said Celia. "Job hunting tomorrow."

"I feel so sorry for Mrs Irvine, Gramps. She can't have any more children. It's so sad. She clearly adores them. Why is it the people who shouldn't have children can have them at the drop of a hat, while others who deserve them don't get their wish?"

"That's how life goes sometimes, my dear. You'll come to know it as you grow up. Life can be unjust, but we must learn to accept it and make the best of what we have. As good Christians, we have a responsibility to care for one another in times of need. When we show kindness to others in their struggles, they will be kind to us when we struggle too."

"I suppose so, Grandpa."

As she went upstairs to share her old bed with Celia, she looked down at Walter, puffing away at his pipe as he made his makeshift bed in the armchair again.

Yes, life was often unfair.

19

SEEKING APPROVAL

The next day, Daphne surveyed the shop's storeroom with a sense of pride. The project had been a much-needed distraction from the troubles she faced at home. Hoping for some well-deserved recognition, she awaited Miss Lillian's final inspection. The boxes were neatly stacked and labelled, the slow-moving and excess stock earmarked for the post-Christmas sale, the drawers emptied, dusted, and restocked in an orderly fashion.

"Goodness, Daphne, everything looks impeccable! I can see at a glance whatever I have come in for," Lillian trilled, eliciting relief and joy in her assistant.

As Miss Lawson went to assist a customer, Daphne allowed herself a moment of satisfaction before refocusing on her duties. It would be short-lived. The little brass doorbell tinkled again. Daphne looked up to see a familiar face, but she couldn't quite place where she had seen the woman before. She spoke to the shopkeeper.

"I'd like to buy some pretty coloured ribbons, please. A yard of each."

As Daphne heard the woman's voice, she realised who she was: the mother of the boy at church she was sweet on. Would the woman recognise her? The girl's heart raced as the customer briefly looked her way, but then turned away without a word. Daphne quickly fled to the safety of the storeroom, and a few minutes later, Miss Lawson followed her in.

"So, this is where you vanished, is it? I just wanted to thank you for all your hard work. You really have transformed my shop into a place of beauty. As you know, it was a chance taking you on, but I am glad I did. That lady was saying only a moment ago what a delightful haberdasher it is."

"Do you know her?"

"No, child. I am good with faces, I'm sure it was her first time in the shop. Your window display drew her in. She said she'd come back tomorrow for some fabric once her husband's been paid. Do you know her?"

"Not really. I think she attends my church with her son."

"I see. Like that is it? Has he caught your eye, then?"

"No."

Daphne blushed and opened a drawer pretending to take something out.

"I've never really spoken to him. He smiles at me sometimes, that's all."

"What's he like, this boy?"

"Well, he looks tall and strong with broad shoulders."

"Go on—"

"His eyes are dark. His hair is wavy and has a natural tousled look."

"And—"

"His jawline, it's so defined, it looks like it was chiselled from stone."

"It sounds to me like you have a crush on this chap since you can describe him in such detail."

As Daphne's face went tomato red, Lillian decided to have a little more fun with the girl.

"I'm still young enough to remember what a crush feels like. Here's a good question. How old do you think I am, Daphne?"

The girl stayed silent, fearing that if she was wrong, Lillian would reprimand her.

"Well? Have a guess, then."

"Erm, twenty-five?"

"Are you trying to humour me, Miss Parker? I left that age behind at least a decade ago."

"Forty? My mama turns forty next year. She jokes that she'll be old and decrepit then, but with the two little ones to care for, she probably feels ancient already. You haven't had any babies yet, I take it, Lillian?"

The fun was over. Miss Lawson gave Daphne a blank look before changing the subject. The girl wondered if her question had upset her employer, or perhaps Miss Lawson was expecting a child and had not told anyone yet? However, Daphne's train of thought was interrupted when she felt the stitching on one of her boots give way. For several weeks, she had been squeezing her growing feet into her best pair. Now, the sole was separating from the upper. She looked down and saw her big toe wriggling. Horrified, she tried to cover the damage by pulling her dress down a little lower. Normally, she would have picked up some second-hand boots from Bert the rag man on Dean Street, but l, for now, she lacked the time and the money.

Later that afternoon, as the stream of customers into the little shop subsided, the two of them finally had a chance to chat.

"Crikey, Daphne. I can't believe how busy we've been. Everyone says the window display enticed them to come inside. You're such an artistic girl."

"Yet my mama calls me a nincompoop because I can't knit."

"You cheeky monkey!" Miss Lawson teased. "You said you could when I interviewed you last week! Were you lying to me?"

Daphne didn't pick up on the joke.

"Erm—more of a white lie, in my defence. I can knit, but I've never really mastered the art."

"We can't be good at everything, lass. I can knit, and spend many an hour doing it. I'll show you one day."

"Thank you. There's another thing, Lilian."

"Go on."

"Do you have any idea how much a smoking pipe costs?"

"Don't tell me you're taking up the habit?" the woman said with a grin.

"No. Gosh! It's for my grandfather. I'd like to get him a new one for Christmas. I don't know if I'd have enough money. His old one is carved like a sailor's head—"

"Let me guess—because he was a sailor."

"Exactly! Do you know where I can get one?"

"The tobacconist on Commercial Road will have some, I'm sure. I would say to pop along now, but I can see some women admiring your display. They might come in. Oh, look, they are," Lillian whispered as all three trotted in.

"Hello, ladies, it's such a fine day. How can we be of service?"

When customers entered the store, Daphne quickly forgot about her broken boot and focused on helping Lillian measure ribbons, look for lace, and match lost buttons. At the end of the day, they stood with hands on hips, twisting to ease their aching spines. The shopkeeper opened the till and counted out some money.

"I'm sure this is my biggest day's takings yet," she said, handing a small coin to Daphne.

Daphne looked down at the money in her hands, shocked and saddened.

"Oh, is this my pay? I thought I wasn't getting paid until tomorrow."

Daphne fidgeted awkwardly.

"What's wrong, girl? Speak up."

"Well, I thought I'd have earned more," said Daphne, glumly.

"Oh, you silly thing. That's not your wages. It's a bonus, a little bit extra for being such a helpful assistant."

"Won't your husband be angry about the bonus?"

"What's he to do with it? He doesn't need to know. Anyway, he leaves the running of the shop to me. He has no interest in it at all."

Daphne lifted her skirt to show her protruding toe.

"I think I'll have enough to get a pair of boots off Bert!"

"You can't go out like that," Miss Lillian exclaimed, closing the door and flipping the sign to closed. "Come on, let's see if I have a pair of boots that will fit you. You won't mind if I give them to you, will you?"

"Mind? Of course not. I'd be delighted, honoured even. But your feet look smaller than mine."

"You can be such a pessimist, Daphne. Let's just see, shall we? And while we're at it, let's see if another dress fits so you can have a change from that one."

Even with a big toe protruding from her battered boot, a gleeful Daphne bounced upstairs to look in the wardrobe again. It was strange, she'd only been working there for a few days, and yet she was so settled, it felt like years. How grateful she was to be earning and not learning stuffy old facts or times tables she knew off by heart already.

Lillian opened one of her luggage trunks to reveal several pairs of dainty shoes, most made out of exquisite satin. She chuckled when she saw Daphne's face.

"These are no good for walking the dirty streets of Whitechapel, are they? These were my dancing shoes."

"You used to dance?"

Daphne took out a graceful pink shoe, encrusted with pretty beads and admired its beauty.

"Yes, and sing. I had a vibrant voice in my youth. I performed at many a soirée."

The girl had no idea what a soirée was. Lillian grabbed the shoe and put it back next to its partner in the trunk, then swiftly shut the lid. Daphne marvelled at the facets of her employer's life. It seemed there was one surprise after another when they had their chats. There were hidden depths to Miss Lawson, that was for sure. The woman bit her lip and her brow furrowed.

"—It must be nearly ten years now."

"I have an Aunt Jessie," said Daphne. "Well, I think I do. I haven't seen her for a good while. Not since I was really little. She came to see us when the first set of twins were born years ago. She married and moved to Cumberland or some other foreign country."

Lillian laughed.

"My dear Daphne, Cumberland isn't overseas. It's still in England."

"Oh!" said the girl, disappointed by the display of her lack of basic geography.

Her mistake made her wonder how much she had learned at school after all.

"By the way, Lillian, I meant to tell you, mama doesn't think we could be related. She doesn't know any Beresfords from Derbyshire."

"Ah, that's a pity. Still, it was a long shot, eh?"

Miss Lawson opened a suitcase, containing more sensible footwear, including some practical leather boots.

"Ever been to Cumberland, Daphne?" she asked as she picked out a boot and began lacing Daphne's foot into it.

"No, I've never been out of London really."

"We really must change that. Now, how does that fit?"

Daphne grimaced. She could feel the instep cutting in the moment they were laced.

"Gosh, I don't want to seem ungrateful—but they are pinching a bit. Maybe the pair next to them? They look a bit wider?"

"Alright. Try these on then, Cinderella," Lilian jested.

At last, Daphne's foot slid in easily. Lillian turned and picked out a blue dress from one of the wardrobes.

"This was my favourite."

She held the garment against her and twirled around.

"I felt grand when I wore this."

"But, Miss Lillian, you always look grand and beautiful whatever you wear," Daphne said as she tried on the other boot.

"Bless you for the compliment. Although I don't always feel pretty, especially since—. Oh, silly me, that one's too bright isn't it. I forgot you're in mourning. How about this charcoal grey one?"

Daphne examined the dress, which was similar to the one she was wearing, with a high neck and full sleeves. Only the colour differed.

"What do you think, Daphne? Is it dark enough? Not many people popping here know who you really are?"

Guilt pricked at her conscience. Would her papa and brother really mind if I didn't observe black mourning dress? Wouldn't they be more pleased she was getting on with her life and supporting her mother? She stroked the material, wanting to say she'd take it, but gave it back.

"May I ask mama and Grandpa first? To see if it's appropriate?"

"Yes, of course, my dear. Fear not," Miss Lillian chuckled as she hung it up, hoping to lighten the mood. "I'm sorry I didn't have the foresight for darker colours when I was younger."

"Lillian, please don't think me ungrateful. I appreciate your kind gesture. I am sure it will be fine. Would you mind if I took a few to show them sometime?"

"That's a bit inconvenient."

Daphne looked hurt.

"I'm sorry, dear. I didn't mean it like that. I meant carrying the dresses all the way to your house and back again. Don't mind me. You do what you want. By the way, how are the boots?"

"Wonderful. Thank you very much!"

Daphne skipped back to Prospect Street, swinging her old boots by the laces beside her. If she got Bert the rag man to take a look at them, they might be repairable for a few pence and her mother could get a bit more use out of them. Full of joy, she felt like singing. She'd never considered what singing voice she might have. She thought back to the conversation about Lillian and her cousin, Jesse and decided to ask some more questions about the Beresfords when she got home. As she turned into her road she saw Ivy at the Leahs' front door.

"Why are you out in the cold?" she asked the child.

"Waiting for ma. She says she'll not be long. We're off out."

"Are you going somewhere nice?"

"Don't know. When can I come and visit again?"

"I'm not sure, Ivy. With all the babies and Grandpa, and Celia. It's a bit crowded."

Mrs Leah came out and shut the door, grumbling.

"You can't trust a man to do anything. I asked him nicely to keep an ear out for the baby crying, and he promises to do that, but the next moment he's dozing off in the armchair, dead to the world. Now my little 'uns in a strop but I haven't got time to change his nappy. McGinty's shop will be closed soon and I don't have anything in for tea tonight."

"We could give you some food," Daphne suggested. "I'm sure we'll have something."

"No, lass, Thank you. You have enough mouths to feed. If we hurry, Jimmy's shop should still be open for a bit."

As Mrs Leah struggled to run while dragging a sullen Ivy behind her, Daphne regretted not offering to take care of the girl herself. She was so preoccupied with Mrs Leah's predicament that she was startled when Mrs Bridges suddenly appeared beside her and the wise woman's issued a warning from under her black shawl

"You'd better put your thick coat on tomorrow. It's going to snow tonight. Maybe sooner. A right blizzard I reckon. I saw it in the tea leaves this morning."

An army of workers appeared to be rushing back for their dinners. The cart men were driving their horses hard as they clip-clopped past much faster than usual. Daphne resisted going back home directly. She was certain that Celia would be putting herself first as usual, warming her bones by the range, like a plump cuckoo in the nest. When Mrs Bridge's weather prediction came true sooner than the girl had expected, Daphne had no choice but to head home. Pinning on a smile, she decided to share the good news about her boots.

"Look at these bobby dazzlers. Aren't I a lucky girl?" she said as she poked a foot round the door.

"Why, they're bonny, lass. Where did you buy those? Bert's? They look like new!"

Baby Johnny was a cheery little soul in his pram, but his mother was nowhere in sight. Daphne hoped that Celia was enduring a long and exhausting shift, retching at the equine horrors of Mr Gould's knacker's yard.

"I didn't buy the boots, Grandpa. Miss Lawson gave them to me. They are grand, aren't they?"

"Where is 'she'?" Daphne asked.

"Who? Your mother?"

"No. You know who."

She pointed to the empty stool by the pram.

"Her."

"You mean Celia?"

"Actually, I meant the lazy selfish strumpet," the girl muttered.

"I beg your pardon, Daphne Parker!"

Being a good Christian was a struggle when it came to Celia. Taking off her coat, the girl changed the subject.

"I bumped into Mrs Bridges not five minutes ago. She said it would snow."

"I could have told you that. You don't need to be going to that old crone for your weather forecasts. Going back to our conversation, Celia has gone to the match factory to find some work. There was a poster up in Jimmy's shop. She left hours ago, so I assume she was successful. I hope she comes back soon. It's getting treacherous out there."

"I doubt she'll do a runner with all the handouts she gets from us, Gramps."

"That's enough! Go and make yourself useful with some chores if you've got nothing nice to say."

Daphne went to the range to check dinner. It was potato soup that night, with no beef knuckle for flavour this time. Her jealousy began to bubble up again.

"I don't know, Grandpa. There's something about Celia. It doesn't make sense Henry going with her. Why would he? I still think she might be spinning a yarn"

Walter said nothing, although his tired sigh could easily be heard behind her.

"How about the fact that little Johnny looks like Henry? Will that do you? If you can't say anything nice, don't say anything at all. I am tired of the bickering between you two. I've got enough to worry about without you acting like a spoiled princess."

His criticism stung, but the girl's envy refused to fade.

"Sorry, Grandpa. Shall I take mama some tea? She must be awake. I can hear the floorboards creaking."

"Yes, that would be preferable to your continual griping. I'll have one as well."

The sound of a crying baby shattered the peace in the house, and then it quickly stopped.

"I bet that's Walter Jr," Daphne guessed. "He's only quiet when he's asleep or feeding. He's a greedy little thing, isn't he? He'll be as round as a football soon!"

Her grandfather didn't reply immediately. Instead, he put his hand on her forearm.

"It's probably little Winnie in distress. She's very poorly, love."

"How poorly?"

"Well, the midwife visited today. She isn't sure the poor mite will make it because she's so weak."

Daphne dashed upstairs to her mother.

"Grandpa just told me about Winnie, ma. She isn't dying, is she? Promise me! We can't lose another one of us so soon."

Her mother looked up from the baby in her arms.

"I'm praying she'll pull through, but she's so small, and refuses to eat."

Her mother unbuttoned her night shirt, trying desperately to get the child to suckle. Daphne knelt beside her and stroked the baby's tiny hand to comfort her, to show her she was very much wanted and desperately loved. A moment later, Winnifred's tiny little fingers clenched around Daphne's thumb.

"Look, she's gripping me ma, so she must be alright. She wants to stay with us."

"Let's pray it will be so, my love. I can't face losing another baby. I just can't."

They fell silent for a minute as Mary did her best to nurse the girl but it was useless. Grandpa came up with a cup of tea.

"How's Winnie faring?" he asked as he set it down.

"About the same. She did stop grizzling when Daphne arrived," Mary replied, smiling at her eldest daughter. "But she still won't feed."

"May I hold her, ma?" Daphne asked. "It'll give you a break."

Mary gently placed the baby in Daphne's arms and adjusted her clothes. The girl held the infant close, whispering in her ear that the Lord would watch over and protect her. Yet, suddenly, Winnie went completely limp like a rag doll. For a moment, Daphne thought the poor child had passed away. She concealed her anxiety as she investigated. Peeling back a bit of the blanket, as she had done with Johnny, she saw the infant's tiny neck still pulsing rhythmically to her heartbeat. What a relief. Mary picked up on Daphne's concern.

"Are you alright, petal?"

Daphne wondered if her unkind thoughts about Celia caused Winnie's health to falter? Was God punishing the baby in response to her own uncharitable thoughts?

"If her illness is my fault, I won't be able to forgive myself," Daphne whimpered.

"How could it be your fault? What makes you think that?"

"Because I've been so mean to Celia and her baby. The Lord is angry with me. Punishing me. And all of us."

"But how could your feelings for Celia make this little one ill?"

"I don't know, but she is so poorly, I can't think what else it might be!" Daphne wailed, looking up at the heavens, imagining God's displeasure bearing down on her. "It has to be a punishment."

Tears welled up in her eyes as her grandfather put his arm around her trembling shoulders.

"Calm yourself, lass. If God punished me for every unkind word I've said about someone, the whole world would be dead by now."

"Oh, Grandpa, you couldn't be that bad," she stuttered, then managed to smile through her tears.

"None of us are perfect, Daphne, except for these little ones who haven't had a chance to sin yet. They soon will when they get walking and talking." Mary chuckled. "If you feel that way, make a promise to treat Celia better and confess your sins to Father Lane on Sunday, and let's not mention this again?"

Mary took Winnie and laid her in her cot to doze.

"This little girl is in the hands of the Lord, and his alone. Merciful father, look after her."

"Amen to that," replied Walter.

A soft voice wafted up from downstairs.

"Ooee? Anybody home?"

"It's Mrs Irvine I'll see what she wants."

Daphne hurried downstairs, but not before noticing a tense exchange of glances between her mother and grandfather. She found Mrs Irvine cuddling Johnny who was squirming and punching her chin with one of his flailing fists.

"Och, I bet this one thought he'd been abandoned."

"We were only upstairs, and he was asleep. Baby Winnie isn't well."

"I hope it isn't anything serious, dearie?"

"We don't know."

"Well, ye know I'd take this one if I could to give ye a break, but his mother's here now. Mr Irvine has found himself a job. It doesn't pay as well as the last one, but we won't lose the roof over our heads. Plus, I could look after him if Celia changed her mind."

"That's wonderful. I'm happy that your husband has a job," Daphne said, ignoring Mrs Irvine's offer. "Was there anything else?" the girl said as she reached to take Johnny back.

Daphne berated herself for being so impolite, wondering if she would ever stop being so unkind.

"Forgive me. It's nice to see you. It's been a long day, and we're all worried about little Winnie."

"Yer fine lass. Don't worry. I just came to see the little lad. Och, he warms the cockles of my heart every time I catch sight of the wee bairn."

She kissed Johnny on the forehead tenderly and then looked outside.

"Perhaps I can take him for a stroll with Celia sometime?"

"Yes, perhaps. Thank you for calling round, and do congratulate Mr Irvine on getting his new job. What a relief that must be for you."

Mrs Irvine seemed reluctant to leave. Daphne held the door open while balancing Johnny on her hip. The lad wriggled wildly and she almost dropped him. Mrs Irvine wanted to intervene, but Daphne held strong.

"Night then," the girl said as she closed the door on the woman.

She felt mean, but she could hear the hiss of the potatoes boiling over on the range. Walter appeared before she reached the pan.

"I'll take care of that. You sit down."

He looked outside at the blizzard.

"I'm worried about Celia. She should have returned by now. She's only gone over to Bow."

Determined to change her spiteful jealousy, Daphne fought the urge to say she was glad Celia wasn't back. The girl sat Johnny on the rag rug in front of the hearth and played with him. At that moment, the front door opened and Celia returned, her face glowing from the cold, proudly wearing Mary's best coat. Daphne wondered if Celia had been given permission to wear it or did she just steal it when mama was dozing? Taking a deep breath, Daphne counted to ten. Her grandfather would be apoplectic if she started bickering again.

"Good evening, Celia," Daphne said as she took the coat off her and gave it a good shake.

"I was getting worried," said Walter. "How did it go?"

Celia warmed her hands by the fire, then gave Johnny's cheek a pinch.

"Evening, little one. Are you still awake?"

The young woman took the best armchair for herself as usual.

"Actually, I didn't find a job. Something far better happened," Celia announced as Daphne snorted in fury.

"Gosh. Whatever could be better than finding a job, Celia? Do tell us?"

"Can you believe it—I bumped into my ma. We had a lovely chat!"

"Oh, that's great news. Did you talk about when you were moving back in?"

Walter tutted at Daphne but she didn't care. She couldn't believe her luck. The cuckoo was about to flee the nest—and soon. However, her joy evaporated when Celia continued.

"Erm, no, not exactly. That would still be difficult. Everyone's talking about me being an unmarried mother, and she can't take it."

"Well, you're welcome to stay as long as you want, flower. It's wonderful news that you've patched things up with your mother. Families shouldn't fall out. Life's too short for quarrels. If and when you want to join your family—or not—then that's fine with us. Little Johnny will always make you part of ours."

Daphne stared at the flurry of silent snowflakes falling and bit her tongue.

20

MIXED EMOTIONS

The next morning, Daphne peered through the frosty ground-floor window at number twenty-two. The snow had formed a thick blanket over the cobbles, making for a treacherous journey to work. Despite the smooth and slippery soles of her boots causing her to slide and stumble, she was grateful for the gift that had kept her feet dry. She had to be at the haberdashers on time, no matter what the obstacles were. Today was payday, and she couldn't afford to miss out on her wages, even if it meant risking life and limb.

Her rate of pay had yet to be agreed upon, so she fantasised about all the things she could get for Christmas presents if her grandfather's gift didn't deplete all of her spare funds. Perhaps slippers for her mother and a new rattle for Johnny, although with luck, Daphne hoped Celia might have got a job by then and could buy him something herself.

Mrs Bradley hadn't sent over the bootees she'd offered to knit for the twins, but Daphne was confident they'd be finished on time. The girl wondered what to get Lillian. Getting something for her seemed the right thing to do. She had been so kind. When she thought of the cost of getting all the gifts, her face fell. What if someone had to do without?

She arrived at the shop almost sliding over an icy patch as she came to a halt, needing to grab the wooden window-sill to keep herself upright. Miss Lillian met her outside the store as snow fell once more.

"How are the boots holding up?"

"Wonderfully, thank you. I'd have frostbite if I was wearing my old ones!"

"You are welcome. I wondered if the leather might have cracked from being unused for so long, but they seem to have survived."

"They're marvellous. I polished them last night twice over. Grandpa said it would keep them supple."

"He's a clever man, your Grandpa."

Lillian hung her coat up in the back of the shop, smoothed her skirts and went out to the counter, leaving Daphne alone. The girl touched the coat. It felt lovely and thick, yet still soft to the touch. It had some delicate beadwork on it and a silk lining. She wished she could own something so soft and luxurious, then realised she would be forever panicking about it getting ruined in the rain. It would live in the wardrobe hanging in the dark like a bat in a cave, if she owned a wardrobe, that is. She smirked at the thought.

"What's so funny, Daphne?"

"Nothing, miss. Sorry, miss."

"Come on. You have work to do. It's time to learn more about selling."

After another quick squeeze of the plush coat fabric, Daphne entered the shop. Customers had already formed a line outside the door. It took over an hour to assist them all. One lady requested to see the entire collection of black ribbons.

"I need something to liven this mourning dress up," she complained, looking down at her outfit. "I know it should be mourning dress, but a little fancy work won't go amiss. My husband was nothing but trouble to me, and now he's making life difficult from beyond the grave, the miserable old toad."

Lillian showed her several reels of ribbon and the entire lace collection but to no avail.

"No!"

"Oh dear, no!"

"Is that the best you have? I need something fancier—but still understated."

The woman was incredibly hard to please. Remembering Lillian's coat, Daphne fetched the complete set of black beads from the drawer and put them out carefully on the counter.

"Would these be what you need, ma'am?"

"How clever of you! Perfect," said the harridan, nodding vigorously. "I'll take a dozen of each style."

Daphne sorted the buttons into pretty paper bags and folded down the tops. Pleased with her initiative, the girl totted up the total sale amount. It was a tidy sum. Her grandfather always told her to use her brain and her new job allowed her to do so daily. Unfortunately, it was so busy, there was no time to chat over lunch about her good sense that day. Daphne's stellar selling moment went unnoticed. Worse, stood up all day, her aching feet made it seem like an eternity until five o'clock. The leather was taking its time to mould to her shape. When the last shopper left Miss Lawson came to talk to her.

"Well, Daphne, it's appropriate that on the day you make your first decent sale, you receive your first wage."

Daphne beamed. Lillian had noticed. Soon, the girl forgot her aching back and feet. Lillian opened the till, counted some coins into her own hand, and then slid them into a small brown envelope. Daphne couldn't see how much she was given. Tentatively, she peered inside. Twenty shillings!

"But that's a whole pound! I can't accept this. It's too much. Especially after you gave me the boots. And lent me your dresses!"

"You are entitled to every penny! You've worked very hard on the display. And took on the challenge of sorting out the mish-mash of stock. And helped with serving customers. But don't expect that much every week, mind. This is to help you and your family after losing your pa. It will be ten shillings a week in future."

Daphne tipped up the envelope and watched the coins jingle into her cupped left hand. She counted them carefully. *'Yes! A whole pound.'* She hadn't expected anything like that much. Even ten shillings was a fortune for a young working-class lass.

"Oh, Lillian," the girl squealed before lurching forward to hug her. "Thank you! I feel as rich as Queen Victoria herself. Do you think she owns a pound?"

"I'm sure she does," Lillian chuckled, "although I hear she never takes her own money out."

"I can buy Grandpa his pipe and my mama the slippers, and you—I have no idea what to get you!"

Miss Lawson shook her head as she counted the day's bumper takings.

"I appreciate the offer, but no thank you, my dear. I've got all I need. Percival sees to that. You need this for your family. I suggest you treat yourself to something nice if you want to splurge. You've earned it."

As Lillian locked the shop door for the night, Daphne noticed one of the window display's paper chains had fallen down. Although she wanted to fix it, she sensed Lillian was in a hurry to leave. While Daphne waited, Miss Lawson gazed up and down the street, as if expecting someone. Soon, the girl heard heavy breathing behind her and turned, fearing an assailant wanting to mug her for her wages. She was relieved to see Mr Johnson emerge from the shadows, puffing and panting.

"What's wrong, dear?" asked Lillian, clutching his sleeve. "You look jiggered."

"Do you have to use such common phrases?"

Although he had to bend over to catch his breath, Mr Johnson still had the strength to scold his wife. It made Daphne feel awkward.

"I am sorry. I'll rephrase that, Percival. You seem— what was that word I heard someone say down at the market? Yes, that was it—knackered? Is that alright or still too common?"

Percival's arm rose, and Daphne feared he was going to strike his wife.

"Never use that type of language in front of me. It's most inappropriate."

The girl stepped back, not wanting to get involved in the domestic dispute, but felt guilty for not standing up for Lillian. Suddenly, Daphne lost her footing on an icy kerb. Her boots slipped out from under her as she went over on her ankle. Her arms flailed as she fought to keep her balance. Instinctively, Percival reached out and grabbed Daphne's coat collar, keeping her upright. Moments later, a heavy wooden cart clattered along the cobblestone street in front of them, the wheels barely missing Daphne's toes.

My dear!" Miss Lillian shrieked, taking the girl's arm. "If you'd slipped any further that cart could have killed you! Are you alright? What a fright. Did you hurt yourself?"

Daphne straightened up and checked that her feet were firmly planted on the pavement. She wriggled free of Percival's iron grip.

"I'm fine, thank you. I'd better be on my way."

"I'll see you in the morning. Thank you for your help this week."

With a backward glance, Daphne was relieved to see the couple walk away arm-in-arm, their quarrel seemingly forgotten. Had her mishap saved her boss from a beating? If it did, it would have been worthwhile, but the further she walked, the more her swollen ankle hurt.

As she limped along Dean Street though, the pain was soon forgotten. The accident in front of her happened so quickly, but for Daphne, it felt like it had unfolded in slow-motion. A girl had run out of a house right in front of her, screaming and bawling, waving her arms. Before Daphne could reach out, the girl dashed into the road and fell under the hefty hooves of a shire horse pulling a fully laden brewery dray. Yanking hard on the reins, the driver screamed at the startled horse to stop, but it careered into the path of a small omnibus approaching. The wagon shed its load and the bus toppled over, spewing all its passengers onto the icy ground. There were screams of terror and yowls of agony from all of them.

Although hindered by her ankle, Daphne hastened to the scene and gasped in horror as she recognised the girl, the one she had befriended a few days before, lying motionless in the road, drenched in blood.

"Finoula, Finoula," she cried, vigorously shaking the girl.

Her eyes remained closed as a woman eased Daphne away.

"Do you know her?"

"Yes, she lives there with—"

Daphne indicated an elderly lady, presumably her grandmother, wrapped in a tattered shawl, who was standing shivering at the front door. Tears trickled down the old lady's sunken cheeks as onlookers shook their heads at her.

"I shouldn't have shouted at her, but I didn't know she'd run out like that."

As Daphne took the old lady's arm and led her inside, a young labourer lifted the girl and carried her towards the house. He placed the frail and motionless figure on the family's kitchen table.

"Is she still alive?" the shocked grandmother whispered as Daphne tried to help her into an armchair.

"I hope so," Daphne said, crossing her fingers since the girl hadn't yet opened her eyes.

Seconds later, Mrs Bridges stormed in and pushed the man aside.

"Out of the way, sonny. Let me see."

As the wise woman examined the child, everyone in the cramped little room held their breath. Daphne realised her fingers were still crossed, but she kept them crossed to avoid tempting fate. The girl felt a small soft hand creep into hers. Daphne looked down and saw that little Ivy had snuck into the house. She clutched Ivy's tiny fingers so tightly that some of the knuckles cracked.

"Is she dead?" she whispered.

Daphne tried to deduce from Mrs Bridges's posture, but she couldn't read her body language. Finally, the old crone stood up and turned to face the crowd.

"Well?" one of them asked, eager to know the fate of the girl.

Mrs Bridges shook her head solemnly and looked down at the floor. Finoula's grandmother screamed and sank further into her chair. The onlookers murmured louder and louder until their voices became deafening. Daphne was shocked and wanted to flee, but Ivy still clung to her.

"What did she say?" the child cried. "Is she dead?"

"I'm not sure," Daphne lied.

Not wanting to be the bearer of bad news, she looked for Mrs Leah, but she was nowhere to be seen in the crowd pushing forward to see for themselves.

"Let's find your ma," Daphne told her as she went through the crowd towards Prospect Street, but Ivy had other plans.

"I want to see my friend."

"That's not a good idea. Let's take you home."

"No." the child protested, stamping her foot. "I want to see her and I will."

Daphne couldn't drag Ivy away, so she let the girl go. Soon a high-pitched wail rang out above the mutterings of the crowd. Seconds later, Daphne spotted her grandfather at the doorway peering over the sea of heads. She forced her way over to him and fell into his arms, her face pushed up against his chest. He stroked her head fondly.

"Thank goodness it wasn't you, Daphne. We heard such a commotion and that a youngster has been badly hurt."

"It's Finoula, the girl I told you comes from the North. This is her grandmother's house. I saw her run out, but I couldn't stop her, Grandpa. And now she's dead."

"It wasn't your fault. Don't feel bad, love," he consoled, but she still felt responsible.

Walter led her outside thinking it would be quieter but he was wrong. A man attempted to direct the cartmen and barrow boys around the upturned bus, but they had other ideas on how to organise themselves. Men staggered, goods tumbled into the road, and tempers frayed.

"Come away, child," Grandpa said as he did his best to steer Daphne home.

She wriggled free. Forgetting her injured ankle, she tried to run between two carts and nearly slipped under another one herself. Grandpa caught her.

"What's the matter, Daphne? Why all the rush? Are you trying to get yourself killed as well?"

Walter helped his traumatised granddaughter back home, his arm around her waist, her arm around his neck. Mary stood at the doorstep, watching and waiting, her shawl pulled tightly around her torso.

"What's happening out on Dean Street?" she asked. "I couldn't sleep with all the racket."

As Walter explained, Daphne could hear Johnny gurgling in his pram and a faint moaning from one of the twins upstairs. The heavy front door muted most of the chaos outside and her tensed nerves eased as she threw her coat on the hook and settled into the armchair.

"Where's Celia?" asked her mother, shoving the poker into the hearth, and making the coals spark angrily. "I hope she's not caught up in all that."

"Who cares?" Daphne muttered under her breath, hoping that no one had heard her, but her grandfather's stern look made it clear that he had.

"She left earlier," Walter replied. "Look, I can't just sit here like a lemon. I'm going to see if there's anything I can do to help the bus driver."

"Pa, there are enough people out there. You're too old to be lifting an omnibus back onto its wheels," Mary snapped. "If you want to be useful, put the kettle on for a cup of tea. We could all use one."

"Good idea," Walter said with a nod. "Would you like one too, Daphne?"

"Yes, please."

"Great. I'll make the Rosie Lee, and then I'll go outside to help."

Mary shot her father a stern look, but he paid no attention.

"I should help too, Grandpa."

"Don't you dare, missy."

Walter wiped a clear spot on the condensated window pane and peered up the street to see if the crowd had dispersed.

"Perhaps you're right. I went over on my ankle earlier and it's killing me."

"Here, let me have a look," said Walter.

She lifted her foot and fought to take the boot off. Her fingers trembled as she tried to unlace it, partly because of the pain, and partly from the shock of witnessing the demise of poor little Finoula. The day's events had taken more of a toll on her than she had anticipated. In agony, she gave up. Grandpa placed her cuppa on the table and stirred in a lump of extra sugar, then sat on a stool just to the side of Daphne.

"Come on. Let me see. Gosh, it's swollen! How did you manage to walk all the way home on this?"

"It wasn't so bad when I first did it, I promise."

"Hmmm, a likely story," said her grandfather wearily.

Her grilling was interrupted when a knock at the door made them all turn. Grandpa went to see who it was.

"Oh, you'd better come in officer."

Mary, in her nightdress, pulled a blanket over her to cover up her modesty, not that she needed to bother, the policeman's gaze was firmly directed at Daphne.

"I understand you saw the accident, Miss Parker?" he said, flipping through a small notepad.

"You're not going to arrest me are you!" Daphne wailed as she looked at her grandfather for support.

"No. Please try not to upset yourself, Miss Parker. I am simply making some house-to-house enquiries to establish the facts."

Daphne told him everything she saw.

"I'm sorry it isn't much. I can't believe poor little Finoula is dead."

"Oh, she's not dead, miss, They've taken her to St. Thomas's for treatment."

Daphne breathed a sigh of relief.

"Thank goodness for that. What wonderful news. You look frozen, constable. Would you like a brew?"

The policeman's face lit up as Walter offered him Daphne's untouched tea. He glugged the hot, sweet liquid down in one go as the girl looked on with gritted teeth. When he left with Walter, Daphne forced herself to her feet and hobbled towards the range to get a refill. Mary offered to help.

"Can I ask a favour, Daphne? Would you entertain Johnny until Celia returns? Just sit him on your knee and make a bit of a fuss of him. He's been on his own for a lot of today. I've needed to concentrate on the twins."

As Mary made her way back upstairs, Daphne didn't reply as she limped towards the pram.

"You'd better not need picking up, young man, I can barely stand myself."

She turned around to find Johnny trying to get out of the pram.

"How long have you been able to pull yourself up like that? Get back down, or you'll do yourself a mischief. We'll have to restrain you from now. Or, your mother will have to take more care of you. Why isn't she here yet again? If she's outside helping with the accident, she's got her priorities wrong. She should be looking after you!"

She sat Johnny on the rug and did the best she could to barricade him in with stool legs. Then she got a tatty old bit of sheet and tried to make it into a bandage for her sprain. As she cut the material she wondered how she'd make it to the shop in the morning if her ankle hadn't recovered. It was then the girl's head snapped up. She hadn't shared her good news about her wages with her mother. How could she have forgotten to reveal her good fortune?

She struggled to get up and hopped over to her coat, then felt in her right-hand pocket. Empty. She tried the left, but it was also empty. Even the secret pocket inside was bare. She racked her brains, trying to recall every detail of the afternoon's events. Miss Lillian had given her the money. Percival showed up and argued with Lillian. Then she slipped but she didn't recall anything falling out of her coat. On the way home, she kept her hands in her pockets to thwart any light-fingered thieves. Then, suddenly, the trail went cold. Naturally, her attention had been focused on the accident, and everything else was a blur. Then reality hit her hard. At the accident site, someone in the heaving crowd could have easily helped themselves to her precious money. How could someone be so cruel and selfish as to steal from her in the midst of such a tragedy? It made her angry to think that there were people who would do such a thing.

As Daphne slumped onto the armchair, tears filled her eyes. How could she have been so foolish? What would her ma and grandpa say now that there was no money coming in that week? What if Jimmy McGinty's men threw them out that night for being in arrears? They had not a penny for the rent. All the spare money had gone on milk for Johnny and food for the extended family.

An icy blast of air hit her face as grandpa returned home, and Daphne dreaded having to explain.

"It's awful out there, Daphne. So many poor people were hurt when that omnibus went over. Broken bones, missing teeth, blood everywhere," said Walter as he bent over to pick up little Johnny off the rug and make a fuss of him.

"It's good you didn't see any of it, young man," he crooned to the baby.

"Is your mother upstairs?"

Daphne nodded, her face anxious to confess the truth.

"What's the matter? Ankle trouble?"

Her injury had completely escaped her mind. She had always been told honesty was the best policy, even if that posed a challenge.

"No, it's—"

She was spared the agony of telling the truth when he put Johnny down and reached into his pocket.

"I found this earlier when you were talking with the constable. I assume it's yours?"

He held out the envelope, with its precious cargo of coins still nestled inside.

"But how did you get this?"

"It was lying on the floor under your coat. It must have fallen out when you flung it on the hook. You were too busy giving your account of the accident to the officer to notice, I suppose."

"My word, Grandpa, I wish you'd told me earlier. I've been frantically thinking some rogue had pinched, and that we'd have to go into the workhouse."

The look on her relieved face tugged on his heartstrings. Walter put his arm around her and pulled her close.

"You softie!" he said, ruffling her hair again. "Even without your wages, things wouldn't be that dire. I still have my savings. I've not frittered them all away at the Drummer Boy! Mind you, my money won't last long if you keep losing yours. Anyway, we'd better get some dinner cooked, or we'll all starve."

"Please may I keep some of my wages for Christmas presents? You did say I could—and there's one pound in there! I got a shilling as a bonus for working so hard."

"Well, aren't you the lucky one," he exclaimed as he closed her hand tightly round her money.

"You keep it all. We'll manage."

"No, I can't do that. Grandpa, please take it. I'd like to pay my way. That's why I got the job."

"This once you may keep it all. You can start contributing next week."

"Perhaps I'll get an omnibus to work in the morning. I don't fancy walking a mile on this ankle."

"Good idea."

"Gramps, I'm so happy Finoula didn't die," she said, counting the coins again to make sure they were all there. "I wish I had stopped her, but she just ran out."

"Don't blame yourself. You're always so lovely trying to look after everyone, but you have to realise other people are responsible for their own welfare, not you. Here, peel these carrots, would you? They're a bit on the turn. We can mash a few up with some butter for his lordship over there."

"But what will I do with this money? Where will I keep it."

"You need to get yourself a money box, my girl."

"Where will I buy one?"

"No need to buy one. You can share mine for now. It's upstairs under my bed, or rather your old bed."

"There are quite a few coins in there that I had left from the navy. Your shillings can keep them company."

She put the wages down on the table in a glittering heap. Her eyes were drawn to them, as if by a magnet, and she kept touching the coins now and again, to make sure they were real.

"I'd put them in the money box now, to make sure they don't disappear, lass." her grandfather said with a grin. "I keep the key on a string round my neck. Here you go. Remember to bring it back."

When she returned, he started on another tale from his youth.

"I remember my first pay packet. It was in a small brown envelope just like that one. About tuppence ha'penny. It was a fortune to me."

He stared into space, reflecting.

"I ran away to sea, without telling my ma first."

"She must have been worried sick."

Daphne knew she was. It was the umpteenth time she had heard the story but she always played along as if it was the first time.

"Yes, but I didn't realise it at the time. I was still a child, really. Thought I knew it all, like all lads that age. I went from training at Dartmouth and then off to India. I soon found out I knew nothing."

With a sigh, he came round from his trance.

"Anyway, all this talk won't cook the dinner. Come over here and give me a hand. Chop, chop."

Daphne looked pained, but not by the chores.

"Silly me. I've forgotten about that ankle of yours. Here, do your chopping at the table."

He steered her towards a stool again and sat her down.

"You can do yours there."

Mary knocked on her bedroom floor with her heel.

"Can you make it upstairs to see what she wants, Daphne?" Walter said, handing her the money box key.

"Just about," she said as her grandpa slid the carrots into a bubbling saucepan of water.

"Good girl."

Daphne collected the money and tackled the stairs. Celia would be in soon, and as her pa had often told her, *'Don't leave temptation in anyone's path'.*

With the meal simmering, Walter opened the door and a chilly blast met his face as he peered up the street. The chaos seemed to have quieted and the traffic was moving freely again. Celia should be back from Bow soon. It was only soup that night, so it would be easy to keep warm until she arrived.

"I wonder what sort of day Celia's had, Daphne?"

The girl growled to herself. The last thing she wanted to think about was Celia, but her besotted grandpa seemed to talk about little else these days. Celia's general attitude to work and her refusal to help with most of the chores was really beginning to grate on Daphne. Little Johnny looked up from the rug and smiled. The girl picked him up.

"Your mother has replaced me in your great-grandfather's heart, I fear," she whispered to the lad.

His face tightened and he bawled.

"No, don't do that," she cooed. "I was just being silly. Please don't cry."

Daphne put the boy down, wincing in pain, as a loud slurp came from Walter's direction.

"The soup tastes wonderful. I am glad about my time in the galley. My cooking skills are coming in handy!"

Walter saw her limp. He kissed his hand and bent over to pat it onto her sore leg.

"You poor thing. Let me rub it better."

Daphne smiled at the kind gesture. Perhaps he still had a place in his heart for her after all.

"It really hurts, Gramps. How will I ever walk to work tomorrow? It takes me nearly an hour if it's busy."

"That's easy. Let me ring the servant bell and summon our coachman," Walter joked.

"As if," Daphne spluttered. "We don't even know someone with a horse and cart."

He stroked his beard as if in thought, and then his eyes lit up.

"How about Celia and I support you on either side and be your crutches. Now, that's a good idea."

"I don't think she'd be willing. Besides, she'll be out looking for work then."

"Not at eight in the morning. There's plenty of time after for job hunting."

"No thanks. I'll manage."

Walter retreated, his movements becoming more forceful as he stirred the soup.

"I'm sorry, Grandpa. You're just trying to help, and all I do is reject your suggestions. I think I am still a bit shaken from witnessing the accident."

He came over and stroked her tousled hair away from her face.

"Everything will work out just fine. Trust me. You listen to your old Grandpa."

She turned as she felt something tug at her dress.

"Johnny, how did you get there?" she exclaimed. "He must have crawled, Gramps. I didn't realise he could do that."

"Me neither. We'll have to watch him closely in future. We can't leave him unattended any more. It's a pity you're not smaller, we could have wheeled you to work in his pram."

"Aren't you the comedian, Grandpa!"

A grin crept up her face as she imagined herself in the pram with a bottle of milk in her mouth.

"Let's get this lad in his pram. We'll have to make his blanket extra snug."

Once the lad was settled, Walter pulled the curtain aside and looked out into the street again.

"Where on earth can Celia be?"

21

A MYSTERIOUS DISAPPEARANCE

When Celia still hadn't returned in time for dinner, Grandpa put on his coat and headed for the door.

"I'm going to find her."

"But your soup will get cold, Grandpa. And it's biting out there."

"All the more reason to start looking. Just turn it down low and add a bit of water if it starts to stick."

"Mary! It's time to come down. Dinner's ready," he shouted upstairs as he put his overcoat on.

The door closed and Daphne watched the old man trudge off. As soon as her mother appeared, the girl expressed her concerns.

"Should I go after him, mama?" He'll catch his death out there?"

Her mother sighed.

"I don't know, love. He's his own man, your grandpa. Always has been. He'll be back soon. No point in all of us having overcooked food too. Let's eat."

Daphne put a chunk of red hot carrot in her mouth and nearly spat it out, but not because it was hot, but because the door burst open and Grandpa sped in.

"Celia is hurt. The carriage that turned over— it fell on her."

"Good grief!" shrieked Mary.

Daphne was wracked with guilt all over again.

"Is she badly hurt, pa?"

A man stepped in, carrying a bloodied Celia. Daphne shuffled away to clear the armchair so he could lay her on it, while her mother ran to the range and filled a bowl with warm water from the kettle to wash her wounds.

"I'm alright," moaned Celia.

"You don't look it," said Mary, wiping off the blood caked on her face and scalp.

Walter stood biting his fingers.

"I am such a silly old fool. Why didn't I see you before? I was there for a while. It never occurred to me to search among the wounded."

"Don't blame yourself, pa."

"Aye. It isn't nobody's fault," groaned Celia, trying to sit more upright. "I was just unlucky."

"How did you happen to be there at just the wrong moment?" asked Walter.

"You were asleep on the sofa and Mary was upstairs, so I thought I'd meet Daphne as she walked back from the haberdashers to surprise her. I was going to take Johnny, but he was asleep, so I left him snoozing. Good job too. I couldn't find the shop in the end, so I turned to come back. I was almost home when all hell broke loose."

Daphne decided Celia's mishap had been her fault. If they hadn't been rowing so much, Celia wouldn't have been coming to see her to smooth things over.

"Have you broken any bones?" Mary asked.

Celia shook her limbs.

"I don't think so."

"It's just my head. That's a bit sore."

"Let me look."

Mary tried to examine her in the gloom of the tiny downstairs room.

"This is no use. I wonder if we should ask Mrs Bridges to help?"

"No, Mary, please. Don't make a fuss. I just want to sleep it off."

"As you wish. But if anything changes, you're to let us know. Agreed?"

There was a weak nod in response. Daphne moved away as her mother covered the battered and bruised girl with her own blanket. Outside, deeper snow drifts covered the street. Only a few foolhardy pedestrians braved the elements. Nothing else moved outside except for the thick swirl of snowflakes. She couldn't tell where the pavement ended and the cobblestone road started. The front doors of the houses across the street were covered up to the handles in snow. Daphne wondered if number twenty-two's was just as bad? She craned her neck to look through their window but couldn't see anything. She slowly opened the door, but the weight of the snow caught her off guard and, in her weakened state, the mini-avalanche pushed it open wide.

"Oh no!"

Walter saw Daphne trying to scoop up the snow and throw it outside.

"What are you doing! Stop!"

Daphne was confused.

"But it's my fault it's here?"

"I know. But you can't beat tea made with melted snow."

"But it'll be dirty, grandpa?."

"Not this top stuff. Pure white, see?" he said as he ran his fingers through it. "Quick, before it melts. Get it in the pan. My dear old father said it was lucky to make a brew out of snow."

She limped to pick up the family's biggest saucepan and they scooped as much as they could with their bare hands. Then Daphne did her best to brush the rest out-side.

"I'll never reach the shop tomorrow. I can only go a few yards at a time before it gets too much. What am I going to do, Grandpa? My ankle seems slightly better now it's strapped up but it's going to take me an age to get to work in this weather. I don't want to waste money on a carriage. Besides, I couldn't walk far enough to hail one anyway, and they never come down Prospect Street."

"The drivers are probably worried someone will have the wheels off it if they stopped," he joked. "We'll worry about getting you to work tomorrow. Come on, let's stoke the fire, we'll all catch our deaths otherwise."

Walter lifted up Johnny, who had wriggled free from his blanket again and was seeking some attention. Daphne's simple task of starting a fire didn't take long, and soon the flickering embers raced up the chimney. It had taken all the coal from the scuttle to get the fire blazing again. She was reluctant to go to the outhouse to fill it for later, wor-ried that there would be as much snow at the back door as the front. Who else might go? Celia was dozing under her blanket in the armchair, and her mother was nursing the twins. Maybe if Daphne hinted enough, Grandpa would fill it for her.

"Gramps, is there enough coal left outside?".

"We're low, but it should last a few days. I hope this snow doesn't stick around."

Despite the hint, Grandpa continued humming to the baby, leaving Daphne no choice but to go and fetch the coal herself.

"Right, I'll go outside now then—even though my leg is sore. Very sore!"

"Good girl."

"I'll go now, then," she whimpered, hoping Grandpa would finally step in to help as she wrapped her shawl around her.

A quick glance showed her that Grandpa wasn't going to budge, so she opened the door slightly at first, then further when no snow fell in.

"I can't go out there, Grandpa. It's about six feet deep. I'll get lost, and you'll find my frozen body, curled up in a ball, in a week's time."

"When will you stop exaggerating? At your age, I had to walk three miles to school and back in worse conditions."

"You told me you only went to Sunday School and left when you were ten. I'm almost sixteen."

"Less back chat, my girl. I need to feed this little guy. How would sir like pureed carrots this evening?"

The boy began to cry. Suddenly, a grimace covered the old man's face. Daphne put the coal scuttle down.

"Are you alright, Grandpa?" she exclaimed, frowning. "You look in pain."

"I'm fine, lass. Just a twinge in the old bones. How about porridge then? Do we have any left, Daphne?"

She offered him a jarful from the pantry cupboard.

"Are you sure you're alright?"

Walter huffed and puffed as he turned to face her.

"Yes. I told you I'm fine. Now, stop twittering. Seeing as you're unwilling, I'll shovel the snow out of the backyard after tea. We need to reach the coal house, and more importantly, the lavvy."

"No, it's alright, Grandpa, I'll do it. You're clearly out of sorts."

"I'll decide what I can do. I'm the man of the house. It's my job to sweep the snow."

"Well, put your coat on before you go out."

"I've been living out at sea for forty years, I can handle a bit of a cold snap."

"But you're not as young anymore."

His eyes flashed at her angrily. Daphne shrugged to show she was not happy with his decision. She also knew he could be as stubborn as her at times, so it was useless trying to get him to do something he didn't want to.

Soon, the piercing sound of a shovel scraping loudly against the flagstones awakened Celia, who gave a wide yawn, and then winced as she felt the gash in her scalp move.

"Cor blimey, it's cold tonight," she exclaimed, as she snuggled further under the blanket.

"How are you?" Daphne asked, looking at her cuts and bruises.

"Alright. We've had a lot of snow, ain't we?"

"Yes, we have, and Grandpa's, clearing a path. We've been busy feeding your son and making some food."

"Thanks. You should've woken me."

In light of her promise to be kinder to the woman, Daphne thought better of pointing out she should volunteer help, and not need to be nagged incessantly. Grandpa came in and stamped the snow off his shoes.

"Perhaps I will take a coat. It's a bit parky out there."

"Told you!" said Daphne.

"Isn't it your bedtime soon? You've got work tomorrow."

"I still need a plan to get there, Grandpa. Do you think the shop will be open in the morning with all this snow?"

"Maybe. Maybe not. But you ought to go over in any case. Miss Lillian lives close by, so she won't have any difficulty making her way there. She won't take kindly to you not turning up."

"But what about your ankle?" said Celia, looking genuinely concerned. "I can't see you making it there."

Celia tried to inspect the injury, but Daphne shuffled away in temper.

"Lillian wouldn't expect you to limp all that way like this, Daphne."

"She doesn't know I hurt myself."

"Daphne? Bed! Now!" Grandpa ordered as he made his way outside again.

The rhythmic scraping continued for a while, and then there was a sickening crash and thump. Daphne forgot her pain and strode outside to see her grandfather, trying to stand.

"I knew I shouldn't have let you. You're too old for heavy labouring."

"Don't you—call me—old," he stuttered as he regained his balance. "I just slipped."

"You look in pain. Are you?"

Her grandfather didn't answer, but she sensed he was struggling.

"Come on. Let's get you inside. I'll finish the job out here somehow."

The pace of progress was slow. Sweat trickled down her back. Her ankle throbbed. She wondered if she should suggest that Celia take over? She felt she had a good excuse to jib out, but wasn't sure Walter would see it that way, so she dug and dug. At least the biting cold was numbing her leg pain. In the chilled night air, clouds formed from her heavy breathing. As she paused to wipe her brow, she noticed a flurry of fresh white flakes falling from the sky and swore under her breath as her path began to fill again. She called time on the task.

Back inside, with a warm mug of tea in hand, she examined her grandfather's face with his attention diverted by Johnny.

"He needed changing and then we realised I had no clean clothes for him."

Daphne hoped that Celia wouldn't ask her to do the baby's laundry and risk starting another argument in front of Walter. Her grandfather remained motionless, staring at the baby as if he was a statuette.

"Grandpa, are you sure you're alright?" Daphne asked, putting her hand on his shoulder.

"Just a bit tired, my dear, don't worry," he replied with half a smile.

"No wonder you're tired, sleeping in the chair night after night. You should be in your own bed."

Daphne gave Celia a pointed look.

"It's not that. I've slept in more crampy places at sea. Did I tell you about when we almost ran into an iceberg, off the coast of Alaska?"

His face became animated as he told the familiar story. Daphne rolled her eyes, but Celia sat spellbound as he told the tale, with its usual set of fresh additions to make it more dramatic.

Daphne peeped out the window. It wasn't snowing anymore, but what about getting to work? As if in answer to her thoughts, a scraping noise came from just behind the front door as a visitor dug their way through the snow. She opened the door and spoke to the man.

"Good evening, sir. Can I help you?"

"Miss Parker?" the young man said, his face partially obscured by his thick knitted scarf. "May I come in?"

"Yes, sir. Give me a moment."

The door creaked as she opened it. Some snow fell in, but far less than before, thankfully. The young man peeled away his thick scarf and her mouth dropped when she saw the caller's face. It was the young man from church with the beautiful eyes that winked at her every Sunday. What was he doing there? How had he tracked her down?

"Miss Daphne Parker?" he said, smiling at her.

"Yes."

"Miss Lawson sent me."

"She did? Do come in."

She closed the door and then looked at the front room with dismay.

"Please excuse the mess."

Dirty baby clothes littered the floor. She tried to grab some but failed. Then she indicated for Celia to budge so the guest could sit in the best armchair, but he remained standing. A frown formed on his face, as he took off his hat. Celia was trying to placate Johnny, who was balling loudly again.

"Ah," he said, turning to Daphne. "The baby isn't yours, then?"

"Gosh no! He's my poor late brother's son. This is his—this is Celia, the baby's mother. And that's my grandfather. I'm sorry, I don't know your name."

At last, she would find out.

"Mr Ryder, Albert," he said with a smile.

"How and why did you come all this way in such awful conditions, Mr Ryder."

"I am made of stern stuff, Miss Parker. Miss Lawson saw me near the shop, and she looked troubled, so I asked if I could help. She sent me to tell you that she won't be opening tomorrow."

He stood twiddling his hat.

"Please, Albert, do sit down. You've come all this way. Let me offer you a hot drink. Tea?"

"I think he deserves something stronger than tea, Daphne, dear," said her grandfather.

Walter dug around at the back of the pantry cupboard and took out a bottle of rum, then showed it to the man.

"You can't beat a drop of fire water. When I was on board ship, it warmed me like nothing else."

"Thank you, sir," said the visitor.

The old man seized two pristine-looking jam jars and filled them halfway with the spicy golden liquid, before launching into another lengthy nautical tale for Mr Ryder's amusement. Daphne turned away, hiding a grin as she watched Albert's eyes grow heavy as the story progressed. In an effort to refresh himself, the young man took a small sip of his drink while listening attentively. She could tell he didn't enjoy the liquor from the grimace he made after the first taste. She reckoned he'd probably never had it before, but he was too polite to say no. He'd know better next time.

At least she didn't have to go to work on her sore ankle, but that didn't stop her from worrying about how to begin a conversation with Albert. She busied herself bringing the coal scuttle from the back door to its place by the hearth. As she staggered about, he jumped up, almost spilling his rum.

"Miss Parker, allow me to assist."

Albert grabbed the handle from her and threw all the contents on the fire. It really didn't need topping up and they all feared the ferocious flames would burn down the chimney.

"Oh, dear," he muttered. "Perhaps I shouldn't have done that."

With the tongs, he fought against the heat to lift off a few coals.

"Please, Albert, don't concern yourself," Walter advised.

Daphne took the tongs from him and felt her hand brush against his, catching his gaze. What a sight those lovely eyes were. Mesmerised, she froze. The girl was glad she was still wearing her work dress and had not changed into her shabby old one. Her grandfather coughed behind them.

"Pray, excuse me, sir. I should be on my way."

"No, stay a while. Are you related to the Ryders of Brick Lane?"

"No, sir, not that I know of."

"Look, it's snowing again, Mr Ryder," Walter warned. "Take off your coat. Rest here for a while."

Reluctantly, with Walter standing over him, the young man relinquished his coat. The old man swept the garment away and hung it on the back of the door.

"Grandpa, what are you doing?" Daphne hissed in his ear.

"Shush, child. I am the perfect host, as you can see."

With raised eyebrows, Daphne shook her head in dismay. Walter seemed to be overstepping the mark of being hospitable by a country mile.

"More rum, go on, Albert. This stuff puts hairs on your chest."

An awkward silence filled the room, but it was soon broken by a shriek from her mother who had retired upstairs.

"Please, God, don't let it be Winnie," Daphne murmured.

She found her mother lying on the floor, crying.

"Is it the twins?"

Daphne checked on the tots, but they both were sleeping peacefully. She touched them to make sure, and they felt warm.

"What's the matter, ma? All this kerfuffle?"

As Celia and Grandpa ventured upstairs, Mary stood up.

"I'm sorry. I was having a nightmare and fell out of bed. Dragons and monsters were climbing all over me. I'm sorry for causing you concern."

Relieved, Daphne helped her back into bed.

"Thank goodness that's all it was, mama. I am sure you're overtired. You really should get some more rest. You're no use to anyone when you're exhausted. How's Winnie today?"

"See for yourself. She's a fighter, thank God. I know you told me not to, but I might come downstairs soon. I've been here too long today. I'm going mad with it again. But I'd better have a little bit more shut-eye first."

"You better had," Walter warned, "else I'll be having words with you."

Mary pulled the blankets and snuggled into them.

"I'll just have another forty winks, and then I'll come down. By the way, did I hear a visitor call or did I dream that too?"

"Crikey, our visitor!" Daphne blurted out.

The three of them left Mary and sped downstairs to find Albert had wrapped Johnny in his woolly scarf and was singing to him, bouncing the lad on his knee.

"Ring-a-ring-a-roses,
A pocket full of posies,
A-tishoo! A-tishoo!
We all fall down."

"Papa used to sing that to me when I was little," Daphne trilled.

"I've several nieces and nephews. The younger ones love that nursery rhyme. It was one of my favourites as a lad too."

"I think I might have seen you with them at church, Mr Ryder?"

"Yes, you have, Miss Parker."

So, he had been eyeing her at church. Daphne's heart was fit to burst.

"Your mother came to the haberdashery shop recently," she added casually.

"Yes, she told me."

"Really? She didn't acknowledge me. I didn't even think she'd recognised me."

"Actually, that was the reason I am here this evening. I came to see you earlier, but I was too late. The shop had already closed. That's when I saw Miss Lawson."

Her face blushed as she caught her breath. Albert gave Johnny back to Walter and then collected his coat. His face looked flushed from all the rum.

"Are you leaving so soon?" Daphne asked.

"Yes, I fear I must. I just remembered my mother asked me to get some groceries. I'm off to Mrs Green's."

"Good. Don't go to Jimmy McGinty's place at the end of the street. He always sells stuff on the turn—at very inflated prices."

Albert put on his coat as Daphne felt an ache in her heart. Her grandfather looked at her with a curious expression. She looked back at him, wondering what he was thinking. He looked mischievous.

"Is something wrong, Grandpa?"

"Yes. We're almost out of food for the little one. Johnny needs a feed. Would you mind escorting Daphne to pick some porridge up at Mrs Green's, Mr Ryder?"

"But what about Jimmy's shop, Grandpa? He'll go mad if he knows I've gone somewhere else?"

"He'll have shut up early because of the snow and gone to warm himself up at the Little Drummer Boy. Besides, he's got better things to do than shout at you."

Daphne wasn't so sure after the argument about the flour but said nothing.

"But—!"

"You don't want the lad to starve do you, Daphne?"

"No, Grandpa."

"Right, that's settled then. Mr Ryder, will you escort my granddaughter please?"

"Yes. It will be my pleasure," the young man said as he offered his arm. "Miss Parker?"

She took her coat, ignoring the fact that she shouldn't be going out alone with a young man, unaccompanied. She decided it was only for a few minutes, to be a good Samaritan for Little Johnny who was cranky and hungry, so what was the harm?

"Just you mind your ankle, lass," her grandfather called down the street at the pair. "You don't want to be making it worse. Make sure she keeps hold of your arm, Mr Ryder, even if she complains. We don't want her getting hurt, do we? Daphne, do as I say. Daphne?"

Gramps muttered to himself as he closed the door that she was still as stubborn as ever, refusing any assistance, even when a little bit of help would make her life a lot better.

22

UNEXPECTED ASSISTANCE

In Daphne's mind, the pain had melted away, lost in the excitement of meeting her heartthrob. She put up a brave face, not wanting him to support her, thinking she could cope. However, her teeth gritted as her limp worsened. She wondered if she should hold his arm after all. It wasn't really the proper thing to do, but, eventually, she decided to seize the moment. Sarah waved from her window as they walked past number five. Daphne nodded back, wishing she had not been seen. Looking for a reason to let go of Albert, the girl fished about in her pockets and found her gloves, but she had already been rumbled by her friend. Thankfully, the weather had caused Jimmy to shut up shop early which offered some comfort. The couple passed the home of Finoula's grandmother near Brooks Road. The door opened and Finoula came out with a younger woman Daphne assumed to be her mother.

"How lovely to see you, Finoula. I'm so glad you've recovered," she said, nodding to the lady.

"Yes. They patched me up soon enough. A bit concussed and a few scratches, but nothing much to worry about. Me mam's taking me to buy a jacket potato as a treat to warm us up."

"That's nice. Enjoy every mouthful."

Finoula and her mother walked in opposite directions with Daphne wondering why the girl should be eligible for a treat rather than sanctions after putting the fear of God into everyone. After a while, though, her thoughts returned as usual to her handsome companion.

"Daphne—about your mother? I hope you don't mind me asking, but she stayed in bed when I visited. Is she ill? I hope not."

"Not unwell as such. She's just had twins and is still lying in."

"I see. Forgive me if I seem nosey. After the heartbreak of your father and brother, I'd hate to see you lose someone else."

From his accent, it seemed he was from a well-to-do family. She wondered how to respond.

"That's fine. You were just curious."

She changed the subject, trying to steer the conversation away from things that worsened her sense of awkwardness. As she stumbled over her words, she couldn't help but regret her tendency to babble and get herself into trouble. Lost in thought, she didn't notice the lamppost in front of her and nearly collided with it. In a quick move, Albert reached out and grabbed her, pulling her away from danger and pressing her against his strong chest.

"Eek! Erm, thank you, Mr Ryder."

She could barely breathe, so close was the moment. He held her for longer than he needed to and it felt lovely.

"Watch your step, Miss Parker. You don't want to hurt anything else, do you? And I don't want your grandfather having words with me for abandoning my post."

His chuckle echoed along the deserted side street. The only other living thing out that night was a mangy black dog, trying to paw at something that resembled a plump dead rat in the gutter.

"I hope the shop's open, Mr Ryder."

"It should be. Mrs Green lives above the shop, so she will hear us. I see a light in the window, which is good news. I should hate to have brought you here for nothing when you've had to struggle so much."

On their arrival at the shop, Daphne was stunned to see it full of customers. Where had they all come from? No one seemed to call in as they were walking towards the shop, and yet there was barely room to stand inside.

"You go first, Miss Parker," said Albert as he ushered her towards the counter.

In her excitement, Daphne had almost forgotten what she came in for. Damn and blast.

"Err—"

"Porridge?" Albert whispered in her ear.

"Yes, four ounces of your best porridge, please."

She placed her order and was pleased to see Mrs Green measured the exact amount into a paper bag.

"That'll be tuppence, please."

Alas, Daphne soon had another crisis to navigate. Her fingertips traced the edges of her coat pockets over and over, but there was no money to be found. Then she remembered in horror. She had deposited every penny to her name in Grandpa's money box. What a fool she felt. The mistake was embarrassing enough, but making it in front of Albert was even worse.

"Tuppence, dear. Can't you see I'm busy here?" Mrs Green demanded, her wiry hand outstretched.

Daphne smiled at her, hoping she would understand, but the lady stood there, looking more ferocious by the second, her mouth set in a severe line. Trying to appear confident, the girl made a suggestion.

"Please add it to our slate?"

"What slate? You Parkers do all your shopping at Jimmy McGinty's, have done for years."

"I came out in a rush, Mrs Green and I forgot my money," she confessed. "I do have the money, just not with me."

"That doesn't help me. You know the rules. Payment up front for people who go to McGinty's."

The ultimate humiliation happened as Albert held up a shiny coin before her cringing eyes.

"Allow me, Mrs Green."

Daphne would have been quite happy for the ground to swallow her up, but all the crimson-faced girl could do was accept his kind offer. He passed the coin onto the shopkeeper who slid her order across the counter.

"Next!" the sullen shopkeeper barked.

Poor Daphne had to stand and wait as Albert got his mother's lengthy list of provisions. The relief when she got out of the shop was palpable.

> "I promise I can pay you back as soon as you escort me home," she whispered, her shamed head bowed and feeling like a laughing stock. "I really can't thank you enough, Mr Ryder. Miss Lawson paid me, and I put my wages in our money box like my grandpa told me to keep it safe. I forgot to keep some out for myself in case I needed it. It's my first week's wage and I've made two mistakes with it already."

> "Don't worry yourself. It's only tuppence."

> "Please don't think this is a regular occurrence. I can pay my way."

Albert turned to face her.

> "Why would I consider such a thing as the norm? Please don't upset yourself. Miss Lawson told me your conduct is exemplary. She speaks very highly of you, Daphne."

Her heart nearly burst with glee when he uttered her first name.

"We shall not speak of this 'porridge incident' ever again," he continued with a warm smile.

"So, we will speak again, Mr Ryder?"

"Albert, please. And yes, I hope so. We are friends now, are we not?"

Daphne's face reddened again, but for different reasons.

"I hope you don't think I am forward, Daphne, but how old are you?"

Daphne wondered if she should lie? He seemed older than she thought. In church, he seemed like a boy, but seeing how he conducted himself this evening, he seemed more manly. Honesty prevailed and she told him the truth.

"Sixteen."

"You're younger than I thought, but it doesn't matter."

Daphne thought it mattered quite a lot if he thought her age important enough to enquire upon.

"And how old are you?"

She bit her lip, wondering if she should ask such a personal question.

"Almost nineteen."

A burly figure stepped out of the shop doorway, making the girl move aside. Her footing slid again, and she almost fell down a small flight of stairs that led to the shop's delivery hatch. Albert grabbed her arm to prevent her from sliding down into oblivion. She looked up at her saviour, who was grinning.

"Thank you for rescuing me—again," she groaned with embarrassment.

"Daphne, you are a walking health hazard. You had better hold on to me the rest of the way home."

He tucked her gloved hand over his forearm, and she prayed he didn't think she had stumbled on purpose to make him do so.

"I'm not normally this clumsy, I promise," she said, hoping her limp was less pronounced now she had some extra support.

On Dean Street, they saw a few figures in doorways and alleys, sheltering from the cold, huddled under piles of newspaper or rags. There were many vagrants in the East End, catching forty winks in the shadows, too proud to go to the workhouse. There they would stay until the police moved them along.

"Do you feel sorry for those people?" she asked. "I do."

Albert stopped.

"I beg your pardon?"

With her finger, she indicated the most recent dark shape they had passed.

"Those miserable people. Shouldn't we give him a few pennies so he can go to a doss house?"

Although she had very little money, her escort appeared to have plenty. For Daphne, life seemed very unfair for the people at the bottom of the heap. Now her family had lost her father's income, she could see how easily a family could sink financially. He swivelled her around.

"No, I don't think we should give them a bean. My mother says you should be wary of such folk. Workshy miscreants the lot of them, in her opinion."

"That isn't Christian. Doesn't the priest say we should help others in distress? Our neighbours have been very kind to us."

Albert said nothing and they walked in silence the rest of the way back.

"This is your house, isn't it," he said coldly.

She looked about her, having not paid attention to their progress.

Yes. Let me get you that tuppence. You could come in for a minute if you like?"

"No, Mother will be waiting for these," he said, lifting the bag of groceries. "Pay me when you see me next time at church. Good night."

He doffed his hat and strode off briskly. Standing at the doorstep, she stared open-mouthed watching his retreat all the way down towards Commercial Road. How had she offended him so soon? How could she have been so stupid? Her mother's voice called out.

"For goodness' sake, come in, Daphne. You're letting all the heat out."

After one last glance, she shut the door, her mood plummeting. Fifteen minutes earlier, she had been in heaven. Now, she was in hell.

"Where did you run off to in such a hurry?" her mother asked.

"Didn't Grandpa tell you?"

"Your grandfather said something about you going off with a young man alone! What did you think you were doing?"

Tears filled Daphne's eyes as she slumped onto the armchair. Her mother sat on the arm and gave her a big squeeze.

"He didn't do anything untoward, did he? Your grandfather shouldn't have let you go alone. I'll never forgive myself if—"

"No, mama, no. He was the opposite, very polite and gentle. He even paid for the porridge."

She pulled the bag of cereal out of her pocket.

"Still, your grandfather should have stopped you."

"He encouraged me to go. I think he knew I was sweet on Albert, I mean Mr Ryder. I've seen him at church. Anyway, I've learned my lesson now. I wish I hadn't gone. Where is Grandpa? And Celia, for that matter?"

"Celia has taken Johnny next door. Mrs Irvine wanted to see him, and your grandfather stepped out for some baccy. He gets through a pouch of that stuff at a frightening pace."

"I could have gone for him. Why didn't he say?"

Her mother shrugged and stood up.

"The good news is I feel so much better this evening, Daphne."

" How's baby Winnie? Is she still keeping food down?"

"Yes, but she still needs your prayers. Compared to her brother, she's very pallid."

Her mother made for the stairs but turned.

"How's your foot?"

"Well, I nearly forgot about it when it got numbed with cold outside, but it's throbbing again now."

Mary lifted her daughter's skirt a little and took off her boots. They examined her ankle.

"It's rather black and blue, but I'll live, ma. What's the expression Grandpa uses?"

"'Worse things have happened at sea?'"

"Yes, that's it."

"Good girl, that's the spirit. Keep your chin up. We'll be just fine."

As her mother retired, Daphne sat alone by the flicker of the fire, watching the flames fade away as quickly as her fledgling romance with Albert.

23

FALTERING HEARTS

On Sunday, Daphne headed downstairs, dressed in her best church clothes. Although some of the snow had melted, it was still treacherous outside and the street looked even more deserted than the day before. Nobody would risk going outside unless they had to. Daphne was convinced she had to. She had to see Albert and beg for his forgiveness. The creaking of the stairs woke her grandfather who yawned and sat up in the armchair.

"How's the leg?"

"Quite a bit better after a night's rest."

"Where are you going in such a hurry? It's barely nine o'clock. Mass isn't until ten."

"Are you coming today, Grandpa?" she asked. "I need to go early. I need to beg for forgiveness from Mr Ryder, for offending him yesterday. I've not slept all night, worrying he might never speak to me again."

"Ah, young love," Walter said wistfully.

Daphne shot him an indignant look. Her grandfather yawned again as he scratched his wiry beard.

"I might miss today, what with the snow and everything."

"You're not poorly, are you, Grandpa?"

She sat on the side of the armchair, looking into his face, gently stroking his beard.

"You would tell me if you were poorly, wouldn't you?"

"Of course. But I'm not ill, lass. Fit as a fiddle I am. Don't worry about me. Oh, before you pop off, can you make us all a cup of tea, would you? I am quite nice and toasty under this blanket."

"Since it's you asking, I will. Now, stop dodging my question. Are you sure you're feeling ok?"

"I'm sure. Now shoo! Oh, by the way, Celia said she'd come to church with you."

Daphne froze on the spot to quiz him further.

"Celia? Going to church? A Catholic church? But she's committed a terrible sin, hasn't she? Having a baby out of wedlock?"

"We all make mistakes, Daphne. God forgives us all if we repent. Now, is that tea mashed? A man could die from thirst in this house."

"Celia had better get a move on. I have to be on my way soon. Where is she?"

"She'll be here any minute. She went to show Johnny to Mrs Irvine in his Sunday best. One of the neighbours lent her some better clothes for him."

Daphne rolled her eyes at the news Celia was sponging yet again. At least it was from another household's coffers this time. Eventually, she reappeared.

"Sorry, I'm a bit late. Mrs Irvine was particularly eager to see Johnny today."

"Are you taking the baby? We won't get there on time if we're pushing the pram in these conditions."

"I hadn't thought of that," Celia said with a frown.

For Daphne, that was Celia all over. She never did think. The young mother bit her lip and turned to Walter.

"Are you going, Mr Beresford? If you're giving it a miss this week, I don't suppose—"

"Give him here," said Grandpa, holding out his arms. "I'll look after his lordship. This wee one's no bother."

"Come on, then, Celia" urged Daphne, eager to be off.

"What's the rush? We've got plenty of time," said Celia checking her hair in the cracked mirror as she put on Mary's best bonnet.

"I don't want to be late. It's going to take much longer in the snow now I'm less mobile."

"Does this bonnet suit me?"

"Yes, now come on," snapped Daphne.

The girl found it exasperating to see Celia wearing another of her mother's precious things, feeling that Mary would have nothing decent left to wear when she comes out of her laying-in period.

"I'm really not sure about the colour."

"It's warm. That's all that matters," said Walter

"My stomach's rumbling. Have I got time for a cuppa?" Celia continued, still preening.

"If you don't come now, I'll go without you," said Daphne, opening the door. "I cannot rush because of my ankle, and I don't want to be late because of you faffing about. Make up your mind. Are you coming or staying?"

Celia blew out her cheeks in defeat and took her coat.

"That'll have to do I suppose," she said, grabbing one last look in the mirror. "Lead on. I have no idea where the church is."

Their journey was fraught. Celia chuntered as she trudged in the snow. Daphne turned to her and took her by the elbow thinking it might speed up their progress.

"Have you ever been to church, Celia? It was a surprise when Grandpa said you were coming, 'cos you're not a Catholic, are you?"

"No, but my ma was when she was a child."

"You can't say someone 'was' a Catholic, silly. Once someone is baptised into the faith they remain Catholic for life."

"Good job I've not been baptised then, isn't it? I can pick and choose."

"It doesn't work like that! Besides, everyone gets baptised. Are you sure you weren't? You probably were, you know."

"I might have been. I can't remember for sure. Ma didn't really talk about that sort of stuff."

Why did Celia have to confess she hadn't been baptised? Daphne wondered whether she was allowed to attend the service because she hadn't been christened, but she decided to give the woman the benefit of the doubt. If she wasn't sure, there was a chance she was, so Daphne clung to that as they lumbered along.

As they neared the church, Daphne saw no trace of Albert, his mother, or his wider family in the congregation. She pursed her lips in fury since the chance to apologise had been taken from her. Thankfully, the Ryders finally came into view in a small crowd by the front entrance. She was curious to see if Albert would acknowledge her. She took a few steps closer and nodded to his mother. The woman returned the gesture, and then, joy of joys, Albert stepped out from behind Mrs Ryder and extended his hand.

"Good day, Miss Parker," he greeted before turning to Celia who smiled sweetly at him and offered her delicate gloved hand.

Albert held Celia's hand for a little longer than Daphne would have liked and she was furious once more. The congregation made their way inside and Daphne stopped at a small side chapel just off the main nave. She lit two candles, one for her father, and another for her brother, and then she said a prayer for them as Celia waited beside her.

"Let's sit near the back, shall we, Celia?"

Daphne was relieved when the woman agreed. The last thing she wanted was to be embarrassed in front of Albert by her companion not knowing the words to the hymns or prayers. It would mean a longer trip to take communion, but it was a small price to pay. Then Daphne clapped her hand to her mouth. Celia wasn't eligible to receive holy communion if she wasn't baptised a Catholic. Daphne pulled her to a quiet spot behind a pillar.

"What's up?"

"I am worried about you receiving communion."

"Oh, that's no problem. I'll just follow what you're doing," Celia whispered.

"No, that's just it, you can't. You're not allowed to accept the sacrament if you're not baptised into the faith. When we go up, just stay here until I'm back. Please don't do anything to draw attention to yourself, I beg of you—especially if Albert's watching."

"What do you take me for, an idiot?"

Daphne thought it best not to answer. She went and chose a spot behind the biggest marble pillar, as far away from the Ryders as possible. When the priest blessed the frankincense, she could see Celia screwing up her face at the smell and hoped she wouldn't say anything. The woman still did.

"Is that the insects they use, Daphne? Ma told me about that."

"Incense? Yes. Shhh."

After that, things went as well as Daphne could expect. Celia sang some of the hymns in tune to both of their amazement. Perhaps Celia wasn't that much of a heathen after all? However, when Daphne stepped up to go to holy communion, Celia secretly sneaked out of the church. As soon as the final hymn ended, Daphne hurried outside and was horrified to see Albert talking to Celia. They seemed to be getting on wonderfully well. Trying to catch his eye, she waved. When he didn't respond, she shuffled across to intervene.

"Ah, there you are, Celia."

"I hope I didn't worry you," the girl replied. "I needed a bit of fresh air. I thought I'd wait here and this man has been entertaining me."

"Has he now?"

Trying to guess Albert's mood, she looked at him and noticed his eyes twinkling at her. She took that to be a good sign after his brusqueness later on yesterday. Clearly, a good night's sleep had helped her cause.

"I was just sharing an amusing story I read in the paper yesterday," he replied, as his mother came over.

"Albert, I'm going. Are you coming with me?"

Mrs Ryder studied Daphne's face.

"You work in the haberdasher's shop, don't you?"

"Yes, Mrs Ryder. I hope you found our merchandise satisfactory."

"Certainly. I've been telling all my friends about Miss Lawson's establishment."

"Thank you, ma'am. Lillian—I mean, Miss Lawson will be happy to hear that."

Albert turned to face Daphne.

"How is your ankle now? I trust it has recovered?"

Daphne tried to think of the most eloquent way to explain.

"It's alright, but I did wonder if the walk here exasperated it."

"I think you mean *'exacerbated'*," he corrected with a grin.

Celia laughed more than she should have done at Daphne's mistake and the girl glared at her.

"Would you like me to escort you ladies back home?"

Daphne's heart was beating harder than a drum. She couldn't think of anything nicer.

"If you're sure, Albert. We wouldn't want to put you out."

"It will be my pleasure. I don't usually escort two such beautiful ladies."

Daphne was horrified when Celia simpered as she took his other arm.

"I hope this snow goes soon, don't you, Albert? Some of us have to make it to work in the morning."

Would he take the hint that her nemesis had no such worries?

"Where do you work, Albert?" Celia asked.

"I work in the office of life."

"Really, where's that?"

"Actually, I mean I work in my father's law business," he said with a chuckle.

"You're a lawyer?"

"I'm taking my bar exams soon, then I will be."

No wonder he seemed wealthy. Daphne had heard lawyers were paid top wages.

"I had an uncle who was a solicitor," Celia added.

"That's not the same thing, I'm afraid, Celia," Albert replied, the correction sending a rush of pleasure down Daphne's spine.

"'Of course not," Daphne said as if she knew all along.

"I never said they were," Celia snapped. "I was just saying."

Albert slowed his pace and the two girls fell into step with him.

"Ladies, no squabbles today. It's a beautiful blue sky after all that greyness of late. Let's listen to the birds singing sweetly in the trees."

"Birds, Albert?" said Daphne looking around, trying to find a single one.

"There was a bird in the tree by the church. Didn't you hear it singing? It's one of the most vivid sounds I know."

"You must be a poet to notice such beautiful things."

"I have my moments. Do you like poems?"

"We read a few at school," Daphne said, "but there isn't time now I am working."

"You should always make time for poems. I would expect my wife to know all forms of literature."

Daphne's face slumped. There was no use in continuing her fantasy. What had she been thinking, to assume that someone like Albert would entertain her company? As they approached the turning off Commercial Road, she stopped the trio.

"Thank you, for escorting us home, Albert. We'll do the last bit ourselves," she said as she fumbled for her purse. "Before I forget, here's the tuppence I owe you. Thank you for helping me. We won't keep you any longer. Good day."

He doffed his cap.

"It was my pleasure, ladies. Good day to you. Please give my regards to your mother and grandfather, Daphne."

For a second, she thought he would say something more, but he disappeared back towards Bow, leaving her heart in tatters.

"That was a bit hasty, wasn't it?" Celia pondered as they walked home.

Daphne nodded.

"You've taken a shine to him, haven't you?"

For a brief moment, Daphne dropped her guard with Celia.

"I thought I did, but there's no point? He's out of my reach. You heard what he said. He wants a wife that knows about literature. I can barely spell the word. I can neither recite nor write poetry. Goodbye, Mr Albert Ryder. It was nice knowing you."

With a heavy heart, Daphne reached for the front door handle. Before she could hide away inside Sarah called out.

"Are you coming over later, Daphne? Mama's finished that knitting for you."

"Yes, I will, Thank you."

Once inside, Celia and Daphne were welcomed by Mary, holding the twins.

"Hello dear, did you enjoy the service?"

Before her daughter could reply, Mary had turned her attention to Celia.

"And how did you enjoy it? I must confess, I didn't really think of you as a churchgoer."

"It was very pleasant, thank you, Especially as I was wearing your beautiful bonnet."

While they were gone, Johnny had played with a toy train on the floor. He looked so happy. Daphne remembered that it had belonged to her brother. He couldn't bear to part with it even as an adult, and it took pride of place on the upstairs windowsill. Daphne wondered if Henry had been so transfixed by it in his childhood. She decided he must have been if he wanted a career with a railway company.

"Mama, I need to change too. By the way, I planned on going to Sarah's later. Unless you need me for anything?"

"You're alright, love. You go and have a bit of fun. If you wouldn't mind checking on Winifred, while you're upstairs, that would be lovely. She was asleep when I came down."

"Is Grandpa out?"

"Yes, he went to the Little Drummer Boy for some ale."

"Can I ask you something, ma?"

Mary nodded.

"Is he alright? He seems quite frail to me. He took quite a tumble yesterday in the backyard and pretended he was alright, but I am not so sure."

"He's fine. Don't you worry. Your grandfather is as strong as an ox."

Something about Mary's tone of voice didn't ring true. Daphne didn't want to dwell on it and instead chose denial and focusing on the positives. She also knew that spending time with his bar room buddies would cheer him up. However, she was aware that excessive drinking wasn't good for him. It was amusing to see him a little tipsy, but it was not pleasant for his family to see him hungover the next day.

Daphne changed into her everyday clothes after checking on Winnie who seemed to be rallying. Celia had changed and was peeling a huge pile of potatoes. Daphne was going to make a snide remark about how delighted she was to see the woman doing something helpful for a change but bit her tongue.

"Do you want any help, Celia?"

"You can peel them carrots if you like?"

"Carrots again, " said Daphne, picking up the knife. "That's all we ever seem to have. It would be nice to have some green beans for a change. I'm going to turn orange one of these days."

"Wrong season for green beans, I'm afraid."

They worked in silence until all the vegetables were done. Daphne wiped her hands on her apron and then saw baby Walter with her mother.

"My, he's growing. He'll soon be as big as Johnny."

"Yes, I'm pleased with his progress."

Despite the good news, her mother's eyes filled with tears.

"If only your father were here. He'd be so proud of him, and Winnie, of course."

The tears couldn't be blinked away and fell down her cheeks. Daphne put her arm around her mother.

"I miss him too, mama. I am worried it'll be worse at Christmas."

"We'll manage, love. You seemed happy when that young man was here yesterday? Mr Ryder was it?"

"I was happy, but not anymore. We're like chalk and cheese, ma, He's much too high-brow. I'll never be up to his standards. Not coming from Prospect Street. Lads like him don't talk to girls like me," Daphne sighed.

"Someone will come along and steal your heart, don't fret. You're still young, remember."

Celia interrupted.

"I was thinking of visiting my mother again this week. See how she's faring. Might not get much sense out of her if she's done down the pub though."

"Good idea," replied Daphne. "Maybe she'll ask you to move back in? Would you like to?"

Daphne realised it was the first time she had asked Celia about how she felt.

"You have all been so kind to me, but, yes I do want to see a lot more of my ma."

"That's perfectly normal, luvvie," replied Mary. "You only ever have one mother. They are precious things. She gave birth to you, gave you life, and you should never, ever take her for granted."

'Thanks, Mary. Whatever she says, I'll make an extra effort to be polite to her. As you said, she's the only mother I have, although you come close to being another. You're such a lovely lady and you've been so kind to me."

Celia's gratitude overcame her and she became visibly upset. After church, Daphne was usually at her most compassionate and so she decided to offer an olive branch.

"May I help?"

"How exactly?" Celia snivelled

"Do you want me to go with you? To see your ma?"

Celia was amazed by Daphne's sudden change of heart.

"I'm sorry I've been so childish," Daphne continued. "Let me help you. I've not treated you well. I think it might be the grief of losing my father and brother so unexpectedly. Can you forgive me?"

Celia wiped her hands across her tear-stained face.

"I shouldn't have dumped my problems on you. I didn't know you were on your own when I left Johnny with you. And I didn't know Harry—Henry—had just died. Nor your pa."

"It isn't that I don't like you, Celia. It's just we are used to living from hand to mouth here, and having two more mouths to feed is a stretch. And what with you not working—."

"I know. I can understand if you thought I'd been acting like a spoiled princess. I was so confused after a few sleepless nights on the streets I didn't really know what I was doing."

Daphne thought about giving a hug but felt that would be going too far, too soon, so she simply patted Celia's arm and checked on the carrots.

"Will Grandpa be back for dinner, ma? Or we'll leave his to keep warm over a pan of water?"

"Let's wait a while, just in case. I like it when we eat together on a Sunday. Pull all the pans off the hotplate a little."

Baby Walter slept in Mary's arms, and she looked like she was ready for a nap too. Daphne took the baby and cradled him so her mother could stand.

"I think I'll go back to bed before Winnie wakes up. I'll have dinner later with your grandfather. You girls can eat now if you want?"

"Are you sure? Mama? I think you should eat something now. Perhaps a biscuit?"

"Go on then."

Daphne found some fragments of Walter's ginger biscuits, which were left in the bottom of the tin.

"We should have bought some more biscuits," she muttered.

Grandpa had still not returned until well after lunchtime, so Daphne and Celia sat together and ate their lunch. How good it felt to have an understanding at last. They chatted about Celia's brothers and sisters and her mother's new man.

"It must be nice to have brothers and sisters around," remarked Daphne, before popping an overcooked carrot in her mouth. "With Henry gone, I've not really gotten to know the twins yet, of course. Poor old ma had a few other babies that died just after they were born, so she says, but I was too young to remember."

"My siblings are a right handful. I've really enjoyed living here. I know you weren't happy about your folks taking me in, but I hope you've changed your mind a bit."

"Let's put all that behind us, eh?" said Daphne as she smiled. "I can't imagine what it was like to be homeless. We don't have much money, but we have more than quite a few on this street, and therefore I consider myself lucky. What was it like living on the street?"

Celia's gaze went off into the middle distance, and she looked troubled.

"You might be surprised to know that sometimes, the ladies were worse than the men for brawling in the street," she said. "I don't want to go through it again. I used to confide in your grandfather on our walks about how horrid it was at night. I didn't want to worry you or your ma. You'd never walk down a dark alleyway alone again."

"So, what was it like then?"

"I never felt so alone and vulnerable in my life, Daphne. The streets were crowded with people, but they were all strangers, and none of them offered any help or sympathy. Eventually, I found a quieter spot to shelter, behind a pile of bashed-up and abandoned tea crates and huddled there with the baby. It was damp and filthy, but it was the only shelter I could find. I wrapped the little one in my shawl and tried to shield us both from the worst of the weather, but there wasn't much point. As the nights wore on, I saw all kinds of people on the streets—drunkards stumbling home, prostitutes plying their trade, and thieves lurking in the shadows. I tried to avoid them all, but it was difficult. They seemed to be everywhere. The only thing I could do was to try to survive, one day at a time, and hope that someday things would get better. Eventually, the only thing I could think of was to keep the little one safe, even if I couldn't save myself. That's when I made enquiries about where your brother lived."

"I'm sorry, Celia. I never really understood how tough it was for you. My parents used to wrap me up in cotton wool, I think, to shield me from the horrors of the East End. Maybe we could move to a bigger place with Grandpa's pension and my wages. It might be nice for ma and Gramps to be free of the ghosts of the past, now my father and Henry aren't here anymore. Grandpa thinks the world of you because you gave him a healthy great-grandson. That is why I was envious, I suppose. I've always felt like his precious little girl. Until you arrived and became the apple of his eye."

"I could never replace you. You are lucky to have such a wonderful family, Daphne. Treasure them."

"Talking of Grandpa, I hope he's fine because his dinner's getting cold. Let me warm it up a little again."

Celia gave up waiting for Walter and went out for a stroll with Johnny to settle him, hoping she might find her mother in one of the neighbouring local pubs. Two hours later, Walter tottered in, singing at the top of his voice.

'What shall we do with a drunken sailor?

What shall we do with a drunken sailor?

What shall we do with a drunken sailor?

Earl-aye in the morning.'

There was the sound of a shoulder banging into their front door and the scratch of a key hunting its hole.

"It's not locked, Grandpa."

The door swung open and hit the wall.

"Eek! Hello! Didn't see you there, Daphne. How are you doing?" said Walter, between the hiccups.

"Grandpa! You're drunk! How many times has ma told you?"

"I'm not drunk. I'm fine! More than fine. Wonderfully fine, actually. I've had a very good time if you must know."

"Hmm. I suppose you're not interested in your congealed dinner?"

He gestured with his thumb for Daphne to get up from the armchair, then slumped down, his breath reeking of ale.

"I don't want anything to eat, thanks, treacle. I don't have the stomach for it. You eat it. Where's your ma?"

"She's upstairs, and Celia has gone out with Johnny. Both babies are asleep and I am here darning some of our socks. I hoped you might help. You're usually good with your hands, but not like this. It's not good enough, Gramps. I really wish you wouldn't keep going to the pub all the time. We need you here."

Walter shrugged, not happy a young girl was laying down the law to him. She shook her head in disgust. Normally, he wouldn't drink that much, but he felt a lively drinking session out with his Navy friends was good for his soul and built him up a bit. Soon, gentle snores came from the armchair. Daphne covered him with his favourite blanket.

"I supposed you're only doing what you have to do to get through the dark days," she whispered. "I think we've all done that at some point in our lives."

With her grandfather settled, she popped her coat on and made for the door. She wondered whether Mrs Bradley would want paying for making the twins' bootees and whether or not to take some money with her just in case. Daphne slipped out to Sarah's as quietly as she could, not that she needed to worry too much. Her mother was flat out in bed, exhausted and given the level of intoxication of her grandfather, he wouldn't hear the world ending either.

"Daphne, do come in. Quiet though. Mr Bradley's asleep," Mrs Bradley whispered as Sarah tiptoed up behind her.

"How's your ma and the babies?" the woman asked.

"Ma's well, Thank you, and the twins are doing well too, although Winifred still isn't as robust as Walter, but she'll get there."

Sarah pulled her friend away from the conversation and dragged her across the smoky room, past her snoring father loudly in his fireside chair, and over to a couple of stools by the range.

"I want to ask you something, You'll never guess."

Daphne played dumb.

"Um—you've won on the horses?"

"No, silly, but I wish I could have. My great-grandfather used to win often. In fact, ma told me he—but never mind. I saw you!"

"Saw me?"

"Yes, with that lad from church. Last night, walking down here arm in arm!"

Daphne's mouth drooped.

"Yes, but it didn't end well. The walk was pleasant enough, but he said, he *'wants a wife who is conversant with literature in all its forms'*."

"Oh, dear! You can't even read, Daphne, let alone recite poetry."

"I can read, thank you. I'm not a complete duffer."

"Well, you'd better get off to that new Whitechapel library then. Find as many poetry books as you can."

"I didn't think of that. But which ones? I mean, there are probably lots of them."

Sarah turned from filling the kettle.

"Did he say he had any preferences?"

"Oo-er. Who's coming over all illiterate now?"

"I think you mean *'literate'*, Daphne."

"You see. I can't even manage normal English properly let alone poetry. I'm doomed! The only poems I've read were the ones we learnt in school. That's assuming Baa Baa Black Sheep is a poem?"

"I think that's a nursery rhyme rather than a poem."

"Argh! Can you remember any poetry?"

"The daffodils one wasn't too bad. Wordsworth's I think?"

Sarah sipped her tea and her eyes glazed over as she gazed out the window.

"How I'd love to live near a lake or a mountain and watch butterflies fluttering around flowers that danced in the breeze, wouldn't you?"

"Instead of London, blackened with smog, Sarah? You bet. Hang on. It's coming back to me. There was one poem I liked. It was about an ancient mariner. I think it used to remind me of Grandpa when he was out at sea for so long."

"See, you do know something about poetry,"

"But how will I manage to go to the library, when I'm at work all day?"

"See if you can go at lunchtime. That's what I do if I need anything."

Daphne hugged her friend.

"Sarah, you're a marvel. Why didn't I think of that, I don't know. Tiredness? Anyway, I'll see if I can pop along tomorrow. That young man, his name's Albert Ryder, by the way. Mrs Daphne Ryder, Doesn't that sound perfect?"

It was her turn to look dreamily out of the window as Sarah stifled a laugh.

"It does have a ring to it. Provided you can recite those verses for him, Daphne."

She dug Sarah firmly in the ribs and she wriggled away in defence.

"Now that your future husband is sorted, what can we do about mine, Daphne?"

"Future husband! Stop pulling my leg. We only walked to Mrs Green's and that was because he was helping me walk after twisting my ankle."

Mrs Bradley interrupted them.

"Where's my cuppa, then, Sarah?"

Her daughter jumped up.

"Sorry, ma," she said, pouring another drink. "Will pa want one?"

"No, he's still asleep. Leave him alone."

Mother and daughter exchanged worried looks. Daphne knew what it meant. They didn't want his foul drunken mood ruining their Sunday. It would be much better if his slumbers were not broken.

"Did Sarah tell you about the bootees?"

"Yes, Thank you, Mrs Bradley. How much do I owe you?"

The lady waved her hand dismissively.

"Nothing. I used wool from an old jumper I had. I hardly needed any yarn, they are so small. I hope the colour suits them. It's a sort of yellow. They're there."

Mrs Bradley pointed towards two pairs of bootees sandwiched between her husband's tattooed arm and the arm of his chair.

"I'll bring them to you when he awakes."

She took down a biscuit tin and opened it beside Daphne. The smell of spices filled the kitchen.

"Peckish? Help yourself, lass."

"Oh, Thank you. You're spoiling me, Mrs Bradley! I love your spicy biscuits. I tried making them, but they never come out as nice as yours."

"It's my grandmother's special recipe. I've never tasted anything like them anywhere."

The trio sat for a while, lost in their own thoughts munching on the sweet biscuits until Sarah suggested a walk.

"That'll be good." answered her mother. "You can't beat a stroll on a crisp day like this. I'll come with you."

The girls frowned. All talk about young men they fancied on their walk was now out of the question.

24

A STARTLING DISCOVERY

In the wee hours of the next morning, Daphne awoke to a strange sound. She sat up in bed, craning her neck, but was unable to pinpoint what it was. The softest of little snorts and grunts came from the dozing twins' drawer at the foot of her shared bed, and her mother was sound asleep. She pushed aside the blankets and crept to the top of the stairs. All quiet. Maybe she'd been dreaming? She thought she'd better check downstairs just to put her mind at rest.

Grandpa was clearly visible when her eyes had adjusted to the darkness. He, too, was fast asleep, with one of his arms dangling down beside him. Daphne went to tuck it back in gently, but something was amiss. When she went to move it, it was stiffer than usual and felt icy cold.

> "Poor old you," she whispered as she manoeuvred the limb under the blanket. "You're so cold your arm's almost frozen solid. Let's warm it up a bit in here."

She tried to breathe life back into the fire, but nothing happened. That was when an awful thought hit her. Instinctively, she knew she had to check on Walter again. She put her fingers underneath the collar of his pyjamas.

His chest was cold. Slowly, she slid her fingers over his collarbone and up to his neck. There was no pulse. She rested her ear on his lips. No breath. Dropping onto the floor beside him, she prayed for his soul to reach heaven straight away. She desperately wanted to tell her mother but knew she was exhausted. And besides, whatever time she told her, the grim fact was the same. Dear old Walter Beresford was no more.

The chime of the church clock signalled it would soon be time to get ready for work. She wondered how to break the news to her mother. What would cause her the least pain? *'Grandpa has gone? Grandpa has passed away? Something else?'*

That morning she didn't open the curtains. The rules of mourning meant they needed to stay closed until Grandpa had been formally laid out. Even though she thought it was absurd to suggest that a dead person would be trapped indefinitely in a reflection, she turned over the cracked mirror and covered it up with a hand-kerchief all the same. She convinced herself that his soul was already in heaven, or at the very least, in purgatory waiting to atone for his sins. He was such a kind-hearted fellow she didn't think he'd be waiting long if he did end up there.

She sat for as long as she could, wondering what to do. Eventually, she approached the stairs and inched slowly upward as she prepared to break the bad news to her mother. She wondered how Mary was going to cope, having only recently buried her husband and son. She was propped up in bed as she stroked the head of one of the twins resting in her lap.

"Hello, my little treasure," Mary whispered with a smile.

Seeing Daphne's sad face, her brow furrowed.

"What's the matter, my love? You're as white as a sheet."

"It's Grandpa, mama. I don't know how to tell you, but I think he's—"

She gulped at the air as the tears began to flow.

"I wish it could be different, but he's—dead. I was with him in the night. I woke up in the wee small hours and had a strange feeling, a sort of premonition, I suppose. You know I get those strange feelings sometimes. Well, I went down and found him cold. Should I get Mrs Bridges to get him laid out? Or do you want to spend some time alone with him first?"

Her mother stared into space as if she hadn't heard. When she did speak, Daphne couldn't believe her ears.

"What were you thinking, spending the night with him when he had passed? You should have come to me right away."

Criticism was the last thing the girl wanted. How was anyone so young expected to know how best to react to a death in the heat of the moment anyway? Daphne couldn't understand her mother's attitude. She'd expected her to wail and cry, not show the cold, unemotional face she was now seeing.

"Do you want me to fetch Mrs Bridges?"

"Yes," hissed Mary. "Now get out of my sight."

Celia stirred and popped her head around the bedroom annexe curtain and asked if everything was alright.

"No, Celia. Things are definitely not right. Stay with mama while I get Mrs Bridges."

"Is there a problem with the twins?"

"No, Grandpa."

Daphne pulled on her plain shift dress. Without taking the coat, she rushed over to the old crone's house on Dean Street and knocked on the door.

"I suppose you need my services," declared the sullen old crone as she peered at her.

"How do you know?" she asked in amazement.

"Ah, that'd be telling," Mrs Bridges said, touching the side of her nose as if 'in the know' about something.

"Come quickly. It's my grandfather."

Mrs Bridges was unaware of the girl's anguish as they dodged the carts and barrow boys hurtling past. An empty hearse passed by. The ominous sight made Daphne gasp for air. When they got to the family house, Daphne looked at Mrs Bridges' cold, craggy face, the wrinkles appearing more pronounced in the dim light.

"How's your mother taking it?"

"When I told her, she appeared stunned and then angry, especially when I told her that I had spent the night with him while she rested. I am sure I did the wrong thing, but I couldn't leave him on his own, could I? Did I do the right thing?"

"I say you should do as you think fit at times like that. If it comforts you, it's the right thing to do."

Daphne gave a grateful smile to Mrs Bridges for the first time in her young life. She watched the lady examine her grandfather:

"Have you called the doctor to certify death?"

"No."

"Get that sorted, and I'll be over within the hour."

Daphne ran to Tynedale Hall and looked for the community doctor. He was just about to leave for a meeting but she managed to convince him to accompany her.

*

After the physician had left, Daphne stroked her grandfather's arm. Despite his bushy beard and sideburns covering much of his face, she thought he looked at peace. The girl wondered if his soul was imagining a beautiful tropical island somewhere, a nice place he had visited in his youth. She took some comfort from knowing he'd had a peaceful and pain-free death at home, and not all alone, drowned after a shipwreck in icy and treacherous waters.

"There will be no more stories now, eh, Grandpa. It's a good job you told me so many times. I always moaned about that, didn't I? Well, you were right. You told me so many times you have made them easy to remember. I promise I'll tell the babies when they are old enough to understand."

Her throat began to tighten.

"I hope mama will let me tell one or two stories at the funeral. That would be nice, wouldn't it?"

She thought back to the last funeral, less than a fortnight beforehand, and she felt the rage build within her. Why did the people she loved have to die? The front door opening interrupted her gloomy self-reflection. She stood up to allow Mrs Bridges and her assistants to perform her duties. She shuffled past the elderly woman and took Mary a strong and sugary tea.

"What shall I do about work today?" she asked her mother. "Should I go? Will you be alright?"

Daphne broke down. Her mother lay Winnie on her lap and enfolded her sobbing daughter in her arms. She kissed the top of her head and tried to soothe her.

"Never again will I sit on Grandpa's knee. No more sea shanties. No more tales where I imagined myself sailing off to those far-off exotic lands. Do you remember that time he said he'd sneak a monkey back for me. Papa was livid!"

"Yes, I do, my love."

Daphne sat up and wiped her running nose on one sleeve and dried her eyes with the other.

"It's alright. I'll pull myself together. What shall I do about the funeral? How can I help?"

"It's alright, dearie. He's my father. I'll sort it out. I've languished up here for too long. It's time I started being your mother again and not just the mother to these two."

Tears flowed down the poor girl's face all the more. However strong she hoped she'd be for her mother, Daphne knew it would be quite some time before she'd be back to her chirpy old self. She tried to speak between the sobs and gasps.

"Are you sure, mama? It's only been a few days since the twins were born, do you feel up to it? There's the undertaker to appoint, Father Lane to see about the order of service, the wake to organise? I'm sure Mrs Bradley, Leah and Irvine would help?"

"No, I'll manage. I don't know how we'll pay for it, mind you. Your Grandpa had money, but where would he have kept it?"

"His money box under the bed. He let me keep my wages in it. I didn't say anything, but I got paid a whole pound."

Mary kissed her daughter on the head and hugged her with relief.

"Well, that changes things a bit! Talking about money, you'd better pop down and keep an eye on

Mrs Bridges. She'll be going through his pockets given half a chance."

Downstairs, the old woman hummed some hymns as she undertook her work. It was almost as if she enjoyed it. Daphne couldn't think of a worse job, other than the night soil men, or the toshers working the sewers. She wondered how she was going to tell Ma Bridges she didn't trust her and wanted to check Grandpa's pockets. Celia came downstairs with a wailing Johnny.

"'Sorry to interrupt, but I need to find him a bite to eat."

Celia's expression soon became one of horror. She walked past Mrs Bridges who didn't pay her any attention, such was her eagerness to wipe down the lily-white body, with a pace that bordered on disrespectful. Feeling bolstered by Celia's presence, Daphne decided to act.

"Mrs Bridges, did you check his pockets?"

"You mean, did he have money on him?"

The old crone reached into her apron and grinned, showing her shiny pink gums.

"No. This is all I found," she explained, with a hint of disappointment.

The old lady held out a brown envelope.

"I can't see his fortune being in there. You'll have to keep looking, lass."

Hardly daring to examine it, Daphne took it in her hands.

"I'll take it to mama, and let her see what it is."

"As long as there's money for my fee, I'm not bothered what happens to the rest of his possessions. I'll have that cuppa now, if I may."

Daphne called for Celia to pour her Mrs Bridges and went upstairs to her mother.

"What did she say?" her mother asked as she gave her the envelope.

"She said there wasn't any money but she did find this."

Her mother opened the envelope. A single pound note fell out, and a handwritten note.

Mary took the note and tried to read the scrawly writing.

"What does it say, ma?"

"Not a lot, from what I can make out. What's this word?" asked Mary pointing to something particularly illegible.

" I don't know. Let's ask Mrs Bridges, perhaps?"

Her mother pursed her lips.

"Do we really want her to know all our affairs, Daphne?"

"But then we won't know what it says. And there's no point asking Celia. She can't read at all. It could be a really important message, especially if he knew his health was failing?"

"True."

They tried to decipher it again but failed, so reluctantly, Mary took the message downstairs where they found Celia and the old lady in the kitchen.

"Um, Mrs Bridges, would you please do me a favour, and read this note, for neither I nor Daphne can make head nor tail of it? You've probably found a few notes like this in your time?"

Daphne handed over the piece of paper and the old lady studied it.

"I can't help. Sorry."

Celia tried to take it, but Daphne snatched it back, speaking, in a sharper voice than she had intended.

"You can't read or write, so there's no point in you looking at it, Celia."

Outside, Mrs Irvine noticed the curtains were still closed and knocked on the door to make sure everything was alright.

"Mrs Irvine, I think you can read, yes?" Daphne blurted out.

Mary looked dismayed at the thought of a loose-tongued gossip like Mrs Irvine knowing her business just as much as Mrs Bridges but agreed that the puzzle would not likely be solved otherwise.

"Och, God rest his soul," muttered Mrs Irvine, making a sign of the cross as her face dropped. "Do you want me to look after the bairns?"

"That sounds good, " said Celia. "I'll come with you. There's nothing I can do, and I am not comfortable sitting here."

"Before you go, Mrs Irvine, please could you look at this note of Grandpa's? We can't make out what it says, and wondered if you can? Especially this word?"

The woman took the paper.

"I think it's the name of a firm of solicitors, I'd say. Yes, Williamson and Parker, or something like that, on Brick Lane."

"A solicitor?" Mary questioned. "Why would he have a solicitor's name on a piece of paper?"

Mrs Bridges posed a solution.

"Maybe he left a will?"

"He said something to me about wills once, ma, but I didn't really understand what he was talking about, I'm sorry. I should have said something."

"Let's not think of that right now," Mary replied. "Not while he's lying there. It feels grubby."

Mrs Bridges lingered, angling for a tip. Daphne turned to face her mother, who was searching the larder for the empty corned beef tin. She shook out a few copper coins and held them out for the woman to take what she wanted.

"I only want my expenses. You know, for my oils and the shroud and stuff. They ain't cheap," said Mrs Bridges as she gathered up every coin.

Her mother sighed.

"I know. I don't expect you to do it for nothing."

The family stayed up all night, watching over Walter. News had spread and some of his sailor pals and drinking buddies came to pay their respects. Everyone commented on the way Mrs Bridges had styled his hair. He looked presentable, but no one thought he would ever have combed it that way himself. The teasing brought a little light cheer to the otherwise heartbreaking scene.

In the morning, the coffin arrived. Eight men took a hold of the fabric, lifted him up and laid him to rest inside it, on the jet-black cloth covering some straw. Beneath the shroud, Daphne saw his hands were crossed over his chest and his eyes closed. He looked so peaceful, even in death. The sadness of the sight was overwhelming. Everyone knew this was the last time they'd cast their eyes on his wily old face.

Mary and Daphne had decided to use some of her wages to pay extra for a better quality hearse, rather than the undertaker's usual rough wooden cart. The two of them followed behind, Celia was alongside them, and the procession of friends and neighbours formed as the cortège made its way to Commercial Road and back up to Bow cemetery once more.

25

A FUTURE NO ONE
IMAGINED

A few days later, on their way home from midnight mass, Daphne hurried along the dark streets with Celia by her side. The lanes and alleys were mostly deserted at one o'clock on Christmas Day morning. At that time of night, only a few vagrants and drunken revellers wending their way to their doss house usually frequented the area.

"We should have brought a lantern," Celia remarked, after almost tripping over some kerbstones.

"We don't own a lantern, silly! Besides, you said the light from the moon would be enough," replied Daphne, looking at the black sky. "But there doesn't seem to be one tonight."

"No, more's the pity. At least the fog that's been over us these last few days has gone. Do you know what? I am still amazed about your grandpa's note. What a turn-up for the books."

The names on the note found in Walter's pocket were indeed those of a Brick Lane law firm. When his will was read, they were astonished to find out that he had left a reasonable amount of money to Mary. She promptly took Daphne and Celia to the dress shop to buy each of them a new dress and a new cot for the twins. There would be no more sleeping in the drawer for them. They all decided Daphne would still need to work, or else the windfall would soon run out. Celia had got a job in a meat canning factory. It meant Mary would have to look after all three babies, but Mrs Irvine had offered to take Johnny as much as possible to give her a break. After a very tough few months, things were finally getting better.

They slipped back into the house. Mary had planned to wait up for them, but she must have been too tired. Daphne lit a candle and picked up one of the prettily-wrapped presents on the mantelpiece.

"When we returned from midnight mass when I was little, I was allowed to open one present. Shall we?"

Celia hung her head.

"I don't deserve one. Your family has been generous to a fault already."

"Don't be silly. I'm sure you didn't plan for your life to turn out the way it did. Grandpa always said we should help those people. Sometimes people are unlucky, and that's just the way it is—"

"—Or stupid," Celia added.

Daphne ignored the comment. In the past she would have jumped on it, but not now.

"I tell you what. Maybe, we should wait till mama and the babies are together. It'll be more fun to open them that way."

Celia smiled as she went towards the stairs.

"Thanks for welcoming me to your Christmas dinner table tomorrow. It was very kind of you."

The woman picked up her sleeping baby from his pram.

"I'll let him sleep with me tonight. I can't give him much else, except for a hug," Celia said forlornly.

Lying in bed beside her mother Daphne took a while to drop to sleep. She decided to say a special prayer for her grandfather and her beloved father and brother before slipping into a deep slumber. When she awoke, she found her mother dressing in her smartest clothes.

"Where are you going?" she asked in astonishment.

"To Christmas mass, of course."

"I hadn't realised you were going. I'm coming too. Are we taking the babies?"

"Yes, I need to speak to Father Lane about arranging their christening. I should have done it already, especially with Winifred being so sick. Still, I'm going today, now she's stronger and that's what matters."

"Celia seemed to enjoy midnight mass, mama. Maybe she'll become a convert. Johnny can be christened then, too."

"He can be christened still, even if she doesn't convert. Pass me another safety pin, please, Daphne. I don't want Walter's nappy falling off in church!"

Daphne did as she was asked and then picked up the little girl from the cot.

"You're going on your first outing, Little Winnie," she crooned. "And it's to a special place. We want you on your best behaviour, so you don't disturb people saying prayers."

Her mother grinned.

"I hope they both behave."

Mary reached over and kissed Daphne's cheek.

"Happy Christmas, darling."

"Happy Christmas, mama."

Daphne, in turn, gave the babies one kiss each.

"And to you two."

"It won't be the same without the men of the house, but we'll make the best of it. What a blessing it is that Miss Lawson has taken you under her wing." ," Mary sighed before a black humour came over her. "Come on, let us go. I'm looking forward to this. It's my first proper trip out in ages apart from funerals! And all our friends will be there."

Celia hadn't come down since she had taken Little Johnny upstairs for his hug hours ago.

"We did get back quite late, and I don't think she'll cope with two masses in one day anyway," Daphne chuckled.

Mary squeezed the tiny twins into Johnny's pram and covered them with their usual woolly blanket. Walter Junior settled down straight away, but, all smiles for once, Winifred didn't want to sleep.

"Look at her little face, mama. She's so excited. She must know it's Christmas."

Daphne looked at Winnie and then pointed to all the decorations in the room. The little girl gurgled with glee.

"This here is called *'holly'*. And this is *'ivy'*."

"For goodness' sake, hurry up, Daphne. We don't want to be late," barked her mother as she smoothed down her black coat and tied the ribbons on her black bonnet. "I'm glad most of the snow's gone," she added as she opened the door. "What a joy it is to breathe in some fresh air after being cooped up for so long."

As they passed the Leah's house, Ivy stepped out, followed by her mother.

"Merry Christmas! Are you off to church?" asked Mrs Leah.

"Yes, and we're late. Must press on."

"So are we," said their friends, but they turned the other way, heading off to another church which swore allegiance to the queen rather than the pope.

"I wonder which one they go to, ma?"

"I don't know and there's no time to think about it now," replied her mother, giving the pram a good shove to get it moving over the cobbles.

"Would you like me to push it?" asked Daphne, worried her mother would tire herself out.

"No, no, dearie. I'm fine. Come on. Less talk, more walk."

They arrived at the church in good time and sat in the back of the nave in case the babies caused a commotion, but they both slept like logs. During the service, Daphne noticed Albert near the front and considered approaching him. In the end, he came to her as she waited with the pram while her mother spoke to Father Lane about the christenings.

"Happy Christmas, Miss Parker."

Her heart raced and, feeling her face flush, she directed her gaze to her feet.

"I trust you are well, Daphne?"

Losing her tongue, she could only nod.

"I'm sorry about your grandfather. My condolences to your family."

"Thank you. Yes, it's been a horrid time these past few weeks. Sometimes I wonder what I have done to upset the Lord for him to punish us so."

The look of sympathy on his face made her eyes sting. Subtly, he reached for her hand and squeezed it briefly. The kind gesture sent her heart fluttering again.

"I didn't tell you, Albert, my New Year's resolution is to read more library books. Every day, if necessary. As many as I can. Especially poetry."

"Is that so? Well, what an excellent choice of pastime!"

She wanted to hug him but she smiled instead, a silent plea for him to wait for her as she moulded herself to be the perfect wife. He smiled back and stood still for a moment, in silence. The moment dissolved as soon as her mother returned and they set off home.

"Farewell then, Miss Parker, Mrs Parker."

Daphne watched him walk off with his mother until he melted into the crowd.

"You're still friends, then?" asked her mother as they walked.

"Yes, mama. I think I want to marry him if he'll have me—when I've read all the books in the library."

Her mother laughed but didn't disagree, giving her hope that someday it just might happen.

*

Celia had tidied up the house when they returned.

"Tea?"

"Yes please, Celia," Mary said. "I am tuckered after that walk. It's further than I remember."

"Not for me, thanks, Celia. I can't stop. I'm popping round to Sarah's."

Before anyone could stop her, Daphne shuffled past the pram by the doorway and was gone. Sarah welcomed her friend inside.

"Isn't Christmas exciting?" she said as she spun around, showing off a dress Daphne hadn't seen before.

"Don't you love my new frock? Ma picked it up for me from Bert. It still looks new."

"It's beautiful," Daphne said, feeling the fabric. "It's so soft and light, but perhaps not suitable for winter thought, is it?"

"Piffle, I don't care. I expect that's why it's cheap. The owner will get pneumonia wearing it in this weather," Sarah jested.

Daphne spotted a small rip under the arm, but kept quiet about it, not wanting to spoil her enjoyment of the moment. They danced around, singing and laughing until Mr Bradley coughed loudly which was Daphne's cue to leave.

"Did the bootees fit?" asked Mrs Bradley, looking up from her knitting.

"The twins haven't had a chance to try them on yet. We'll unwrap them later before our meal. But I'm sure they will fit perfectly. I hope you all have a lovely day," she called as she made to leave.

"We were sorry to hear about your Grandpa, Daphne. Send our condolences to your mother."

Daphne gave a solemn nod as she closed the door. Back at her family house, the three women opened their presents. Celia had embroidered a couple of handkerchiefs for the Parker women with a little sunflower in one corner. Where she got materials from or had the time to get it done, Daphne didn't like to ask.

Daphne had bought her mother a bonnet from the shop along from the haberdashers and hoped she wouldn't see the small hole at the back. For Johnny, she had bought a tiny wooden tractor to go with his train. Celia ended up with a pair of knitted mittens since she didn't seem to own a nice pair of gloves and her hands got so cold pushing the pram handle.

Miss Lillian had given Daphne a present—a lovely diary, leather-bound with a small lock and key.

The present she was looking forward to most was the one from her mother. What could it be? Quite large, and round. She tore off the paper to reveal a box. On opening it, she gasped. It was an exquisite dress.

"Mama, it's gorgeous."

"You won't be able to wear it until mourning's over, but do you like it?"

"I love it. I can't wait to wear it to church."

"For Albert?" Celia teased.

Daphne ignored the jibe and held the dress up against herself. Much as she liked Miss Lawson letting her wear her dresses, they never really felt like her own. This dress, however, was definitely hers.

The girl helped Celia set the table and, after finishing settling the twins, her mother joined them.

The minuscule joint of beef brisket was boiled to perfection, and there was just enough to go around. Mary cut it into three tiny pieces, and then scooped out the vegetables from the pan. Daphne was not best pleased to see a proliferation of carrots yet again. They raised their mugs and toasted lost loved ones. For a few moments, all remained silent, each one savouring their own bittersweet memories of the year.

"Who wants one of the baker's mince pies?" chirped Mary, lifting the mood.

"We are pushing the boat out today, mama"

"Well, I thought we deserved a treat. My inheritance could stretch to three of Mr Horowitz's finest."

"What a wonderful day we've had," Daphne pronounced. "After all the sadness this year, I am sure next year will be brighter for us all."

EPILOGUE

Two years later

In their cosy home, Albert wrapped his arm around Daphne and gave her a gentle squeeze.

"Are you happy, dearest?"

"Blissfully, my love," she replied, standing on the tips of her toes to plant a kiss on him.

Since their whirlwind wedding, life had been hectic. But even amidst the frantic activity, Daphne felt grateful. Lillian and Percival's tragic train accident on the continent the year before had cut their lives short, but their generosity had left Daphne with the shop and home in their will. The turnaround in her life since her time on Prospect Street was incredible. She tickled Albert's beard.

"Do you mind if I help mama move from the flat above the haberdashers today? I know we still have a lot to do here."

"Of course, I don't mind, my love," he replied smiling.

As she rested her head on his chest, listening to his steady heartbeat, she asked a question quietly.

"Would you have married me if I was still a Prospect Street girl? Admit it, your mother would never have allowed it, would she?"

"Perhaps not," Albert said with a chuckle. "But let's focus on brighter things. When are the cook and maid moving in? I still can't believe we have staff, Daphne."

"They're both arriving tomorrow," she said. "I'm glad I agreed to your suggestion. I can't run the haberdashery shop and keep up with the household here."

"Speaking of visitors, don't forget that Celia and her husband will be coming to see us next week, along with little Beth and Johnny. And Mrs Bradley, Leah and Irvine are coming for afternoon tea next week."

"I think it would be quicker if you told me who isn't coming, my love," Albert joked.

Daphne nestled into Albert's arms, enjoying the comfort of his strong embrace. She gazed up at him, a soft smile playing at the corners of her lips.

"Celia's little Beth is a treasure. I wonder if our little one will look like us?" she mused.

Albert's eyes widened at the unexpected comment.

"Are you telling me what I think you're telling me, my sweet?" he asked in disbelief.

Daphne nodded, her grin growing wider by the second as she felt her own belly.

"I think so. Are you pleased?"

Albert's face lit up with pure joy, and he pulled Daphne even closer to him.

"Pleased? I couldn't be happier!"

"Even if it's twins?" she teased, her eyes sparkling mischievously.

"Well, that will be double the joy," he said before kissing her softly twice.

———

Enjoyed The Shop Girl's Secret? Here are some more books in my 'Victorian Whitechapel Girls' series you'll love. Have you read them all?

- https://mybook.to/WhitechapelGirls

GET ONE OF MY BOOKS FREE

Hi! Beryl here. You can download your free short story with this link.

- dl.bookfunnel.com/2jkv8e1qoq

Thanks for all your support. It means everything to me.

If you would consider leaving a review or rating that would be greatly appreciated. It helps more readers enjoy the stories.

Printed in Great Britain
by Amazon